RISING HOPE

Rising Hope

RISING HOPE
HALF MOON BAY BOOK 3

ERIN BROCKUS

Copyright © 2021 Erin Brockus

This is a work of fiction. Names, characters, businesses, places, events, locales, and incidents are either the products of the author's imagination or used in a fictitious manner. Any resemblance to actual persons, living or dead, or actual events is purely coincidental.

All rights reserved. No part of this book may be reproduced or used in any manner without the prior written permission of the copyright owner, except for the use of brief quotations in a book review.

Cover design by GetCovers

Edited by Misha Carlstedt

Ebook ISBN: 978-1-957003-00-9

Paperback ISBN: 978-1-957003-01-6

Hardcover ISBN: 978-1-957003-03-0

CHAPTER 1

March...

IT WAS A SEA SLUG. Patiently exhaling the bubbles from her regulator, Hope Collins waited in the line of divers to see what Alex Monroe had discovered. As owner of Half Moon Bay Resort in St. Croix, she insisted guests be first to see any discoveries.

Also, being last had one important benefit.

As the diver in front of her moved off, Hope approached the dive guide. Alex drew her forward and removed his regulator to kiss her hand. His blue eyes held a humorous glint as he replaced his regulator, but kept hold of her hand, squeezing as he indicated the treasure he'd found.

The sea slug, otherwise known as a nudibranch, sat motionless like a three-inch lump on the tan-colored coral shelf. Hope admitted it was a very pretty lump, bright blue and yellow, with two stalks on one end sticking up like horns. She turned to Alex, who pointed at it with his other hand and grinned around his regulator, waiting for her reaction.

Smiling back, she was struck by a vivid memory of when he had taught her about nudibranchs during her open water scuba class.

"Sea slugs?" Hope had curled her lip, shivering at the thought. "That's disgusting! Do they leave a trail of slime?"

Alex stiffened and shot her a dirty look. "No! They're beautiful. I'm always on the lookout for them. They—"

Her laughter interrupted him. "Oh, I'm so sorry! I had no idea you were so passionate about slugs. Please forgive me."

He narrowed his eyes, then stood and reached on the scuba classroom's bookshelf for a ratty, dog-eared book titled *Marine Invertebrates of the Caribbean*. He opened it right to the section he wanted and held the wall of pictures out to her, each depicting a different slug. "Here, see? Look how beautiful they are. Ms. Collins, you need to show more appreciation for marine life if you're going to be a diver."

Hope peered at the pictures in the book. The nudibranchs were incredibly varied—blue, green, and white; some were flattened, and many had fantastic alien stalks growing out of them. "Ok. I have to admit they are very colorful, and a couple might even be . . . attractive." She met his eyes. "But do *not* expect me to get excited about slugs."

She had come across many on dives since and seen photographers get positively rapturous over them. But she made it a point never to admit to Alex she was impressed by any of them, no matter how striking they were. It had become something of a joke between them.

Now, glancing at his expectant face, she refused to give in, even to this beautiful specimen. Hope rolled her eyes, using her free hand to shove him in the shoulder before letting go and swimming away. With a final squeeze of her hand, Alex laughed as he moved off, and she couldn't help the smile that rose to her face.

I bet that marine biology degree is handy for a dive guide, huh, Alex?

He swam back to the group and beckoned everyone to follow. Today they were a group of two couples plus Hope, so she stayed close to Alex as he always buddied up with any extra diver in the group. Never dive alone was a fundamental rule.

They swam over a flat reef top that abruptly dropped to a sheer vertical wall of dizzying depths. Beneath them on the flat was an expanse of tropical hard and soft corals, with impossibly bright fish darting about.

The two dive groups on the boat had headed in opposite directions, both planning to end the dive back under the boat. Before starting, Alex had told his group to watch closely on this section of the dive. Sometimes larger animals, such as dolphins or rays, swam by in the deep water next to the drop-off.

He stopped to peer intently at a coral outcropping, completely motionless except for the tilting of his head back and forth, and Hope crossed her fingers. Alex was familiar with every inch of the reef. To her disappointment, he looked up and shrugged, not finding what he'd been looking for. Continuing, he turned to his left, glancing at the deep-blue water.

And froze. He studied the water with blazing intensity.

Squinting, Hope followed his gaze, but couldn't see anything. Alex exploded into motion, finning and beckoning frantically for the group to follow.

Ok, obviously he sees something, but I sure don't.

He was swimming hard and had distanced himself from the group now. Hope was following as fast as she could and urging the others on, but concern crept up at how hard they were working to keep up with him. When he turned around, she gestured for him to slow down. Alex softened his eyes but shook his head, urging them to hurry.

Ok, this better be a manta ray. Hope and the group continued after him. They were out in the featureless depths of the ocean now, with no bottom in sight.

Then, facing away from them and still fixated in front, Alex held both arms out, pressing his outstretched arms down repeatedly in a slow-down gesture.

Huh? Now we're stopping?

Hope snuck a glance at the divers on either side of her, relieved their expressions were eager and not stressed from all the finning. With wide eyes, Alex looked back to make sure everyone was there, gesturing once again to stay in place. She'd never seen him so animated about something underwater, though she couldn't see a thing except the deep void of blue water. Hope shrugged emphatically at him, both arms out. *What?* He widened his eyes, and with a smile, jabbed his finger in front of him.

I can't see anything! She was ready to give up on the whole thing when she detected movement.

An immense, elongated shape slowly emerged toward them from the hazy depths. She spotted the huge vertical dorsal and tail fins, her heart going into overdrive as a primitive part of her brain screamed *shark!* But then she smiled at the glimpse of the flattened head and white spots along the gray body.

She beheld a whale shark.

The largest fish in the ocean, the giant was a gentle filter feeder and a danger to no one. It was also considered a holy grail of scuba diving and very rare in the waters around St. Croix. Hope hovered motionless, nearly forgetting to breathe as she inspected the mammoth fish.

Oh my God! Alex, how on earth did you spot it?

It continued on its same course perpendicular to the dive group. Alex swam with it, matching its speed but not approaching as he beckoned the divers to come closer. It was nearly thirty feet long. The whale shark slowed, as if it were curious about these strange creatures blowing bubbles next to it.

The group swam with the massive shark for nearly twenty minutes, and Alex moved back to let the other divers approach it. Hope finally took her turn, swimming hard to match its pace while holding her distance several feet from its head. Its tiny eye regarded her with curiosity, and her heart soared as goosebumps broke out on her arms.

The shark maintained its leisurely pace, swimming forty feet below the surface, and Hope exchanged wide-eyed glances with the other excited divers. Finally, it angled downward, its great tail fin gently weaving back and forth as it continued on its way and disappeared into the indigo depths.

Alex checked his dive watch and gave the group the three-minute safety-stop signal, indicating the dive was over. He deployed his surface marker buoy from its reel while the group hovered at fifteen feet, eliminating the nitrogen their bodies had accumulated during the dive before finally surfacing. He locked eyes with Hope, both of them breaking into smiles.

The couples spit out their regulators and whooped in unison, and the entire group exchanged high fives. Alex laughed and reeled in his SMB while making sure it stood well up from the gentle waves, making them easily visible.

Hope squinted at their dive boat, barely able to see it. "How are we going to get back to the boat?"

"We're not." Alex turned his smile to her. "Tommy can pick us up. He knows which way we went by our bubbles. I can see the other group getting on the boat now, so it shouldn't be long. Enjoy the sunshine." He tipped his head back and closed his eyes, his mask around his neck. Hope peered at the distant boat but couldn't see any of that. However, she was perfectly willing to accept Alex had better eyes.

A few minutes later, *Surface Interval* motored over to them. Tommy Williams grinned down from the elevated wheelhouse, his white teeth shining against his dark skin. "Did you get lost again, Alex? You gotta stop doin' that, man!"

The two couples in Alex's group shouted in unison, "Whale shark!"

Tommy's smile disappeared as his mouth dropped open. Hope

grinned as he scrambled for a pair of binoculars, scanning the ocean surface in front of the boat.

Alex laughed, shaking his head. "Don't bother, Tommy. She was headed into deeper water. I'm sure she's long gone."

Their divemaster, Robert Davis, had led the other group of six divers, who all stood on the boat wearing matching disappointed frowns.

Once back on board, Hope tried to console them, though her group couldn't conceal their excitement as they made the short trip back to the resort. Alex's laughter drew her attention. He was pulling off his wetsuit as he talked to one diver in their group. He tossed it on the growing pile at the stern, standing tall in his dripping board shorts. She tried not to stare at his sculpted chest, grateful for her sunglasses as he replaced his staff shirt. *Oh, those abs!*

"Hope!" Robert yelled at her side, making her jump.

"Oh, sorry. I was distracted." She darted a glance back to Alex. He grinned at her, fully aware she'd been staring. Hope lifted her chin in a haughty display, which only widened his smile.

"Here," Robert continued, handing her an empty plastic airtight container. "I thought you might want your case back. You know, so you can bring us more cookies tomorrow."

"They must have been a hit. There are none left."

"Don't worry. I made sure Tommy didn't eat them all."

"I can always count on you, Robert." She had always enjoyed cooking and baking, and now that the resort was doing well with its general manager Patti Thomas overseeing day-to-day operations, Hope had been baking more and providing snacks for the daily dive trips. They had been a hit with the divers. And the dive crew.

"I'll make sure Alex brings reinforcements tomorrow. Don't worry." Hope patted him on the shoulder before sitting next to Maggie, a seasoned diver from his group, who sat forlornly on the side bench. She'd never seen a whale shark. "It was just luck, Maggie. It could have just as easily been Robert who found it."

Privately, Hope's thoughts were very different.

Ha! Nobody but Alex would have seen that whale shark.

She turned away to hide her smile as she gazed back at Alex, who was busy unhooking the scuba equipment. *Did you have occasion to use those eagle eyes when you were a Navy SEAL, Alex?* He likely hadn't spent many missions looking for whale sharks, so probably not.

But it certainly made him a stellar dive guide.

CHAPTER 2

The water lapped gently against the hull of the boat as Hope gathered her things. Robert secured the lines to the pier and jumped back on board as the divers returned to their bungalows, leaving the crew alone.

Tommy descended the ladder to the main deck and stood next to her. "I'm starvin'," he said, patting his broad stomach. "I'm gonna head up to the kitchen for lunch. I'll finish washin' down the boat after."

"What, my baked goods weren't enough for you?"

Tommy parked a hand on his hip. "No. Not even close. Robert and Alex kept takin' them away from me." He turned to Robert. "You joinin' me, or what?

"Yes!" Robert popped his dark shaved head up from a tank at the stern. "Wait for me. Otherwise the food will all be gone."

Their laughter echoed across the water as they made their way up the pier, making Hope smile.

"I really love having you on the boat."

Hope glanced up. Alex was unscrewing a regulator from its tank and watching her.

She approached and wrapped her arms around his waist. "Oh?

I have to admit it's a fun part of the job. Though this morning I came along strictly in a business capacity. Personal feelings had nothing to do with it."

His short, light hair was still neat even after spending most of the day underwater, the opposite of her rat's nest, now contained beneath a Half Moon Bay Resort baseball cap.

Alex pulled her closer and bent his head, pressing his lips tightly to hers. A jolt went through her as he unexpectedly opened his mouth and deepened the kiss. "Maybe I can make it more personal," he whispered.

"Settle down, sailor. There's still work to be done." But she didn't make any effort to move out of his arms.

With a smile, he brushed a lock of hair from her brow. "You sure were a good-luck charm this morning."

Hope beamed, bouncing on her feet. "That was incredible! I'm so glad I got to see it."

"Me too. I've only seen a few in all the dives I've done here. And she hung around for a long time too."

She cocked her head. "How did you know it was a female?"

Alex's smile widened. "No claspers. Only boy sharks have claspers, you know."

"Oh? Claspers?" She pressed against him again, breathing in his ear. "And is there an equivalent on human males, Mr. Monroe?"

"Well, we might just have to investigate that together." He brushed her lips again before stepping back with a sigh. "But we can't get too carried away, can we? We're pretty visible right now. And you're usually the voice of reason, Boss Lady. I'm surprised you're not cracking the whip to get me back to work."

Hope thought of a retort to his comment, but let it pass. With Alex's quick wit, they'd be there all day. "It's nice to know you retained some leadership qualities, Mr. Monroe. Maybe I was testing you."

He glanced at her breasts and then a gleam formed in his eyes. "Is that what you call it?"

Hope followed his gaze and scowled. Her bikini top was making an abject liar of her. Drawing an arm across her chest to hide the evidence, she moved to the covered bow to replace her shirt, proclaiming, "It's cold here in the tropics."

"Uh-huh. Freezing."

After wrapping a swim skirt around her hips, Hope returned to Alex. "I'm working from home this afternoon, so I'll see you later." She pressed the length of her body tightly against him for a quick kiss and laughed as she gave him a private squeeze. "Well, you're definitely not cold. Perhaps you shouldn't be casting stones."

"I'll have you know I'm perfectly behaved as long as you're not around."

"Since you're so eager to get rid of me, I guess I'll be off." She was moving away when Alex grabbed her, pulling her into his arms and kissing her deeply as he ground his hips against her. Then he pushed her away with a smug wink, moving back to the scuba tanks and leaving her weak-kneed and dizzy.

Fanning herself with her hand, Hope stepped off the boat. As she walked up the pier, she waved to Selena and Patti, who were coming down the stairs from the spa.

"Oh, good. You're back," Patti said. "I need to talk to Alex."

The general manager continued down the pier, and Hope smiled at her newest team member. "How's your day been?"

"Busy mornin', just how I like it," Selena said, lighting up. She was a Cruzan native in her mid-twenties who had recently graduated from massage school and was thrilled to be the resort's first massage therapist. "I still have more work this afternoon. Several divers are booked."

"Glad to hear it. Keep up the good work."

Wanting to ask Patti how the new dishwasher was doing, Hope turned toward the boat. She and Alex stood in the open-stern section, and he had his arms wrapped around her. Patti's shoulders slumped as she rested her head on Alex's chest, and he shot Hope a sheepish smile. Heart melting, she nodded and let them have their private moment.

Hope continued toward the beach. Patti had known Alex for years, but had learned a lot about him in just the past few months. And she was still processing her guilt over the Charles ordeal. Patti and Alex had always been close, and his opening up about his past had made them closer.

Hope stepped onto the powdery white sand beach, walking another quarter mile until she reached the house she shared with Alex. As she climbed the steps onto the cool covered porch, a medium-sized yellow dog lay curled up on his bed in the corner. He raised his head and yawned, raising his hindquarters into a luxurious stretch.

"Hello, Cruz. You've been hard at work this morning, I see." Hope's skittish stray dog had become downright lazy and domesticated since deciding she was the lesser of two evils during a hurricane last September. Cruz and Alex had moved in with her at the same time after Alex's apartment had been destroyed.

At first, there had been a bit of a turf war as both protective males competed for Hope's affections. But Alex demonstrated his good sense by coming home from nearby Frederiksted one afternoon with two dog beds. One was for their great room, and the other for the corner of the porch. Cruz accepted this peace offering, and the two had been fast friends ever since. Her elite soldier boyfriend was a creampuff.

But a chill trickled down Hope's spine as she recalled several instances when she'd seen the SEAL side of him firsthand. He'd fought a much larger, armed man and knocked him unconscious, getting shot in the process, though he was fully healed now.

Recently, Hope had caught another glimpse when Alex became angry on the witness stand, proclaiming that Charles, their former co-worker and unreformed thug, was only alive because Alex chose for him to be.

He was a mass of contradictions, but there were two things Hope didn't question—that Alex would never harm her, and that he would stop at nothing to protect her.

The short-coated dog now padded over to join Hope inside the air-conditioned house. A small smile replaced the icy frown as she turned on the shower in their bathroom. Alex's protectiveness could occasionally manifest into coddling her. When his unconscious condescension crossed the line, Hope wasn't shy about letting him know. It was a delicate balance they were still working on.

Though you weren't exactly complaining when he took a bullet for you, were you?

Hope couldn't deny her inner voice was very logical today.

After a quick lunch, she proceeded to her home office to do battle with her email inbox. Cruz curled up on the floor next to her desk, happy to spend the heat of the afternoon in cool comfort. She was just opening her email when Sara's ringtone sounded in the quiet room. Hope answered with a smile. "Little sister. How's life in Charlottesville?"

"Same old, same old," Sara replied. "My life isn't one big adventure like yours."

"Whose fault is that?"

"Hey now, drop the snark. You wouldn't even be there if it weren't for me."

"Guess I can't argue with that. Any particular reason you're calling, or do you just miss me?"

"No reason. Just thought I'd catch up. I was reading Alex's article again this morning and thinking about you guys."

"That explains the shooting pains all over his body."

Sara laughed. "No voodoo dolls, I swear. Actually, I was feeling kind of bad for giving him the third degree when I visited."

Hope's smile widened. She'd never let on that Alex had come

up with the nickname Hurricane Sara. "Really? I didn't think you were capable of regret."

"I was just trying to make sure he wasn't hiding a wife or family somewhere. I had no idea he'd turn out to be a damn hero."

"I agree he hides it well. Don't worry, your secret's safe with me. I'll never let him know you think he's ok."

"You better not. There are still ample opportunities for him to screw up, you know."

"Of course." Hope refrained from mentioning her own screwups. Like running out into a raging hurricane to rescue a dog.

"You two have quite the little home together. Any talk of the future?"

And . . . the fishing line comes out! "We're very happy, Sara. Why risk that? I don't want Alex getting all weird on me."

"Neither of you has a traditional background, but I hardly think he'd get upset about it. In fact, I don't think he's the one with the weird attitude about this subject."

Hope heaved a sigh. "Oh, stop with the psychoanalyzing. Alex's marriage wasn't a happy one. And we've been a little busy surviving shootings and hurricanes to discuss the future, ok?"

"Uh-huh. Sure. But as long as you're content, so am I."

"That's you and me. One big happy family." Sara laughed as Hope's email pinged for the fourth time in the past few minutes. "I gotta get back to work. My inbox is overflowing. Love you."

"Love you too. Wriggle your feet in the sand for me."

CHAPTER 3

Sunbeams danced through the clear, tropical water as a school of goatfish stirred up the sandy bottom, looking for a meal. Alex hovered motionless just over them, inspecting the scene before him with an expert eye. He was diving in forty feet of water, just off the resort beach and north of the pier. The construction before him was tent-shaped and massive underwater, more so than his prior experience with it suggested. He slowly finned to one of the open ends and peered into the dim interior. The other end beckoned fifty feet away.

Unable to resist, Alex swam underneath the roof of his old apartment, effortlessly controlling his buoyancy to avoid stirring up the sand or scatter fish resting within the dark confines. The roof rested on the sandy bottom, fully intact. He emerged on the other side in a short time, full of the childlike wonder that came from exploring a dark tunnel and making it out safely.

But Alex wasn't here to play.

He continued along the outside of the roof, stopping midway. Before him, six PVC treelike structures were secured to the structure at even intervals. Each tree was four feet tall, and a multitude of coral fragments hung from the plastic branches, each dangling from a piece of fishing line tightly tied to the branch. In addition, different varieties of coral were attached to the roof itself.

Alex was pleased. He'd only drilled the trees and placed the coral transplants a few months ago but could already see progress. Coral was notoriously slow growing, but small pieces such as these were stimulated to grow more quickly.

He approached a tree of staghorn-coral fragments, the brown and tan spiky branches showing nearly enough growth to be transplanted to the nearby house reef. That was the next phase of the project. He continued, inspecting each tree and measuring the growth of the pieces hanging from each as well as those growing on the roof itself.

Finally, Alex back kicked some distance away and took a long look at the expansive project, very satisfied. A multitude of small fish flitted about the scene, cleaning the young corals. They were already attracted to the artificial coral nursery, making it their new home.

Alex made his way back to the pier, climbing the ladder onto the wooden planking. Tucking his fins under one arm, he walked to the gear room where he removed his kit, opening the backpack-like canister and removing a small cylinder he set next to the air compressor to be refilled.

He set his pony bottle in the corner—the additional air source used whenever he dove alone. He regarded the room, neatly organized and looking brand new after repairs, though it was still hot and stuffy in the afternoon sun. After rinsing his gear, he was hanging the large backpack device on its hanger when a voice called out from behind him.

"Well, hello there, handsome."

A grin spread across Alex's face as Hope slid her arms around his waist from behind. He turned around and gave her a lingering kiss. "Hello, yourself."

She turned to move around the perimeter of the room, running her hand over the resort regulators as she passed. "I thought you had this organized well before the storm, but it looks really good now." The room was bright and clean, with the bulky air compressor on the other side of the room, attached to its water bath to fill scuba tanks.

"I wanted more separation between the resort gear and the guests' personal gear. More people are using their own now."

She nodded and stopped in front of the section where he kept her equipment, studying it. Wrinkling her brow, she picked up her regulator and took it back over to the resort section, holding hers next to a resort regulator as she compared the metal first stages.

"How come my regulator looks different?"

He crossed to look over her shoulder, trailing a finger over the tattoo peeking out from under the strap of her sundress. Its turquoise and yellow colors were muted in the dim room. "Because that's not one of the resort regs—old or new. You use one of mine. The resort equipment is good quality. I make sure of that. But my regs are top of the line, and I wanted you to have one of those."

Hope beamed at him, holding her regulator close to her chest. "Really? I had no idea. How long have I been using one of yours?"

"Since the very start, your first pool session. I wanted Boss Lady to have the best experience possible." She gazed up at him, and he drowned in her beautiful hazel eyes—they were a sunburst of gold, brown, and green.

"Careful," she warned in that low, husky voice he loved. "Your reputation as a battle-hardened warrior is in serious jeopardy here."

"What can I say? You bring out the kitten in me."

That brought out a roll of throaty laughter. "A kitten is generally not the animal I think of when I'm around you."

She continued on her little tour, stopping in front of his personal equipment. "Ok. I see two BCDs here, three regulators, and various wetsuits. But I've always wanted to ask you, what on earth is this thing?" She pointed to the still-dripping black rectangular canister and attached vest he'd just returned to its hanger next to his buoyancy compensation device.

Alex approached to stand next to her. "My rebreather. I started diving with it again—I've hardly used it since you arrived." He sent her a smoldering stare. "It's like I've had other things on my mind."

She gave him a sideways glance that made his heart race, but ignored his comment. "And what is a rebreather?"

"Well, that's going to require a bit of an explanation. It's a little late, but have you had lunch yet?"

"That's actually why I came down here. I was going to see if you wanted to join me."

He held his elbow out to her, flashing her a broad smile. "Well, come with me and I'll explain the finer points of closed-circuit underwater-breathing systems to you over lunch."

THEY TOOK their customary seats at the corner table in the restaurant. Since both were done working for the day, Hope ordered a bottle of white wine, which resort bartender Clark Bailey poured for them. She took a sip of the delicious cool wine, enjoying the soft breeze that fluttered the potted red and yellow bougainvillea nearby. Her attention wandered to the empty section of wall and she made a note to order more of Robert's prints to display. It had been on her to-do list, but the project had gotten delayed due to the trial.

"Did you have a good day?" Alex asked.

"Yes. I'm very happy with the remodel of the bungalows. We're nearly done with the final one. The design ended up just how I was hoping—modern tropical, yet keeping the romantic, classy touches."

"Well, you know something about being romantic and classy."

Half Moon Bay's primary server, Charlotte, came by and took

their orders. After she returned to the kitchen, Hope turned back to Alex. "Ok. So what is that rebreather thing hanging in the gear room?"

Alex leaned forward and put his elbows on the table, tenting his fingers together. Hope managed to keep a straight face—he was officially in instructor mode now.

"You learned to dive using a standard scuba setup. Do you remember what scuba stands for, Ms. Collins?"

"Yes, Mr. Monroe, as a matter of fact, I do. Self-contained underwater breathing apparatus."

"Excellent. Though I should probably point out that rebreathers are technically scuba also since they're even more self-contained."

"Do tell."

"This is serious, Hope. Rebreathers are a totally different animal." His smile was gone now. "A standard scuba tank is what's called an open-circuit system. You breathe in air from the regulator, which is attached to the tank, and exhale it into the water. As you dive, the air in the tank gets depleted and eventually it runs out."

"Got it. Don't see the serious part, though."

"I'm getting there. A rebreather is a closed-circuit system—air is never released into the water. That black rectangular case you saw contains an oxygen cylinder, a carbon-dioxide scrubber, and two counter lungs.

"When you breathe in from those lungs, instead of exhaling into the water, your exhaled air goes into the scrubber, which eliminates the excess carbon dioxide. From there, the air goes back into the counter lungs, and oxygen gets added from the cylinder to bring it back to optimal levels."

He paused for a sip of wine. "So, the air you breathe gets continually recirculated through the rebreather, no bubbles are exhaled, and you have a much larger quantity of air available for the dive."

Hope tried not to get lost in his explanation. "That sounds really complicated."

He softened his eyes. "It is. It can also be dangerous if you don't know what you're doing. If the oxygen level is off or the carbon dioxide doesn't get removed, bad things can happen. That's why I said it was serious. People have died using rebreathers."

Hope sat up straight, tightening her shoulders. "Then why the hell would you want to use one?"

"Like I said. There are no bubbles, so you're completely silent, and you can have greatly expanded bottom time. That's why I've been using mine with the coral-restoration project. The extra dive time has come in handy as I built the skeleton of the nursery and started my fragments."

"I guess that makes sense."

His face burst into a grin, and he leaned forward. "Best of all, they're super cool looking. When you wear one, you can pretend you're a Navy SEAL."

Hope rolled her eyes. "It still sounds dangerous. I worry about you sometimes."

"Don't, baby." His smile fell as he regarded her seriously. "With the type of diving I did in the past, being silent was important, and I don't take unnecessary risks. I'm an expert on rebreathers."

He swirled the wine in his glass before looking back at Hope, the glint back in his eyes. "Believe it or not, I'm actually pretty good at this diving thing."

That made her smile as she took his hand. "Yeah, I know you are."

CHAPTER 4

"I'm feelin' a lot more relaxed than the last time we walked down this pier." Hope's friend Cindy Pearce high-fived her as the two walked toward *Surface Interval*. It was a chamber-of-commerce kind of morning—soft, fluffy clouds in the sky and a light breeze drifting through the palm trees.

"I'm very glad to hear it," Hope replied with a laugh.

Even after their disastrous last trip, Cindy had wanted to dive again, and Alex had recently given her a refresher class in the resort pool. Then she informed Hope today was the only day she could go. Naturally, Hope had smiled and agreed immediately, though she'd had to rearrange her morning to make it work. But diving with her love and her new best friend was the best possible way to celebrate.

This was an enormous day for Hope.

One she hadn't said anything about. To anyone.

She and Cindy were last aboard and were getting settled prior to leaving the resort. They had a full load of sixteen divers split into the two groups. Alex stood in the middle of the tank area at the stern and raised his voice.

"Can I get your attention, everyone? I have an announcement

to make." Everyone turned as Alex's natural authority asserted itself. "Today is March fifteenth, and this is a very important day for our little resort."

Hope's jaw dropped as he came up behind her and placed his hands on her shoulders. "One year ago today, Hope arrived in St. Croix. I won't bore you with the details, but she took over the resort in pretty much the worst circumstances possible. Those of you who are returning guests can see the incredible changes she's made in the past year. She's had an enormous impact on all of us who work here."

He leaned to the side so he and Hope could smile at each other. "Well, on some of us more than others. Please join me in giving her a big round of applause to celebrate her one-year anniversary!" An animated round of cheering rose around the boat, with Cindy leading the way.

Alex tipped Hope's chin up and gave her a kiss for all the world to see.

The applause increased, along with several whistles. Her heart was about to melt into a puddle on the fiberglass deck. "How did you know? I didn't say anything!"

His grin lingered. "Oh, I have ways of getting information. No secret's safe from me." He turned back to the crowd. "Ok, let's go dive!"

The other divemaster, April, a friendly thirty-five-year-old with braided honey-blonde hair, tightened her mouth at Alex's announcement. Hope suspected she hadn't been able to shut off her feelings for him like a light switch, but she'd made no overtures since learning he and Hope were together, and the two women had always gotten along well.

She approached Hope with a smile. "Congrats! You've accomplished a lot in a year's time. I might just have to get a massage sometime. The spa's in a pretty convenient place."

"Well, it's been a big hit, and the massage therapist is fabulous. You won't regret it, I promise." Hope grinned as Alex tossed her the lines, climbing back aboard. Then, Tommy eased them away from the dock and off to their morning adventures.

After the dive trip, Hope and Cindy sat down in the restaurant for lunch. "Well, that was a lot more successful than our first dive trip," Hope said, holding up her iced tea in a toast.

Cindy laughed as their glasses rang together. She had beautiful ebony skin and long, thin braids tied into a long tail. "Definitely! No eels and no horrible boyfriends. Just good people to hang out with."

The dive trip had been a resounding success. She was much more confident after her refresher with Alex and a different person in the water. Hope couldn't help but think Marcus's absence helped too. Cindy's ex-boyfriend hadn't been a supportive dive partner, to put it mildly.

"I didn't see you at the group run last Saturday." Cindy oversaw the weekly group run sponsored by the local running club. "You comin' this week?"

"Yes, I'm back at it. Just three-milers, though. I still feel tired after the triathlon." *Maybe the race took more out of me than I thought?* She made an effort to brighten. "Speaking of the sports festival, you sure smoked your half-marathon."

"So did you. I was so excited you guys won!"

"I was shocked. Didn't expect that at all. Alex and Gerold were good teammates." Alex had beaten several pros out of the water, and Half Moon Bay's chef Gerold Harrigan had turned in a blistering time on the tortuous bike leg. Hope had anchored their team and handily beat her half-marathon personal record.

Cindy raised her glass again. "To happy endings."

AFTER LUNCH, Hope made her way to the lobby and had just sat down at her desk when a thunderous Patti marched in. "Well, I take it your day isn't going well," Hope said.

"It's the new dishwasher I hired. He's terrible! He's been late —I mean half an hour late—for three out of his last five shifts. I just told him if it happens again, he's fired." She rested her head on her hand. "It's worse because I'm related to him."

Hope had to laugh. "Patti, you're related to everyone! And you do a great job managing the staff—if he doesn't work out, we'll find someone else. People seem to want to work here."

She spent the rest of the day paying bills and catching up after her rearranged morning. Since implementing the new booking portal on their website, the resort was seeing more revenue from longer bookings. And longer vacations also resulted in guests having more interaction with the staff and the island, leading to excellent reviews and noticeable repeat bookings.

The afternoon passed quickly, and soon she was saying good night to front-desk clerk Martine, who gave her a half-hearted wave. Hope was impressed she'd made it through her shift. Her pregnancy was progressing normally, but she still had some miserable days.

There was a steady breeze, and her butterfly wind chime rang in deep tones as Hope climbed the stairs to the porch. Alex was relaxing at one end of the couch, sipping a beer, with several more buried in a bucket of ice on the coffee table.

She drank him in.

He was dressed only in cargo shorts, a button-down shirt draped over the couch arm. Hope zeroed in on his muscular chest, increasing her step. Since she wore capris, it was a simple matter to straddle him and sit on his lap. "What am I going to do with you? This is the second time today you tempted me by not wearing a shirt."

A smile spread across his face while his eyes sent an entirely different message. "I'm completely innocent here—it's too hot out here to wear a shirt. I was just enjoying an adult beverage after a long day. You're the one taking advantage of me here."

Hope scooched closer, feeling his response growing between them. "Innocent, huh? I don't think so."

She took a drink from his bottle. "One year. It's so strange—all the changes." Then a thought occurred to her, resulting in a smirk. "I wasn't too sure about you that first day. I thought you were a bit of an asshole when Patti told you about Steve leaving."

"Is that why you took such a dislike to me right off the bat?"

"It wasn't dislike, really. More like I was scared to death of you. Especially after your charms started working on me."

He pressed his hips against her. "Oh? Are my charms still working?"

"What do you think?"

He became serious, running a finger down her face. "You never need to be scared of me."

"I know that too." She brushed a feathery kiss over his lips, then pulled back, poking him in the chest. "How did you know today was when I arrived, anyway?"

"I keep logbooks of the dive sites we go to each day, so we don't repeat too often. And I make notes of other important things going on too. It was just a matter of looking for the exact day in mid-March when you arrived—I knew I'd made a note of it."

Hope shook her head, slowly shifting from knee to knee as Alex's nostrils flared. She was distinctly warmer than a few minutes ago. "You're full of surprises. I wasn't expecting that kiss in front of everyone, not that I'm complaining."

"Well, after I declared under oath to the entire world that I loved you, I didn't see much point in depriving myself anymore."

"Yes, you are terribly deprived. But I think we can do something about that right now." Hope set his beer on the coffee table and, still straddling him, pushed against him hard. She ran both hands through his hair, then pulled his head close, opening her mouth to run her tongue slowly across his. Alex rumbled deep in his chest, drawing her tighter.

He pulled her shirt from her capris, lifting it off. "Told you, it's too hot out here for shirts. Bras too." In a second, he had her bra off, tossing it on the floor as he took a firm hold. The cool afternoon breeze swept over her back.

Breathing hard, Hope leaned forward and pressed her breast into his mouth. As he began to move his tongue, she closed her eyes and arched her back. "Mmm, you make me feel so good."

"That's the general idea."

"Don't talk with your mouth full."

He laughed, then gave the same treatment to the other breast.

Without warning, he moved his hands to her hips, lifting her off him and tossing her onto her back. Hope caught a sense of his strength and power in how effortlessly he moved her.

Leaning over, he kissed her relentlessly with a hot, wet mouth. Desire arced through her—knowing with certainty he would do whatever she asked, or stop immediately if that was her wish.

Which it most definitely was not.

Hope groaned, pushing him away as she raced to unbutton his shorts.

"Feeling a bit feisty, are we?" he asked, then snapped his mouth shut to inhale sharply as she wrapped her hand around him.

She curled her lips up as she stroked him. He was already highly aroused. "Apparently I'm not the only one."

Hope grabbed what she could of his short hair with her other hand, yanking him back to her mouth as their teeth crashed together. Now it was his turn to fumble with removing her shorts, and his own too.

She lay on her back with her knees bent together. After removing his shorts, Alex placed both hands between them, parting her legs and kissing the inside of one knee before moving up her inner thigh. But Hope wanted something else.

The other part of him. "I need you. Now."

Waves splashed on the beach as she grabbed his upper arms, pulling, and he scrambled up her body as she opened wide for him. Desire throbbed throughout her body, and sweet, tender sex was the last thing on her mind. Alex was a large, powerful man, and she wanted that side of him.

Their mouths were inches apart, both breathing the same air back and forth with their eyes locked. Sweat had broken out over his torso as Hope smelled his maleness, his unique scent, which sent more blistering heat through her.

"Hard, Alex. Now."

He gave her what she wanted.

Hope cried out and arched her back as he slammed into her, more than ready for him. She wrapped her legs around his waist, letting him in even deeper. The skin of their chests slid against each other as she gave back as hard as he was giving her.

She knew it wouldn't last long like this, and from the sounds Alex was making, he was as close as she was. The thought caused her to peak, and she bit hard onto his shoulder, trying to be mindful of their outside location, though their house was well separated from the resort.

Alex collapsed on top of her, his back a sheen of sweat as he breathed in gasps. She ran one hand across his shoulders, luxuriating in the slick feel of it.

"Oh my God, baby. I need to have a beer on the porch more often."

Hope's laughter rose, and soon they were both laughing together.

He rolled onto an elbow and frowned at his shoulder before glancing back at her. "Hey, you need to stop leaving bite marks. It makes me look unprofessional. How would you like it if I left a bunch of hickeys on your neck?"

Still grinning, she leaned forward until their faces were nearly touching. "I can cover them with makeup. Knock yourself out."

"Mmm. You're very naughty, Ms. Collins."

She gave him one final squeeze that made him yelp. "Yes, I am."

They redressed and entered the house. Hope moved to a wicker basket sitting on the kitchen island as Alex set down the bucket of beers.

"You going to pick mangoes?" he asked.

"Maybe later, after it cools down a bit."

There were two large mango trees in their front yard, one with a healthy crop currently ripening. She had ignored them last year, overwhelmed by the work of taking over the resort. But she had been fully enjoying its bounty recently, which had led to her adventures in baking, including the mango tartlets she had been perfecting.

Just as Hope reached to move the basket, the first twisting pain in her abdomen came, and she closed her eyes. "Oh, shit."

"What's wrong?"

She started giggling. "I guess actions have consequences. My period just started."

Alex's look of concern turned to a smile he tried but failed to hide. "I'd say I was sorry, but I'd be lying."

She laced her fingers around his neck. "Agreed. It was worth it. Why don't you open a couple of those beers? I'll be back in a minute."

After a trip to the bathroom, she returned and accepted a beer to swallow three ibuprofen tablets. Not even the growing ache could dampen her wonderful mood. "Today's been an incredible day." She brushed her lips over his. "I love you."

Alex brushed a lock of hair from her brow. "I love you too. A year ago was one of the most important days in our lives. We just didn't know it."

CHAPTER 5

A week later, gentle morning light shined through the double windows of Hope's home office as she sat at her desk, sorting a pile of business mail. The first envelope was from the St. Croix County Treasurer, and Hope was highly suspicious it was her property-tax bill. She immediately moved it to the bottom of the stack.

Next was an envelope from her insurance agent, so she opened that one and was rewarded for her courage. It was a final, delayed settlement check for the hurricane damage. Smiling, she set that on a desk tray to be deposited later. Eventually, she worked through the whole pile except for the ominous treasurer envelope. With a deep sigh, she opened it.

Hope read the letter three times, her pulse pounding louder in her ears with each read through.

"This can't be right."

Patti had paid the taxes for the previous year, so Hope hadn't seen them until now. The amount was outrageous. She ran her finger down the letter once again, pausing at the property-size listing and narrowing her eyes. She'd never investigated how much land she owned but had always guessed it was ten to fifteen acres. This letter described it as more than fifty.

She leaned her forehead on the heel of her hand.

Had Steve and Patti been overpaying the property taxes for years because the stupid county entered the acreage wrong?

She stood up, turning to the tall filing cabinet behind her as she tapped her fingers on her crossed arms. "I know that plat map was in here somewhere when I went through everything after I first arrived."

With a shudder, a vivid scene came to mind of the mess the former owner, Steve Jackson, had left when he'd exited the island unannounced the night before her arrival. Even though she had organized everything in the filing cabinet, there were still four drawers to investigate. Pulling open the top drawer, she got to work.

Half an hour later, she slammed the drawer shut with a curse. Cruz lifted his head, giving her a doggy frown for interrupting his nap. She stood up to stretch her cramped legs, her muscles protesting after her thirty-minute treadmill run in the resort fitness center. As soon as she'd seen the insurance check, she had mentally spent it—on new fitness equipment. The current equipment needed replacing, plus she could get an additional treadmill installed here in the house and alleviate her guilt about tying up guest machines.

Hope walked around the office, shaking out her legs while glaring at the filing cabinet. Finally, with a groan, she sank back down and opened the bottom drawer. She flipped through one file after another, growing more frustrated with each passing second.

She skipped right past the document before some part of her mind started ringing alarm bells.

Hope's heart leapt as she froze, then thumbed back a few files until she found it. With a loud whoop that sent Cruz into a tizzy of barking, she pulled the plat map out of the drawer and returned to her desk. She inspected the oversized piece of paper for the next ten minutes. Finally, she sat back in her chair, stunned.

The tax assessment was correct.

Her property was fifty acres. The oceanfront parcel was roughly twenty, but the majority of the property was on the eastern side of the highway—over thirty acres. The mountains rose steeply on that side of the road, but there had to be some good, flat land there.

"Huh, how about that? Not all oceanfront, but still a very nice bonus I didn't know about."

Cruz cocked his head, and she returned his look. "What do you say? You up for a little adventure?"

He woofed and wagged his tail, which she took as enthusiastic support.

Fifteen minutes later, Hope walked out the front door dressed in hiking shoes and long pants and covered in a cloud of insect repellant. She walked down the resort road to the highway with Cruz trotting at her side. As they approached the busy road, Hope frowned at him—she'd never attempted to put a collar or leash on him. The dog was edgy, and she didn't want to push it.

But crossing the highway was another matter. She stopped, and he obediently sat down in front of her, tongue lolling as he looked up at her. Hope scooped him into her arms and marched across the highway during a break in traffic.

"I'm glad you're not a big dog. At least I can carry you. You stay away from the road, ok?"

She put him down on the other side and walked along the edge of the jungle, parallel to the road. Cruz loped ahead of her, then turned into the foliage and disappeared. Hope followed and discovered a faint path, really just bent grass and a thinning of the foliage, leading into the jungle.

As good a place as any, I guess.

She turned to follow him. Once out of the sunlight, the temperature dropped and the humidity increased. Cool beads of sweat ran down Hope's back. She tried not to think what animal might have made the trail, or if she was about to come face-to-face with a wild boar or something else equally terrifying.

Then she relaxed, confident Cruz would alert her to any danger. He was having a wonderful time, confidently bounding ahead over the vines and fallen trees covering the path, and she was enjoying the adventure too. He scrambled up a sizeable fallen tree blocking the path and stood on top, surveying his domain. He glanced at her, then hopped to the far side. She followed, climbing over the fallen tree herself.

They continued for nearly half a mile as the jungle closed in around them. Hope brushed vines out of the way, petrified of stepping on a snake. She was far from the highway now, and unease prickled down her spine.

No one knew she was here.

She'd watched local-news reports about the drug activity in the Caribbean and had experienced an attempted armed robbery firsthand. With effort, she pushed the thought away.

I'm safe on my own property, for heaven's sake.

She was thinking about turning around when the tree line ahead thinned out. The path opened into a large clearing, and as she took a long drink of water from the bottle she carried, her misgivings were forgotten.

They were replaced by sheer wonder.

In front of her was an enormous natural pool of water, Cruz lapping at its edge. The pool was surrounded by large boulders for most of its perimeter, but the area directly ahead had a gentle, sandy entry. "Well, I guess that explains the animal track. This is a great source of water, and it must be fresh."

Hope approached and inspected the water, which was a vivid blue and extremely clear. The rock formations continued underwater, and the pool looked deep. The side opposite her was around fifty feet away, and the pool was nearly two hundred feet long. The area was silent except for the occasional birdsong and exuded a peaceful aura. Ample sunlight drifted in, creating a perfect temperature.

To her left, the rock formations rose into a sheer, dark gray wall that was part of a bigger hillside, but there was no waterfall or other source of water for the pool. She started toward the rock wall, trying to keep to the edge of the clearing so she didn't need to scramble over the boulders. She only got halfway before the jungle butted right up against the rocks.

Hope inspected the gray wall. Moss grew abundantly, and rivulets of water ran down it, turning it nearly black. Then she saw something else.

It wasn't solid.

There was a considerable black opening in the middle of the rock face that plummeted straight into the pool. She studied it but couldn't find any way to access the cave except through the water.

Taking in the scene in front of her, a smile spread across her face. "This is amazing! What an incredible spot."

Hope picked her way back to the sandy beach entry and removed her socks and shoes. She took a few steps into the water, surprised how cool it was, but it had a wonderful effect on her hot feet as she wiggled her toes in the sand.

Still smiling, a thought occurred to her. "Alex would *love* this. I need to come back with him."

A colorful blue and yellow bird flitted over the still surface, and Hope swept her gaze around the tranquil, remote pool, the possibilities of her lucky discovery turning over in her head. Which were quickly replaced by possibilities involving Alex and their own private oasis.

Cruz had curled up on the sand and closed his eyes. Hope left the water, sitting on one of the big flat rocks and swiping the sand off her feet before replacing her footwear. "Sorry, Cruz. It's not naptime yet. Back we go."

He popped his head up at his name, and as she started toward the trail, he jumped up to take his place in front of her. From the way the dog acted on their little trek, he had likely already discovered the pool. She didn't like the idea of him crossing the highway.

But who knows where you lived before you found me?

It was already 3 p.m. when she opened the front door, greeted with a welcome blast of air-conditioning. Sweat saturated her clothes, and she peeled the collar of her shirt away, curling her lip. "Yuck. Shower first, for sure." Cruz hurried to his water bowl as she headed into the master suite to get cleaned up.

After dressing in a floral sundress, she took a glass of iced tea onto the back porch as Cruz trotted down the stairs to the sand. She was standing at the open windows when a voice came from the beach. Alex bent to rub Cruz's belly as the dog lay at his feet, tail thumping. "Hey there, buddy. How are you doing?" Alex had a big smile on his face. Hope laughed quietly, enjoying the sight. She leaned against the window frame as Alex approached.

I'll never tire of looking at him.

He moved with a strong, graceful confidence, and she responded just to the sight of him. Smile lingering, he climbed the stairs onto the porch and saw her. As their eyes locked, his smile faded, and without a word, they crossed to each other for a long, delicious kiss.

Eventually, he moved his mouth to her hair and inhaled deeply. "You smell incredible. How do you do that?"

"It's no mystery. I just got out of the shower." She rested the side of her head against his chest, taking a breath of her own. "You smell pretty good yourself."

"I had a refresher this afternoon, and they wanted to do it in the ocean, not the pool, so I showered after." He broke their embrace and led her over to the patio couch. "Think my days of that are numbered, though, with the spa open. I was lucky it was empty this late—no way I'm showering with other people around."

"Sorry to disrupt your routine. I just love Selena. She gave me a massage yesterday. The guests are going to love her!"

Cruz padded to his bed and sat down. Pointing a hind leg in the air, he started licking his testicles. Hope frowned at him. "I really need to make an appointment to get you neutered."

Alex crossed his legs. "I sincerely hope you're talking to the dog right now."

Her frown was replaced by a smirk as she turned to him, his hands clasped protectively over his lap. "Yours can stay. I've grown rather fond of them just where they are."

"Good. So have I."

They shared a laugh as Alex put his feet on the coffee table. Three white pelicans flew by at the waterline, but Cruz was too engrossed with his ministrations to bark at them. "I suppose I should wait a bit more on the vet appointment," Hope said. "I don't want him running off now that he's finally settled in."

"Well, that would do it." Alex breathed out an easy sigh. "Tomorrow's my day off, and I'm really looking forward to it. You know, I never cared about days off before you came into my life—the more I worked, the better. Maybe we can do something fun."

He widened his eyes as she started laughing, both hands over her mouth. "What?"

"Funny you should say that. I think I can deliver on your request." Hope pursed her lips to keep from spilling the beans. "I have a surprise for you, but you're going to have to wait until tomorrow morning. I'll tell you this, though. You and I are going on a little adventure."

Leaning his face to hers, Alex drilled into her with his eyes. "Is that right? I'm looking forward to it." He traced a finger from the hollow of her neck to her breasts. "But what if I don't want to wait until tomorrow for an adventure?"

"Well, I think we can come to an interim arrangement until then."

CHAPTER 6

After they finished breakfast the next morning, Alex headed for the shower while Hope straightened the kitchen. She was loading the dishwasher when he called out behind her.

"So, am I dressed appropriately for our adventure?"

He stood there naked, both arms held out from his sides as she laughed, leaning against the counter. "Although I'm enjoying the view immensely, after my prior investigation, I think shorts and a T-shirt would be fine—definitely bring some swim trunks. And solid footwear too."

"Combat boots, maybe?"

"That might be overkill. I think sneakers or hiking shoes will suffice." When he came back fully dressed, she was putting the final touches on a picnic lunch.

Alex broke into an enormous smile. "Oh, a picnic! Now we're talking. Did you get the bottle of champagne too?" He came up behind her, resting his hands on her hips as he peeked over her shoulder.

Hope raised the knife she was using to cut the sandwiches.

"Mr. Monroe, you need to behave yourself. This is strictly a precautionary measure. I don't know if we'll need it or not."

He grabbed the knife out of her hand, setting it on the counter out of her reach and nuzzling her neck. "Hmmm. Are you planning on us working up an appetite?"

"You didn't hear a word I said about behaving, did you?"

"Of course I did. Why do you think I took the knife away from you?"

Hope slapped his arm before packing their lunch into a backpack. Then they both applied insect repellent. "I'll even carry the food this time." She held up the backpack.

"Not a chance." Alex grabbed it from her. "At least let me be a gentleman and carry the backpack."

Hope stopped and leveled her gaze at him. "Oh, Alex. I think you've proven you can be very un-gentlemanly when the situation calls for it." She smiled as she circled her hair into a messy bun. "But you're welcome to carry the backpack. Come on, Cruz!"

Alex opened the front door for her, and the dog trotted along at their heels.

"We're bringing the dog?" He looked down as Cruz smiled up at him.

"Oh yes. He was instrumental in this discovery. Let's go. We're burning daylight."

"We're walking?"

"Yes, we're going on a little hike. That's why I said you needed good footwear." She took hold of his hand as they walked up the narrow road toward the highway. "Did you know the resort property includes a huge parcel on the other side of the highway?"

"I never heard Steve talk about it. I wouldn't know anything about that. I just work here."

"Oh, don't give me any of your 'I'm just a lowly employee' crap."

He laughed as Cruz ran in a circle around them. "Trust me.

Steve never discussed any of the financial aspects of the resort with me. I have no idea how big the property is."

Hope explained her investigation leading to the discovery of the other property parcel, and Alex gave a low whistle.

"I admit, that's intriguing." He lowered his brows. "I'm not sure you should have gone off exploring on your own, though."

Hope shrugged and they continued.

Mr. Protective . . .

Soon they reached the highway, Hope picking up Cruz as they crossed the road and turned to the north. After she put him back down, the dog once again ran ahead and disappeared down the overgrown path.

"Here it is. We go down this path a half mile or so."

Alex stood still in front of her. She started to move around him, but he held his arm out, blocking her movement.

"Hold on a second. Let me look this over."

"Alex, I went down this in both directions yesterday. I promise, there are no booby traps. We're next to the highway, for crying out loud."

He frowned at her. "I'll go first."

"Fine, go right ahead."

They entered the jungle, and once again, the temperature dropped and the humidity skyrocketed. It was also much quieter and darker, but even that couldn't tamp down her impatience. He was going to love the pool!

Come on, Alex! Hurry up.

He made nearly no sound as he slowly moved in front of her with light, balanced steps, his head on a swivel. No doubt she sounded like a herd of elephants by comparison. She fanned the neck of her shirt as sweat dripped down her back.

Cruz bounded back down the path to them, apparently not pleased with Alex's deliberate progress.

"He wants to know why you're so slow, Alex."

"Tell him I'm making sure there's nothing suspicious here."

Hope rolled her eyes but held her tongue.

They crept on, Alex completely silent, until finally they came to the large fallen tree she had scrambled over yesterday. But he just stood and assessed it, studying the area carefully. They were far from the highway now, and the jungle around them was silent except for the occasional bird. It was humid and oppressing as steam rose from the plants.

Hope lost her patience. "I scrambled over this tree twice—it's solid as a rock. Would you please get a move on already?"

Alex spun around, his eyes narrowed and his mouth a thin slash.

She stepped back, shocked at his change in mood.

"Hope, you can't just go wandering around in the jungle by yourself. You live on an island in the Caribbean. God only knows who you could have run into out here! This is just the kind of terrain drug runners like to hide out in. I didn't realize you'd been hiking down a damn animal track in the middle of nowhere. You should have *never* come out here alone!"

Hope held both hands up, trying to control her irritation. "It's fine—I was perfectly safe. I'm not some damsel in distress you have to constantly save, you know. It's broad daylight with no shabby buildings in sight. Let's move on."

If anything, that made him more tense. He towered over her, hands on his hips as he spoke through clenched teeth. "We're hell and gone from the highway now. Look, you have no idea what people are capable of—people who could be on this island at this very moment. And I will do my best to make sure you never find out."

He stared at her, breathing hard. "We're not taking another step from here until you *promise* you'll never come out here again without me."

Hope stood there dumbfounded, staring up at him. As much as she didn't want to admit it, she'd had the same thought yesterday about the danger. Maybe he had a point. "Ok, I promise."

Alex was a man who took promises very seriously.

The tension eased as he clutched her into a tight embrace. "I love you so much. I need to keep you safe." He kissed her deeply, then pushed her back and met her eyes with a steel gaze. "I spent *years* of my life witnessing the absolute worst of humanity. I can't bear to think what might have happened if you'd come across some assholes out here."

Her breath hitched in her chest as she blinked rapidly. "I'm sorry. I just wanted to have a fun adventure with you."

Alex drew back, closing his eyes before taking a deep breath. When he opened them again, they were much softer. "I know. Let's keep going. So far I haven't seen any signs of people except the trail you left yesterday. We're safe."

He turned around and vaulted over the fallen tree in a single jump before turning and helping her scramble over it.

They continued down the path, Alex moving at the same slow, deliberate pace, with Hope just behind. Only now, instead of a grand adventure, Hope saw threat and danger in the close foliage around her, though she still couldn't decide if Alex was being overprotective or if she was underestimating the danger.

Unbidden, an image of Charles stepping out of the shadows of the alley rose to her mind. It was quickly followed by the memory of him reaching for her throat in the courtroom, and she fought back a shiver. Alex had intervened both times, though she'd kept Charles at bay the second time until he'd reached her. She firmly pushed the images away.

As they continued, Hope got hold of herself, and her natural eagerness to show Alex the pool reasserted itself. He would see the possibilities immediately. The trees thinned ahead and she stopped.

"Alex." He turned around, and she gave him a hopeful smile. "What I wanted to show you is just ahead."

He held out his hand. When she took it, he moved her in front of him, facing the clearing. He wrapped both arms around her shoulders, pulling her back against him.

"We'll see it together. I know this means a lot to you." He squeezed her, kissing her neck. "I'm sorry I snapped at you." Then he looked forward, resting his chin on the top of her head. "Whatever it is, it must be big from the size of the clearing ahead."

"It is. Let's go."

They entered the clearing as he took her hand, and they approached the pool together. Hope didn't say anything as Alex evaluated the area, his eyes in constant motion. Appearing satisfied for the moment, he stepped forward and turned his attention to the pool. They stopped at the sandy beach, just shy of the water's edge.

"The pool is really big, and it's deep," Hope said. "Look over to the left. There's a cave, and I think it's only accessible from the water."

Alex turned toward her, a smile growing on his face. "Ok, you're right. This is pretty spectacular." He put a hand on her shoulder. "Wait here, ok? I'm going to check around the pool perimeter." She nodded as he shrugged off the backpack and edged away.

Alex scrambled onto the rocks on the far side and worked his way to the vertical rock wall. He stood still, inspecting the cave entrance for several minutes. After returning to the sandy beach, he repeated the maneuver on the opposite side, approaching the cave from the left this time.

His posture was less tense now. He returned and jumped off the last boulder onto the sand. "I didn't see any signs of people, so I don't think anyone's been here for a long time. Just some animal tracks around—a lot of what look like dog tracks. And you're right. There's no way into the cave except through the water."

He climbed onto a flat boulder nearby and hunkered down on

his heels, just studying the pool and cave. Hope smiled, watching his tactical mind turn over the possibilities and scenarios. He chewed his bottom lip, excitement growing on his face.

After several minutes, he stood up and hopped off the rock. He returned to Hope, his smile getting bigger the closer he got to her.

He didn't slow down as he got close, and she shuffled backwards, a grin spreading across her face.

His face lit up. "Oh, no you don't. You're not going anywhere."

Laughing, he lunged out and embraced her, then bent her over backwards in his arms and gave her a blistering kiss. Hope giggled, sure they looked just like the photo of the World War II sailor and his sweetheart. She appreciated the symbolism.

He broke off the kiss, his eyes on fire. "I can't *wait* to dive this!"

"Well, that was my first thought when I found it, but I was thinking maybe a swim today might be nice?"

CHAPTER 7

Hope wore her swimsuit under her clothing and Alex already had his board shorts on, so they quickly got ready for their swim. Though more at ease now, he was still alert, moving his eyes around the area. She quickly gave up on her idea of repeating their picnic at Horseshoe Key. With a sigh, she understood now that their previous idyll happened because Alex was very familiar with the islet.

Hope dove into the pool, shocked at the chilly temperature, especially compared to the ocean.

"My guess is it's spring fed, coming up from the bedrock," Alex said. "Come on, let's check out that cave."

The dim interior was even more chilly. A sheer wall plunged into the water on their left, but a series of stepped ledges led from the water on the right side. The cave was much bigger than it appeared from outside. They treaded water in the middle, and Alex craned his head around, examining it.

"I don't think Steve knew about this," he said. "He would have asked me to investigate it. It could be a real draw for guests too. The tricky part would be controlling access, so not just anyone could get in here."

"I thought about that too." Hope swam to him and laced her fingers around his neck as Alex darted his eyes back to hers. "But I like the idea of just keeping it between us for now." She drew closer and gave him a long kiss.

"Oh, me too." He went back for more, then pulled back with concern. Her teeth were chattering, and he swiped a finger down her nose. "Come on, let's get back in the sunlight before you freeze."

Hope didn't argue and swam toward the bright light. When they reached the middle of the pool, she flipped over on her back with a happy sigh, the sun once again bathing her in its warmth. Alex gazed down into the clear water below.

"How deep do you think it is?" Hope asked.

"I wish I had a mask, but I'd guess at least forty feet."

"I actually thought about bringing one today but didn't want to give too much away."

He turned a delighted grin to her. "My rebreather will be perfect for exploring this! Come on, let's get out."

Once out of the cool water, Hope removed her towel from the backpack and wrapped it around herself, teeth chattering. Alex enfolded her tightly, turning them in a slow circle as he rubbed her upper back.

Hope sighed, her eyes closed and her head resting against his chest as she absorbed his warmth. "I'd like to think you're being romantic right now, slow dancing with your girl. But I bet you're looking around as I speak, making sure no one's sneaking up on us."

"Ok, you caught me." He laughed, giving her a quick kiss. "But it's still romantic."

"Do you want to go back now, maybe have our picnic on the beach?"

"No, I want to stay right here. You found a great spot." He picked up the backpack and soon they had their lunch spread out with a nice view of the pool, though Alex kept the boulders at their backs.

"I'm afraid my sandwiches aren't in the same league as Baxter's," she said with a laugh, referencing the sweet restaurant owner she had purchased *Surface Interval* from. "And there's no champagne. Just water."

Alex smiled at her, his eyes sultry as he ran them down her body. "We'll just have to save the champagne for another time." He picked up a grape and popped it into her mouth. "When we get back, can I look at that plat map? I'd like to reconnoiter the whole parcel before I come back with my dive gear. I want to make sure there's no one around."

"Sure. It's still on my office desk." That reminded her of the filing cabinet in her office and the disaster she'd inherited when she arrived. "You mentioned Steve earlier. Do you think about him?"

Alex widened his eyes. "No. Why should I?"

"You told me the two of you were close." She shrugged. "He left me with a mess when I arrived, but he kind of betrayed you by disappearing during the night. It would be natural to think about it once in a while."

"He's long gone, and I doubt we'll ever hear from him again. For his sake, I hope not." He turned his gaze back to Hope. "And why are we talking about Steve, anyway?"

She handed him the rest of her sandwich. "I guess there are more exciting things, aren't there? Like that big cave over there. Too bad you don't have another day off for a bit. I can't wait to get in there. When you're ready to dive, we're bringing an extra tank for me, right?"

"Not right away. Maybe after I check it out and determine it's safe, we'll talk about it."

Her expectant mood fell like a landslide. Alex turned to her, serious now as he pointed back to the cave. "Look, that is a wet cave over there. A totally *unknown* cave. This is just about the most dangerous situation in diving. You're not going anywhere near it until I check it out first."

Her blood pressure rose even as Alex held a hand up. "And before you get your hackles up, I'm not just saying that because I love you and am being protective. Cave diving can be deadly. I wouldn't let *anyone* else near that cave right now without the proper credentials."

She wasn't happy but couldn't argue with his logic. Trying to moderate her scowl, she said, "And I suppose you have those proper credentials?"

Alex cracked a smile, but it fell from his face. "Yes. This isn't the first unfamiliar cave I've been in. Wet or dry." His attention drifted to the black opening, his eyes far away. "At least this time I'm fairly confident there's no one inside waiting for me."

Their walk back to the resort was more relaxed than the outbound trip. Alex was still alert, sweeping his head back and forth as Hope walked behind him. When she'd started their trek by stepping in front of him, he'd gently grasped her upper arm, saying, "I'll take point," and moved in front of her. He'd said it casually, without thought. This type of situation came up between them from time to time.

It was a stark reminder that their former lives had been very different.

After her disastrous relationship with Caleb, Hope had walled herself off, going through the motions of life in a fruitless effort to keep safe. At the same time, Alex had spent long stretches in covert operations overseas, and she would likely never understand all he had experienced. His trauma was much more recent than hers, partly the reason she was able to help him. She had the advantage of distance and time from her ordeal, giving her perspective.

It was their only source of friction—her need to prove she

wasn't under any man's thumb against his deep commitment to protect her, even at the cost of his own safety. Hope widened her lips into a smile as he walked alertly ahead of her.

A couple could have worse problems.

CHAPTER 8

Alex tried to concentrate on the BCD spread open before him, but finally sat back with a relaxed sigh at the blast of cool air hitting his back. The air conditioner installed near his workbench was heaven. A few days ago, he'd returned from the morning dive trip to Hope bouncing on the balls of her feet as she waited for him under the palapa. She'd grabbed his hand and practically dragged him to the gear room, her face nearly splitting from her smile.

They'd walked into the dim room, and she'd moved to a freshly installed modular air-conditioning unit high on one wall and already cooling the stifling area. "Ta-da! I thought this would make equipment repairs more comfortable."

The room had always been stuffy and miserable to work in, even with the single window open. But Alex had never considered adding an air-conditioning unit. He stared at it, stunned.

Hope's face fell. "You don't like it?"

He turned to her, swallowing a lump in his throat. "Like it? I *love* it."

It made an enormous difference to his work environment, but he'd needed Hope to realize it.

After basking in the cool air, he shook himself and got back to work, quickly getting the sticky inflator valve fixed. He placed the BCD back on its hanger, then turned back to his workbench. He zeroed in on his phone and sat back down.

I should make that call now.

But his mind was still full of Hope, and he turned his attention to the shelf mounted above his workbench. On both ends were several three-ring binders full of schematics for servicing scuba equipment, but Alex's eyes were drawn to the large brown and aqua glass octopus sculpture displayed front and center.

The octopus was Hope's birthday gift to him during a hasty, impromptu celebration caused by Charles's trial being moved up. A celebration she had felt terribly guilty about for some reason. As if Alex cared about birthdays anymore. Forty-one was old enough to stop being excited by another year.

They'd shared a dinner at the restaurant, and after returning to the house, Hope had presented him with the octopus. She frequently passed by a glass artisan's shop in Frederiksted, and one day last month she'd gone in and commissioned the glass octopus for Alex.

It was a beautiful work of art, the colors blending seamlessly to suggest the color-shifting properties of the animal. It was presented propped up on its eight legs, each one in a slightly different position.

Alex placed his elbow on the workbench, resting his chin in his palm as he examined the implications of the sculpture. The years after he'd arrived on St. Croix had been a dark time, and he had spent years with no female companionship—of the intimate type, anyway. He'd started rubbing his right hip without thinking about it and snorted, pulling his hand away.

Yet here he was now, living with Hope.

After scraping back his chair, Alex stood and stroked a finger over one of the octopus's smooth cool legs, then stepped outside. He breathed in the salty air as he walked down the wooden pier, grateful for the lessons of a simple birthday gift. Alex kept the octopus prominently displayed so he could remember what a lucky man he was. Especially since there were times he hadn't felt very lucky recently.

After spending five years trying to bury the pain of the disaster in Syria, Hope had helped him tremendously in starting to face it. But just last month, an inquisitive reporter had uncovered it and printed an article for the whole island to see. By sheer force of will and love, Hope prevented him from surrendering to despair. Her words had poured into his soul as he'd clung to the kitchen countertop, literally hanging on to keep it together.

They were engraved indelibly in his memory.

"A year ago, you saved me from drowning," Hope had said, staring deep into him. "Now it's my turn."

Ironically, the altercations with Charles, followed by Alex testifying against him, had brought vivid reminders of the man Alex had once been.

A man he'd thought was gone forever. Now he wasn't so sure.

And that was a very good thing.

Alex blinked rapidly, bringing himself back to the present as he strolled to the side of the pier and watched the fish below. Once again, the need to make that phone call nagged at him. He'd been mulling it over since Christmas, and with the trial over, there was no reason to delay any longer.

He returned to the gear room and locked the door behind him. Sitting down, Alex glanced at his octopus before picking up his phone. He opened his contacts, staring at the name. With his gut a tight ball of squirming eels, Alex pressed the green button and lifted the phone to his ear.

"Hello?"

So much came across in that simple word she uttered. Her careful tone of voice indicated Alex's name had come up as the caller. There was shock, and also fear—that something was wrong.

"Hi, Katie. It's me."

At first, there was no response, and Alex could picture her with the phone to her ear and her mouth open. "Alex? Is . . . everything ok?"

He couldn't help the nervous laughter that bubbled up. "What? You just assume something's wrong because I haven't talked to you in several years and hung up on you last time?"

"Um, yes. That's it exactly."

"Nothing's wrong, little sister. I'm calling to say I'm sorry I've been such an asshole."

The smile was clear in her answer. "Well, that is something you're an expert at."

"I'm doing better now. Trying to be less of an expert."

"I am *really* happy to hear that you're doing better." Her words came easier now, and her voice was more animated. "What's changed?"

Like a magnet, his gaze was drawn back to the octopus. "I've decided life's worth fighting for after all."

"It is. I've missed you."

"Me too. How are Dave and the kids?"

She gave him an update on her husband and two kids. In short, Katie Fletcher's life was still incredibly busy, and he was still blown away by how she managed it all. And handled her own successful career too.

"We're usually running in four different directions at the same time. So tell me, what made you decide to start living again?"

"It's been a combination of things. But I'm with someone now." Alex was almost shy as he gave her a recap of the last year and his relationship with Hope. In general terms that skipped the boat sinking and the shooting. He didn't want to dump too much on her.

"You deserve to be happy, Alex. You've carried this survivor's guilt for so long. Having a full life isn't a betrayal of your men."

"Thanks. I've had to deal with a lot the last six months, but Hope has really helped me."

"She's lucky to have you. And it sounds like that might go both ways. I'm really glad you called me, Alex." Katie sighed, and the longing in it made Alex smile. "I bet you're sitting on a white sand beach underneath a palm tree right now, aren't you?"

His smile widened. "Nope. I'm in a dark cave of a room that smells like wet neoprene. Jealous?"

"Of the beach, maybe. We haven't had a family vacation in over a year. Dave and I were just talking about taking the kids to Washington D.C. for a few days over spring break."

Alex's heart sped up. "If you guys are looking for a getaway, I might be able to help you with a location."

"Oh? Is that an offer to come visit?"

"Yes. I'd love to see you. And I'd like you to meet Hope too."

"Let me see what we can work out. I'll get back to you." There was distant shuffling, like she was writing things down. "Thank you for reaching out. It means a lot to me."

"Me too. It's time to be your big brother again. Dave's had it easy for way too long."

Warm laughter sounded from the phone. "I'll warn him."

After ending the call, Alex returned his eyes to the octopus as a slow smile crept across his face. This was the perfect way to end his day. Digging the keys out of his pocket, Alex locked up and headed home.

∽

Frederiksted was a bustling hub of activity as Hope ran through it with her usual Saturday group-run friends. She turned around to complete the six-mile run at a much slower pace than her half-marathon, but she was still pleased with the effort.

After finishing, Hope met up with Cindy and they proceeded to Tropical Bean, their usual after-run spot overlooking the pier. Hope took a sip of her iced coffee, which was wonderful after her run. "How are things? Life after Marcus going ok?"

"Yeah. Now I have no idea why I stayed with him so long. I've been out on a couple of dates, but there's nobody I'm really interested in."

"It's better not to rush into anything. Just enjoy yourself."

Cindy flicked a glance at her. "You and Alex have been together a while. You happy just livin' together?"

Hope suppressed a sigh. *At least Cindy won't pry like Sara . . .* "Yes. We're both happy with things as they are. Before Alex, I had never lived with a man, so this was a big step. I didn't make the best choices with men when I was younger, and it made me pretty gun shy."

Cindy nodded. "You've mentioned that before."

"I admit I like the idea of a happily-ever-after. Alex is all I've ever wanted—and more."

"He's pretty lucky to have you too, you know."

Hope threw her a grateful smile. "Thanks. Children are pretty much off the table for me, and he knows that. He's ok with it, and that's enough for me. A piece of paper and a ring won't change what we have together." She swallowed the lump in her throat as she said the words. Their relationship was as much a miracle to Alex as it was to her. Perhaps he was just as reluctant to break the spell.

"A good man is hard to find. Maybe someday I'll find mine. But right now work and school keep me busy enough."

"How much longer before you can get your physical therapy-assistant license?"

"Another two semesters until I graduate, then I have to pass the test. I'll keep workin' at the running store for now, but I'm startin' to think about a job in a PT office, even if it's just as a receptionist."

Hope leaned forward, warming to the subject. "A foot in the door always helps. I started at the Chicago hotel as a front-desk clerk and made my way up to front-desk manager. I thought I'd keep climbing the corporate ladder there, but instead I'm here in the Caribbean. You just never know where life will take you."

∽

Hope and Alex ate dinner outside, and she filled in pauses in the conversation as he stared at the ocean, furrowing his brow occasionally. She gave him a quick recap of her day. "It seems like Cindy is getting along just fine without Marcus."

Alex pushed food around on his plate, staring at the tablecloth before lifting his head. "Sorry, what?"

"You've been preoccupied all evening. Is something wrong?"

A corner of his mouth quirked, and he squeezed her hand. "I'm sorry. Nothing's wrong. It's actually a good thing." He took a big swig of beer before darting a glance at her. "I called Katie."

Hope nearly fell off her chair. "Your sister Katie? How long has it been?"

"It was the first time we've spoken in a couple of years—we've texted on and off. The last time we talked, I shut her down." A red flush crept up his neck. "I've felt bad about it ever since, and now it's time to make amends. She really tried to help me after I came back to the States . . . I made it hard for her."

"Did your call go ok?"

He smiled. "Yeah, it did. I apologized and explained I was doing better now. I told her about you. It was good to talk again, and her family's doing well. Jason's twelve now, and Monica is nine. Her husband, Dave, is a vice president at some biotech company in Baltimore." He met Hope's eyes again, staring steadily. "I asked if they'd be interested in coming down for a visit."

"That's a great idea! How long has it been since you've seen her?"

He fidgeted in his seat before setting his fork down. "Not since I moved here. It's been a long time."

"Do you want them to stay in the house, or should I block a bungalow for them?"

"I think it would be pretty crowded in the house with all of us, and they'd probably like their own space. Let's plan on a bungalow. She's going to get back to me, but she was thinking about coming down for a few days during spring break in April."

"Well, let me know the dates they're interested in. Spring break is a busy week, but I don't care. We'll make this work."

CHAPTER 9

April...

Golden morning sunshine streamed through the wall of windows as Hope and Alex re-entered the house through the slider after finishing breakfast. It was his day off and he'd eaten a huge meal to prepare for exploring, nearly vibrating with anticipation throughout.

Alex headed straight for their bedroom to change while Hope retrieved her laptop from the office and sat at the kitchen table. She verified the dates for Katie and her family's visit, less than two weeks away. As soon as Alex had told her about their visit, she'd blocked the availability of a bungalow with two beds for several weeks. Now that their dates were finalized, she released the unneeded days. They had just bought their flights, and Hope was excited to meet them, though Alex looked worried when they discussed it.

But he wasn't worried now.

She looked up, widening her eyes as Alex entered the kitchen, tucking something into the back of his pants as he pulled his shirt down. "When you said recon mission, you weren't kidding, were you?" A laugh escaped as she took in his olive-green T-shirt and camouflage pants. At least he had hiking shoes on, not combat boots.

"Dress for success, right?" he said with a smile.

"And what would be a successful mission today, exactly?"

He put on a baseball hat and added a pair of sunglasses to the brim. "Finding nothing, that's what."

"How long do you think you'll be?"

Alex moved to the kitchen table and opened a plastic bag, transferring a length of climbing rope and several other strange objects into his backpack. "Most of the day, I'm sure. Sometime in the afternoon. I'm bringing my phone, so I'll text you when I'm heading back."

"Thank you. Are you planning on climbing mountains today?" She was trying not to laugh. "Climbing rope?"

He shrugged into his backpack, a small smile cracking his face. "You know how I feel about being prepared."

"I do. Give me a kiss goodbye."

He did. A very thorough one.

"Be careful!" she said to his retreating form.

"Yes, ma'am."

Then he was gone.

She couldn't help feeling a bit left out that Alex got to explore the land around the cave, though she understood his reasoning. And she would only slow him down.

Climbing rope? "Not exactly my area of expertise," she muttered.

There was no doubt Alex had skills she didn't. Not for the first time, her thoughts took off as she imagined him performing heroics as a SEAL. Eventually, she brought herself back to the present and shut her laptop. She didn't have much on her schedule for today workwise, but there were a few projects to fill her day.

Maybe I should tackle the closet.

After Alex had moved in following the hurricane, Hope had quickly cleared a large section of the master closet for him. Many of his clothes had already been there, but she wanted to make sure he had his own space. Now her things were jumbled together, and she'd wanted to reorganize her part for some time but kept putting it off.

Hope entered the bedroom and leaned against the doorframe of the closet. Looking at his side, she smirked at the few pairs of pants he had. She'd been here months before realizing he even owned them since he was always in shorts. All his clothing was neatly arranged. Hope had always been organized herself, which was why her portion of the closet bothered her. But in the neatness department, Alex might have her beat.

Her smirk turned to a full smile at the sight of a zipped garment bag in the far corner, next to a built-in dresser they split the use of. Hope had been treated to the rare sight of Alex pulling on a suit jacket prior to the trial. She'd also glimpsed some old Navy uniforms behind the suit jacket—a flash of camo, dress blue, and white.

Her eyes were drawn to the floor on his side. Alex kept several boxes tucked into the corner under the garment bag and two were pulled out now, as if he'd needed something in the stack this morning. Hope had never been compelled to snoop through his things, but couldn't help being drawn to the two boxes sitting out in the open.

The bottom one was a flattened rectangular box made of a dull-gray metal, about three feet long by two feet wide. It was padlocked shut. Above it was a somewhat smaller box, also rectangular, made of the solid, light-colored material she recognized as being waterproof and fireproof. There was a lock on it, but no key was inserted.

Hope hesitated.

Alex was a private person, yet she couldn't stop her curiosity. She knelt in front of the boxes, fully expecting the top one to be locked.

It wasn't.

She opened the heavy, protective lid, and her breath caught. She scanned from left to right across a jumble of items. There were two official Navy photos of Alex, and an assortment of large jewelry-type hinged boxes took up the right side of the box. She'd seen him brooding over two of these—and the medals contained within—after a conversation they'd had about his education and officer status.

She picked up one box at random. A sizeable gold pin of an eagle with spread wings carrying a trident in its talons was nestled inside, and she smiled. It looked like the Budweiser beer symbol.

Hope closed the box and picked up another, revealing his Purple Heart. Her breath hitched as she regarded it for a long moment. She'd never completely understand what he'd been through.

She opened another box to reveal Alex's Navy Cross.

Hope shook her head. This was the highest honor bestowed by the Navy. Alex had never felt he deserved it, though she couldn't feel more differently.

There were more boxes, but she put the medal back and turned her attention to the two eight-by-ten photos of Alex, a smile spreading across her face. His hair was very short. He'd always kept himself neat and clean, but he had a military haircut in these pictures. And his hair was much darker in both. The sun had bleached it substantially since moving to the island.

Hope picked up the one on the left, an official photo of a young Alex, and her smile widened. Without a line on his face, he was seated in a Navy blue-dress uniform in front of an American flag and a Navy flag, his hands clasped on a table in front of him. His left breast held a bar of ribbons with a gold pin above and below. Hope sharpened her gaze. The upper pin was the eagle pin in the box she'd just held. She stared at his eyes—his look of pride was unmistakable.

He's so young!

Still smiling, she put it back and picked up the one next to it. It was a very similar pose, but now Alex was older. This picture must have been taken within a year or two of his injury. Many more ribbons now, rows of them, and the same two pins above and below. He now had a star and several gold stripes on his lower sleeves.

"Well, hello there, Commander Monroe. You don't look so bad."

She moved her gaze to his face. This was more like her Alex, and a warmth swelled through her as she brushed two fingers down the picture. His eyes still held a look of pride, but now there was a weariness there too, as if he was thinking, *time to do photos again?*

Hope started to put the picture back when she saw a third photo underneath.

She picked up this one with one hand, riveted, as she absently replaced the second back in the box.

The smile fell off her face, and her heart began pounding.

This eight by ten was more of a candid photo. Taken at night, it was a close-up from head to mid-chest. The man wore a mass of tactical scuba equipment, nearly all his exposed skin enclosed. His head was covered by a neoprene hood, and he wore a dark exposure suit with a rubber neck seal and a valve in the middle of the chest with an attached hose.

An enormous regulator mouthpiece covered his mouth, and large black corrugated hoses on both sides led to a rectangular black canister on his back. She recognized it as a rebreather. The regulator was part of a full-face mask which completely covered his face. His eyes were the only identifiable part of the man in the photo.

But Hope would know those crystal blue eyes anywhere.

Just as clearly, this man wasn't *her* Alex.

He glowered at the camera. His eyes were cold and deadly, shooting daggers of freezing menace. She broke out in gooseflesh, and a fine sheen of sweat formed. A trickle ran down her back, causing a shiver.

The photographer was very talented—the image was beautifully presented. Taken in ambient moonlight, bright stars lit the sky behind his head, and one side of his mask reflected the pale light. Several inches of a rifle extended into the picture along the left side of Alex's chest.

Inexorably, she drew her gaze back to those eyes.

The piercing intensity of his stare and its lethal intent made her blood run cold. This was a man ready for battle and whatever he might face, completely confident in his abilities.

Enemies didn't stand a chance.

Hope had seen the barest glimpse of this man in the courtroom. The full version was before her now. A veteran SEAL at the pinnacle of his career—ready and willing to kill for what he believed in.

Hope couldn't focus on the photo. Her hands shuddered so badly she couldn't hold it steady, and her heart nearly pounded out of her chest. She rushed the photo back to the box where she had found it.

Slamming the lid down, she wrapped her arms around herself and sat on her knees, taking frantic, gasping breaths.

CHAPTER 10

Hope scrambled to the corner of the closet, curling into a ball as she pounded her hands on the carpeted floor. Each huge breath made a loud, whooshing gasp as her heart raged. Her vision narrowed to a dim tunnel, so she closed her eyes tightly.

"Stop it, stop it, STOP IT!"

She screamed the last two words, wrenching her throat. Digging her fingernails into her palms, she beat both fists on her thighs as sweat rolled down her back. She hadn't had a panic attack in years and wasn't going to start now.

"He's not Caleb!"

No, he's a thousand times more dangerous.

"You know he would never hurt you. You *know* that!"

Distantly, Cruz barked outside the sliding glass door. Her screaming must have been loud. She swallowed, her throat dry and strained.

With her eyes clamped shut, Hope concentrated on taking deep, slow breaths, and the panic subsided. She dug her fingernails in more, focusing on the distracting pain.

Calm. Calm—you know *him.*

Finally, she opened her eyes, and her gaze immediately fell on Alex's box. Gritting her teeth, she growled and scrabbled back to it, flipping up the lid again. She grasped the photo of the older Alex in uniform—*her* Alex—and raised onto her knees above it. She held on to it, gripping it with both hands as her fingers became whiter.

Hope stared at his face while taking deep, slow breaths. She studied every angle, every nuance. Her body calmed as she studied the picture, focusing her entire being on this man she loved. Though this man wasn't *quite* her Alex. There was a confident, almost cocky, glint in his eyes missing from the man she knew. The man in this picture hadn't been devastated by life.

She lifted the picture and set it on top of the photo of the younger Alex, so it was side by side with the nighttime photo. Looking back and forth between the two, she tried to reconcile how they were both Alex.

They are two sides of the same man. One can't exist without the other. His eyes are so different!

Eventually, her heart rate slowed, and her breathing returned to normal. Her shoulders were nearly cramping with tension. Hope sat up and stretched her arms before bending back over the box with a deep sigh, finally calm.

She could look at the nighttime photo without panic. It still gave her chills, but now her response was surely like anyone else's. It was an alarming photo—the man in that picture would scare anyone.

Even though Hope had seen a hint of him during the trial, there was a yawning chasm between Alex in a courtroom and the deadly operative captured in the moment. He had thrown the much larger Charles off Hope, subduing him easily. Yet even when he whispered his deadly threat, he'd been in full control.

That further calmed her. Alex wasn't a man prone to rages.

He'd told her he viewed himself as a professional. The deadly

SEAL was a facet of him used at necessary times. To be called upon when needed, then put away again. She put the picture of the older Alex back on top where it was originally, stroking the frame with her index finger.

"You know he'd never hurt you. Never." Her voice was raspy in the small room.

Hope shifted her eyes and opened one of the jewelry boxes. She stared at Alex's Purple Heart, then flicked her eyes back and forth between the medal and the photo.

The emotion and tears built once again, but they were different this time.

Now they were for Alex, and all he had fought for—and lost—in an instant. Not pity, but grief for a man who had spent years blaming himself for something that wasn't his fault.

She cried herself out, finally putting the medal back and closing the box. As she wiped her face with her hands, her palms stung. She lifted her hands in front of her face, surprised at the dried blood crusted around four half-moon cuts on each palm.

"Oh, no!"

Hope scanned the box. There were a few smears of blood on the top of the lid, which she wiped off. She opened the box and inspected the contents, but there was no blood on them. With a deep sigh, she closed the box and rose to her feet, walking to the bathroom to wash her hands. She was exhausted, yet strangely exulted.

As if she had worked through something she hadn't realized was so necessary.

Hope padded to the bathroom and studied her reflection. Her eyes were red, and her face was puffy. She filled a glass with water and drank, wincing at her sore throat. Her watch said it was early afternoon and her breath caught. She'd left her phone on the kitchen table.

As she left the master bedroom and appeared in the great room, Cruz began barking and leaping against the sliding glass door. Hope let him in as he whined and jumped on her legs.

"Sorry, boy. Did I scare you? I kind of scared myself." She knelt to scratch his ears. "I'm doing better now." She picked up her phone, but there were no texts or calls from Alex.

She searched for something to distract her—to help her regain her emotional footing. Her gaze fell on a bundle of ripe bananas she'd taken with Gerold's blessing from the kitchen. She was moving before she knew it, pulling out her stand mixer to make banana bread.

It was an easy task, just what she needed. She didn't even need a recipe. Twice she went back to Alex's box and opened it, looking at what she now thought of as the Night Photo. There was no panic anymore. She could hold the picture in both hands, though she much preferred the other two, especially the older Alex.

Immense pride washed over her when she saw him in uniform. But she was still coming to grips with the third picture. Hope knew in her soul Alex was a man of deep honor and always true to what he believed in, including her.

At three o'clock, as she was setting the two loaves of bread on wire racks to cool, Alex texted that he'd be home within the hour. She went to the bathroom to check her appearance. The face looking back was more normal now, and pride rose in her eyes.

Nope. Not succumbing to panic. Not ever again.

She wasn't sure how Alex would feel about her looking through his box, but she wasn't going to keep it from him.

∽

ALEX WALKED in the door just before 4 p.m. He held out a hand, palm forward as Hope approached him. "You don't want to get too close, baby. I'm covered in sweat, and you can probably smell me a mile away. Let me take a shower first." He laughed, his excitement shining through, and she couldn't help smiling back at him. As he headed into the master bedroom, her mind turned back to the Night Photo.

How can he be the same man? My sweet, funny Alex?

Today had brought home that there were aspects to him she might never fully comprehend, but she at least had the equilibrium to accept that now.

Hope gave him ten minutes before bringing an open beer into the bathroom. He smelled fresh and clean as he pulled on a new T-shirt, and Hope's love welled up, along with her nervousness. He hadn't moved the boxes.

His face lit up when she handed him the beer. Hope aimlessly straightened hangers while he drank the whole thing in one long shot. She walked up and slid her arms around him with a sigh, eyes closed as she prepared herself.

Alex glanced at her with a creased brow as he set the empty bottle on the vanity. "Everything ok?"

"I did something today, and I'm not sure how you're going to feel about it. You might be upset with me."

He tilted her face to his. "You can tell me anything. What's up?"

"Your box in the closet. It was just sitting out in the open." Her breath increased in lockstep with her anxiety. "I let my curiosity get the best of me and looked through it. I'm sorry I didn't ask you first."

Alex raised his brows as he turned toward the closet. "You mean my Navy stuff? I don't mind you seeing that. You want me to show you?"

She nodded. Relief flooded through her, though she was still concerned about discussing her reaction to the Night Photo. "It doesn't bother you to look at it?"

"It's time I did. A big part of who I am is in that box." He paused, turning to her. "And I'm learning to come to terms with it."

"Of course," she squeezed his waist. "I didn't look through the whole thing, just what was on top. If you need to stop, just say so."

He studied her, his head cocked. "You're not getting sick, are you? Your voice sounds scratchy."

"No, I don't think I'm getting sick. I'd like to learn more about your SEAL days."

"A lot of the stuff in there wouldn't interest you. Lots of ribbons for marksmanship and campaigns and stuff. Come on." He walked into the closet, and they sat down on the floor together.

As he opened the lid, Hope was curious about what would draw his attention first. Alex zeroed in on the box with the large pin she had first looked at.

She smiled at him. "I saw that. It looks like the symbol for Budweiser. Is that something the Navy gives sailors?"

He laughed, trailing an index finger over the pin. "Actually, its nickname is The Budweiser." He turned his smile to her. "They don't hand these out to just anyone. This is the Navy SEAL insignia."

"Oh." He offered it to her, and she examined it with new eyes now.

Next, he picked up the box with his Purple Heart, his shoulders tensing as he opened it. He snapped it shut and tossed it back in.

Hope quickly replaced the SEAL insignia and reached for his Navy Cross. "Have your feelings about this changed at all?"

Alex hesitated. "Not really. I understand what you said about it not being my fault, but that doesn't make this something I should be proud of."

"Maybe you should think of it more as a way of honoring the men you lost." Hope touched his arm. "It doesn't have to be a symbol of pride. It could be one of acknowledgment of their sacrifice. An acknowledgment of the lives you saved that night too."

He lifted a corner of his mouth, accepting her response even if he didn't believe it. "Maybe someday. Not now, though." He closed the box and put it back.

Alex picked up the two photos of him in uniform as Hope took a deep breath. He took them out of the box before seeing the third one below, absently laying both down on the carpet.

He burst into laughter as he picked up the Night Photo. "I forgot about this! I had this one guy on my Team who was always taking pictures." He glanced at Hope with a raised brow. "You do *not* take photos during an op. At least he had the sense to knock it off once we got going—this was before. I don't remember the location exactly, but since I'm wearing a drysuit, it must have been cold."

A slight smile remained as he studied the picture. "I always had a ritual I did to get ready. To get my mind right. I had just finished when he called my name and took this damn picture as I looked over. I was *so* pissed! I really laid into him. You probably can't tell any of that from the picture—I'm pretty covered up. Afterwards, he presented me with this framed copy, the bastard." His smile widened. "He was a good guy."

Hope sat frozen, stunned.

It's just a fond memory for him.

Her face must have given away her thoughts, because his smile faded as he watched her. "What?"

Hope forced her tight muscles to relax. "Well, you're wrong about one thing. Your expression comes through crystal clear in that photo." Her eyes were drawn back to it. "In fact, that's one of the most terrifying pictures I've ever seen. I had a pretty major reaction when I saw it."

Alex watched her closely, concern on his face now. "What's wrong?"

He took one of her hands and squeezed, making her wince. Turning it over to expose the cuts left by her fingernails, he took the other and discovered the matching set.

"What happened to your hands?" he nearly whispered, staring at her with wide, shocked eyes.

CHAPTER 11

They faced each other on the closet floor, the house silent around them. Hope gazed into the same pair of blue eyes as the photos, yet they weren't the same. She needed to assure him she was all right.

Now the work began. "I'll tell you."

The last thing she wanted was to hurt him. She leaned back against the dresser as Alex pivoted next to her. Taking his hand gingerly, Hope stroked it with her fingers.

"I used to get panic attacks . . . after Caleb. They happened without warning." She shook her head. "One time, I was in a department store shopping for jeans and this couple nearby got into a huge fight. He started yelling at her, and the next thing I knew, I was curled up in a ball on the floor of the dressing room with no memory of how I got there." She stroked the backs of his fingers, needing to keep contact with him. "Eventually, the panic attacks went away. For years, I've never even had a close call . . . until today."

Hope picked up the Night Photo and leaned her head back against the dresser. "I've been having some silly romantic fantasies about what you used to do. But this picture makes it very clear you were deadly out there. I couldn't stop looking at your eyes—how different they are in this picture. I started hyperventilating and curling up, and I'm *done* with all that."

She cleared her throat, still sore and scratchy. "So I screamed a few times, dug my nails into my palms, and then got it under control. I forced myself to open that box back up and look at those photos until I understood—deep down inside—that there were times you needed to be this man." She held up the Night Photo. "And doing that allowed you to be this man." Once again, a smile brightened her face as she picked up the photo of the older Alex in uniform.

Alex was still pale, and his pulse throbbed in his neck. "Hope, this is who I am. It's a deep part of me." Finally, he whispered, "Are you ok with me?"

"I've never been surer about anything. I love you." She kissed him, his cool lips telling her how shocked he was. "The last thing I want to do is cause you pain, but I *needed* to see this and work through it."

She touched the center of her chest. "This is about me and what I'm still dealing with. And I *am*—I'm fine, love." She smiled, but he still looked stunned. "You and I both have some heavy things in our past we need to work through. If this past year has taught me anything, it's that I've only avoided dealing with my pain, and burying it doesn't work. That's why I wanted to talk to you about this."

"You've helped me so much since you came here. I feel like I just make your problems worse. I can't change who I am."

"I never want you to. This just drives home how completely different you are from Caleb. He was a coward of the highest order. You risked your life every time you went on a mission, and I know you didn't join the SEALs because you wanted to hurt or kill people."

"No, not at all. There are truly evil people out there—I fought them for years. And I have no regrets about that. None."

"And you shouldn't. I told you when we were on Horseshoe Key that I *know* you. You couldn't be more wrong to say you make my problems worse." She stroked his cheek. "You gave me the courage to finally take the leap. You helped me come alive again."

"I wish I could have been here to help you with this."

"You were. Maybe not in person, but you're the one who got me through it. I'm ok—really. And what I want to tell you most is how incredibly proud I am to be a part of your life."

His composure broke at that, and he pulled her to him. "Thank you."

They held each other in silence, Hope cradling his head on her shoulder and stroking it.

Finally, Alex straightened and placed a hand on her cheek. "You're really all right?"

"One hundred percent." Hope leaned forward for another kiss and he pressed his lips tightly to hers—he needed the reassurance now.

Then Alex's stomach announced itself with a thunderous growl and they broke apart, both laughing.

"Oh, you poor thing. You've been gone all day and I drop this on you as soon as you walk in the door. I haven't even asked you how your adventure went." Hope checked her watch. "The restaurant isn't serving dinner yet, but I can whip up some hamburgers for us."

She stood up and held out her hand to him. "Come on, sailor. Let's eat."

∼

IT WAS A BEAUTIFUL EVENING, warm with just enough breeze to make the nearby palm trees whisper their secrets. Hope had set the table on the porch so they could both enjoy the ocean, and Alex was now on his third hamburger as she opened two more beers.

Throughout dinner he'd asked her more questions about her near panic attack, slowly becoming more at ease with her assurances that she was fine.

That *they* were fine.

His face relaxed as the meal proceeded, and as his tension eased, so did hers. Their usual easy banter reasserted itself.

"So, tell me," Hope said after a sip of beer. "How was your day playing Davy Crockett?"

"Well, I'd like to think of it more as being Rambo, but that entire section seems secure." His smile was back. "I covered almost the entire thing according to your plat map and only found evidence of one camp, and it was really old."

He stopped for a drink. "Oh, one other good thing. I found a small cave near the sandy beach area. It was just about covered with vines—I almost missed it. But I think that will be a good place to store equipment, so I don't have to hump it in and out every day."

"I never even thought about that. Scuba equipment is *heavy*. How are we going to get it over there?"

"Do I look that pathetic?" He straightened. "I admit I'm not in combat-ready shape anymore, but I'm sure I'm still capable of hiking a few scuba tanks and a rebreather a couple of miles."

She frowned at him. "I happen to think you're the opposite of pathetic, thank you very much. But are you sure you don't want to use a cart or something?"

He grinned, shaking his head. "I want to keep that path as unobtrusive as we can. I might start some parallel paths close to the highway just to hide it a little." He sat back and his grin became a laugh. "I don't need the cart, baby. I used to do ten-mile marches in full gear, including tanks."

Hope's mouth hung open. She snapped it shut and said, "Ok, then. I insist on helping. I'll carry a regulator."

He took another swig, his eyes sparkling. "Deal."

Hope brought out a plate of the banana bread she had baked that afternoon, and Alex attacked it. She had to admit, it was pretty tasty. Pleased he had been so willing to open up, she leaned forward in her chair. She had been comparing him with his younger picture all night. "How old were you in that photo, Alex? The young one."

He shrugged. "Twenty or so. I don't remember exactly. It was soon after I made SEAL Teams."

"Was that your goal from the start?"

Alex pushed his plate away. "No. Like I told you before, I enlisted in the Navy right out of high school and was stationed in San Diego. After a few months, my CO asked if I'd ever heard of BUD/S."

Hope sighed—the military was a maze of abbreviations. "What's buds?"

"Another acronym. Basic Underwater Demolition/SEAL training."

"And had you heard of it?"

Alex grinned. "*Everyone* in the Navy's heard of it. He wanted me to do the pre-testing for it, so I thought, why not?" Her face must have looked blank because he explained, "I did a bunch of sports in high school and was in good shape, so I wasn't too worried about the physical tests. They also put you through a pretty heavy battery of mental and psychological tests. And I liked the idea of the challenge and whether I had what it takes."

"So, if you pass the tests, you're selected for BUD/S?"

"No. If you pass, you get the *opportunity* to get selected. Not everyone does. And if you are chosen, you receive the honor of getting the living hell beaten out of you for the next twenty-four weeks." He was laughing now, pride gleaming in his eyes.

"Yes, even I've heard that SEAL training is rather difficult."

The smile faded somewhat, but the pride remained. "My class had an eighty percent dropout rate."

She held up her bottle, glowing inside, and they clinked them together. "I meant what I said, about how incredibly proud I am of you—and to be with you."

He became serious, and now his look made her breath quicken. "Thank you. But I'm the lucky one. The day you came down here was one of the luckiest days of my life."

Her face was getting warmer by the second, so she paused for a drink of beer. "I'd like to ask you another question. You had another box underneath the one with your pictures and medals. It was padlocked. What's in that?"

He lifted his bottle and sat back in the chair, watching her under lowered brows. "I guess it's my turn to tell you something I'm not sure you're going to like. Once on a Team, guys tend to specialize in one or two things. My specialties were dive ops and overwatch." He stopped to look at her.

"I don't know what overwatch is."

He nodded. "It's a sniper. That padlocked box is my sniper rifle."

Hope's eyebrows flew skyward. "You have a sniper rifle in our house?"

He leaned forward, setting his bottle on the table. "Yes, but don't be alarmed. It's broken down and fully locked up, completely safe. I don't take unnecessary risks." He shrugged. "I haven't even had it out of the box since I got discharged, but I won't part with her."

"Your sniper rifle is a she?"

He smiled. "Yeah, her name is Betsy."

She took a deep breath. "Ok. I didn't realize they just gave you guys those things when you left the service."

The smile widened, but it didn't reach his eyes. "They most definitely do *not*. My CO pulled some major strings to get me that rifle and my favorite service pistol when I left."

He shifted in his seat and rubbed the back of his neck. "He thought it might . . . help me work through things. When I was at Walter Reed and could walk again, I used to go to a nearby range a lot—it helped me relax. It was something I could still do. But I've never even unlocked Betsy's case since I was discharged."

Hope's head spun with all she had learned about him in just one day. She scooped up a piece of bread. "I can understand that. So, you have a pistol somewhere, too?"

"Yes, that's why I pulled out the boxes this morning. I took my pistol with me today, just in case."

She dropped her banana bread on the plate.

"I have a concealed-carry permit, Hope. I've had it for years." Alex spoke in a soothing tone. "And after what happened in Frederiksted, I'm not going into any potentially dangerous situations unarmed again. Ever."

The heat crept up her neck again as Hope finally understood why he'd been so upset on the way to the rock pool.

"After I got back today, I moved my pistol to my nightstand, which is where I kept it in my apartment. I keep it in a gun vault, so it's secure. Is that ok with you?"

She thought for a moment. "Yes, it's fine with me. I'm not thrilled about guns personally, but I appreciate that you're an expert. And after our experience with Charles, a little extra protection isn't such a bad idea."

"That was my thought exactly." He leaned forward and took her hand. "You're sure it's all right? Say the word and I'll find somewhere else to store them. I never want you to feel unsafe around me."

"Keep them here—they're a part of you. And you can't imagine how safe I feel around you."

He gave her a small smile, but his eyes were serious. "Thank you. I love how well you understand me. After I got discharged, Katie wanted to keep them for me. We got in a big fight about it. She couldn't understand that I needed to have them, even if I couldn't look at them."

Hope leaned over the table and pressed a soft kiss against his lips. "I understand you pretty well, Alex."

. . .

Hope laid awake long after he had fallen asleep, a montage of the day's dizzying highs and lows spinning through her head. She studied him now, his face smooth and relaxed in sleep, and had no qualms whatsoever about the type of man she was living with.

But getting used to who he used to be might take a little longer. Her gaze was drawn to their closet and what it contained.

CHAPTER 12

Alex watched *Surface Interval* motor away from the dock as he and Hope climbed the steps to the pier. They had just finished breakfast, waiting for the busyness of the morning dive trip to subside before heading to the gear room. Alex slipped an arm around her waist without even thinking about it. They were back on solid ground after working through Hope's reaction to his night-op picture. In fact, it had brought them closer.

Ever since telling her he'd been a SEAL, Alex had suspected Hope didn't quite understand what his job had entailed. Given her past with a violent, abusive son of a bitch boyfriend, he'd been surprised she'd never had more of a reaction to him—being a SEAL, specifically. He wasn't sure exactly why the picture had brought it home for her, but he was relieved.

They had talked about it more in their great room a few days following the incident.

"I GUESS I didn't really understand what SEALs did," Hope had said. "I feel kind of dumb now."

He squeezed her shoulder. "You shouldn't."

Her cheeks were pink. "Yeah, I kind of should. I pictured you rushing from the ocean in dive gear and rescuing people from burning buildings."

"There was some of that. But there was a lot more. Some of it pretty dark."

Hope shook her head. "You flat out told me you shot people. Killed them. Seeing that picture finally brought it home—you were a very elite-level fighter. Even when you told me you were in Syria hunting a terrorist cell, it didn't really hit me. That you were there to kill them. You, personally."

He gave her a faint smile. "They don't generally send SEALs on humanitarian missions. I've rescued hostages, but I've killed my share of terrorists too. And I meant what I said. I don't regret any of it."

"Good. You shouldn't. The other thing that brought it home for me is the fact that you were a sniper. I'm sure you were a good one."

"I was."

She smiled at his simple admission, and his own grew in response. Reaching a hand to his face, Hope gave him a quick kiss. As she pulled away, they locked eyes for a long moment. He couldn't resist her, and their mouths came together. Softly at first, but quickly becoming ardent. Her mouth was hungry and searching as he slid a hand to her breast, discovering she was very turned on.

"Come on," she said in a low growl. "I want to explore some of your other talents." Taking his hand, she led him to the bedroom.

"What are you smiling about?"

Alex jumped, turning back to Hope, who looked at him with a small smile and both brows raised. He was grinning like an idiot, completely distracted, as he pulled out the key to unlock the gear-room door. "Um. Sex."

She tipped her head back, laughing. "Figures. At least you're not scowling."

"No chance of that."

He winked at her before entering the room. There was one other reason they had waited until the pier was deserted before coming down—their purpose. They were keeping the rock pool to themselves for now as their own private oasis.

Alex's gaze fell to the corner as he entered the room. There was now a section of his work area dedicated to the supplies he needed for the coral-restoration project. He had just checked on his baby corals the previous day, pleased with their growth. Both Tommy and Gerold had expressed interest in helping him transplant the first fragments to the house reef, though both needed to tune up their diving skills first.

He removed his wetsuit from the hanger, handing it to her to carry. He was fully focused again, and an electric current ran through him at the prospect ahead.

Alex couldn't wait to explore that dark passage in the cave.

After another glance around the room, he turned to her. "Let's head back to change."

"You've got everything?"

"My rebreather is at the house, and I already hiked over most of the gear to the small cave. This is the last of it. I just need to get changed, then we're off."

∼

A LIGHT MIST swirled through the jungle as Alex walked down the faint trail. Hope followed just behind, sounding like a bunch of stampeding horses, and a faint smile crossed his face.

At least I know where she is.

He was far more relaxed this trip, having determined the area was secure. Hope had made a teasing comment about him overreacting to the whole situation, since it turned out fine. But he wasn't about to disappear into that cave and leave her alone without making sure the coast was clear. If that made him overprotective, so be it.

He shrugged his right shoulder, adjusting the position of the rebreather on his back.

"Are both the cylinders on your rebreather oxygen tanks?"

"No, only one is. The other one has air in it right now, but a variety of gas mixtures can be used in the second one." Cruz darted out of the brush and back onto the path in front of him. "When I explained rebreathers to you in the restaurant, I kind of gave you the kindergarten version. Mine is quite a bit more complicated than what I described."

"That doesn't surprise me, Alex."

He grinned and turned around, walking backwards. "You should consider yourself lucky. I didn't even get into semi-open versus closed-circuit rebreather diving."

"You have my eternal gratitude. Why are you using that instead of a regular tank, anyway?"

He turned back around so he didn't fall on his ass. "I plan on keeping the unit in the small cave I found. That way I only have to take the two small cylinders back and forth to refill them, instead of big scuba tanks." He stepped over a small rock formation and helped Hope over. "Plus, I don't need to worry about running out of air, at least for the dive times I have planned."

They broke out of the jungle and approached the sandy beach area of the pool. Alex removed his rebreather with a sigh and stretched his shoulders as Cruz lapped at the water, then found a shady spot to curl up in. Hope carried Alex's thicker 5 mm wetsuit over one arm. He anticipated the temperature of the water would be in the mid-70s, much cooler than the ocean, and he wanted the extra insulation.

Alex had intentionally not brought any regular scuba equipment out here yet, so Hope wouldn't be tempted to follow after him. She could be more than a little unpredictable.

And a cave was no place for that.

"I need to do some pre-dive tests and checks, so I'm going to be busy for a while. You brought something to keep you occupied while I'm diving?"

She unslung her backpack and patted it. "Yep, I've got a new book right here. I'll probably go for a swim too if I get hot."

Alex couldn't resist that. "You're always hot." He laughed as she rolled her eyes at him. "You might want to get yourself settled. I'll let you know when I'm done with my pre-dive checks, and we can discuss what I'm planning."

She nodded and pulled a blanket out of her backpack as he got busy.

Thirty minutes later, he was satisfied everything was ready to go with the rebreather and studied the pool, his blood pumping about the prospect ahead. Hope sat on the blanket and closed her book with a smile after he sat down next to her.

"Ready?" she asked.

"Yes, just need to get changed. My plan is to dive the pool first, but I don't think that will take too long. Mostly, I want to see if there are any passages leading off it. Next I'll move into the cave." He reached for her hand. "I'm not planning on doing anything extreme, and I'm setting a maximum dive time of three hours."

He watched her carefully, but she was relaxed.

"I've got a reel over there on top of my wetsuit I'll use to lay down a guideline so I can find my way out. I told you before, this isn't my first unknown cave. I'm very qualified to do this, ok?"

She furrowed her brow, sitting up straighter. "Is this safe? What happened to never diving alone?"

"Instructors are qualified to dive alone. And I've got a hell of a lot more training than that. I've taught a lot of divers in overhead environments—military divers." He leaned forward and kissed her. "I'll be back on time, ok?"

Fifteen minutes later, he was geared up and ready to enter the pool. He shifted his pony bottle a bit and tucked his fins under one arm before drawing her in for a kiss. "If I'm gone longer than three hours, you can start worrying. But not before that, ok? Remember when I told you I was pretty good at this diving thing?"

She had been biting her bottom lip, but that made her smile. "Yes, I remember."

He leaned his brow to hers. "I am. I'll be back to you soon."

He kissed her again, then turned to enter the cool, clear water.

It took him thirty minutes to explore the pool, during which he saw one passage leading away but didn't explore it, wanting to use his time in the cave. He sank to the bottom and determined it was nearly fifty feet deep before following the contours of the floor toward the cave.

Despite worrying Hope, Alex was excited but not nervous about penetrating the cave, his heartbeat slow and steady. Passing into the dim interior, he turned on his headlamp. Two handheld lights hung from the rebreather, but he preferred to keep his hands free as much as possible. He checked the display, which indicated over three hours of dive time remaining, much more than he needed.

Alex headed left first, finding the sheer wall he'd noted before continued underwater with no openings. It turned a corner with a jumble of rocks piled up. He skirted around those and continued along the back of the cave, maintaining the same distance from the bottom.

There were several holes in the wall, but nothing big enough to get into. Alex was about three-quarters of the way across when he saw a void above him. He ascended to fifteen feet and studied it. The opening was a good six feet tall and about five feet wide.

This looks promising.

Making a mental note to return, he continued along the back

wall and eventually turned right to face the cave entrance. There were several rock shelves and steps on this side, which led up to the flat plateau above water they'd seen on their first trip.

Finning to the cave entrance, he followed a three-feet-wide shelf which continued alongside the edge to the cave entrance at a depth of ten feet.

I wonder how much the water level's fluctuated over the years. The cave could have been more accessible in the past.

Back at the entrance, Alex continued toward the center where he unclipped his reel with hundreds of feet of white line. He tied the loose end securely to one of the bigger rocks sticking up from the floor and tugged on it, making sure the end was secure before swimming up toward the passage he saw earlier, unspooling the line as he swam. Another outcropping of rock protruded near the floor of the large passage, and he wrapped the line several times around it, creating a taut course from the tunnel to the entrance of the cave.

Alex let a smile creep across his face as he regarded the black unknown passage before him, a delicious shiver sliding down his back.

CHAPTER 13

Alex tilted his head, the beam of his headlamp bouncing around the dim passage but not illuminating the expanse of it. He needed better light to determine what he was getting into.

After unclipping his powerful handheld dive light, he carefully inspected the floor, pleased to find it made from solid rock with little to no sediment. Angling the light up revealed the passage was a different color than the main cave, more of a reddish brown. As he turned the light off and returned it to a D-ring on his rebreather, a thrill rippled through his gut as he entered the unknown passage, using only his headlamp for light.

He continued on, ensuring the line remained about a foot off the floor as it unspooled from his reel so he didn't disturb any residue on the tunnel floor. He grinned—he'd begun frog kicking without even thinking about it, moving his fins sideways instead of up and down to avoid any sediment. A careless fin kick could turn crystal-clear water like this into zero visibility in an instant, given enough sediment. *We'll see how my hip likes it.*

Around fifty yards in, Alex's headlamp illuminated an opening to his left, much narrower than the passage he was currently in.

After inspecting the narrow entrance, he disregarded it for now, instead wrapping the line around another rock several times before continuing down the main passage, clearly marking which direction he took.

Exploring side passages was a job for next time.

Alex swam another thirty yards before his shoulders slumped as a sheer wall rose before him—a dead end.

But he hadn't come this far to turn around without a thorough inspection. He approached closer and excitement flared again as his beam swept up. There was a narrow opening in the reddish-tan rock about two-thirds up the wall in front of him, and he drifted up to look into the opening. The entrance was roughly square, about three feet wide and three feet high at most.

That's a little tight—gonna need to take the rebreather off if I crawl through that.

Alex took out his handheld light and shined it through the narrow opening. The squeeze was a good fifteen feet long. The top of it angled up at the end, but he couldn't detect any far wall beyond, making him wonder if there was another open area on the other side. He checked his computer—he had been down for ninety minutes now.

Still plenty of time left. This is worth checking out.

Turning off his light and re-clipping it, Alex smiled as he unbuckled the rebreather, took it off, and placed it on the narrow shelf in front of him, exhilarated to be performing technical maneuvers once again. He pushed it through as he followed behind, the mouthpiece still firm in his mouth as he inched along the narrow tunnel on his elbows and knees.

The squeeze was definitely tight, and there was one section where the back of his right shoulder scraped against the cool ceiling, but he made it through without mishap. Looping his right arm through the arm straps of the rebreather, he pushed it out of the squeeze, then followed, replacing it on his back as he hovered in the water.

He took a look at his new surroundings.

It was another room, much smaller than the dry cave. Alex glanced up, able to see the mirror-like surface above without any rock protruding down.

I think there's air up there.

He ascended to the surface and established positive buoyancy, the beam of his headlamp bouncing around the confines. The room was roughly circular and a good size, with a curved ceiling soaring overhead. The rock here was the same reddish brown, with streaks of tan across the ceiling.

Several fist-sized holes punched through the ceiling, letting in light. Two bats hung upside down from the ceiling, indicating there was a good connection to the surface here. Removing the regulator from his mouth, Alex took a breath, finding the air somewhat stale but perfectly breathable.

He lowered his mask around his neck to survey his find. The walls were sheer above the waterline except for an accessible rock ledge sloping up from the water's edge. "Cool. Time to check that out."

His voice echoed in the cave, making him smile as his heart beat faster. He swam over and took his fins off, then climbed out and set them on a flat rock, setting his reel on top as he shrugged out of the rebreather. He moved his gaze around the area, the beam of his headlamp following. The dry portion of the room was sizeable, about the size of a large living room.

Alex stepped to the back wall and turned left to follow it, coming across an opening just over halfway down the back wall. His neoprene booties left wet footprints on the ground as he checked the footing on his way to the tunnel. The air pockets above must have let in weather over the years because there was a layer of dirt on the ground.

The opening in the back wall was plenty big enough to get through, and he was eager to explore it. As he neared, his headlamp picked up a glint of something shining on the ground.

He kneeled, and carefully digging with his thumbnail, Alex freed a gold-colored, irregularly shaped disc from the floor. He brought it closer to his headlamp. It looked like an old gold coin, and he couldn't stop the bark of laughter that escaped.

"Are you kidding me?"

He brushed both hands over the area, freeing another small object, which he held up as his jaw dropped. Alex stared intently, its possibilities clear immediately. Biting back a grin, he unzipped his accessory pocket and placed the item inside a secure interior pouch.

Returning his searching hands to the dirt, Alex caught another glint and curled his index finger around a gold chain. His breath quickened as he slowly pulled it free from the sediment, inch by inch. The ground finally relinquished a golden oval pendant the size of his palm inset with an enormous emerald, its green facets sparkling in the dim light. Immediately below where the necklace had lain were two more gold coins.

"Oh my God!" His heart nearly pounded out of his ribs.

He quickly brushed his hands over the area but didn't find anything else, and his display informed him two hours had passed. Alex sat up on his knees and sighed, casting a longing look at the black tunnel ahead. His desire to keep exploring was at war with the need to get back, so Hope didn't worry too much.

"Besides." He studied the gold objects in his hands, running a thumb over the emerald pendant. "I can't *wait* to show her this."

He laughed, shaking the coins in his fist.

He rinsed the three coins and the necklace in the clear water, and there was almost no tarnishing. The pendant was engraved on the back, and all four pieces were brilliant gold, glimmering in his headlamp.

While no expert, even he knew silver tarnished while gold didn't. He placed everything in an empty pocket and made damn sure it was securely shut. Looking at the area again, he gazed once again at the passage that beckoned just beyond as awestruck wonder raised goosebumps on his arms.

Alex re-entered the water, double-checked the display on his rebreather, and once again sank below the surface. He tied off his guideline just below the water's edge and cut it with his dive knife, creating a clear trail from the big cave's entrance to this point, then clipped the reel back onto his rebreather. The white line led to the squeeze and out.

After returning through the constriction, Alex quickly made his way back through the passage to the big cave. With his dive time well under the three-hour deadline, he swam to the entrance and surfaced, floating in the dim cave as his eyes adjusted to the bright sunlight ahead.

Hope floated on her back in the middle of the pool. She lifted an arm, looking at her watch, and a warmth spread through his chest, knowing she waited for his return.

Then a huge grin spread across his face.

She'll kill you if you do this. You know it.

He stopped to assess the consequences.

Yeah, totally worth it.

Alex toggled the switch on his rebreather from semi-open to closed circuit and descended again, totally silent now, with no bubbles. *Time for stealth.* He slowly approached her from a depth of ten feet and enjoyed the view of her enticing body from below as he planned his attack.

Finally, he tipped back and raised both hands. Kicking gently, he rose and tickled both her feet.

Her reaction was everything he'd hoped for.

She let out a deafening scream and thrashed in the water, spray flying everywhere as she furiously kicked.

He surfaced and removed his regulator, laughing so hard he couldn't talk.

"Goddammit, Alex! That's not funny!" She glared at him, lips pursed in a thin line before finally laughing herself. "You are *such* a jerk."

"I really am sorry, baby, but I just couldn't help myself." He toned down the laughter enough to swim over and gave her a proper hello. "Let's get out of the water. I'm ready to get dry."

He ducked as she threw one last splash at him, then they made their way out of the pool. He unbuckled his rebreather and pony bottle, facing away from Hope as he bent over to open the pocket.

"Don't keep me waiting! Did you find anything interesting?"

Smiling, Alex turned around toward her. "Well, that depends on what you mean by interesting." He lifted the necklace he had looped over his finger and dangled it in front of her face. The gold pendant swung back and forth in front of her wide, stunned eyes. "Fancy a treasure hunt?"

∽

Later that evening, Hope turned over the intricately engraved pendant in her hand, running her thumb over the emerald. She and Alex sat at their kitchen table. Both had their laptops open, Hope looking at Spanish coins while Alex read about local pirate lore. The three coins were spread out between them, each stamped with a cross, all four arms of equal length.

"I got interested in pirate stories when I first moved here," Alex said. "St. Croix was a hotbed of pirate activity for centuries. There were a lot of pirates and buccaneers on this island preying on the Spanish treasure fleet."

"Do you think there might be more in that cave?" She still couldn't believe what she held in her hand. The emerald was enormous. The thought of more was almost beyond comprehension.

Almost . . .

"No way to tell. I searched the area where I found this stuff, but there could be more scattered around." He drummed his fingers on the table. "And there was that dry passageway just behind where I found this—I can't wait to see where that goes, if anywhere."

Hope leaned forward, her voice rising. "So, when can we go? After Katie's visit, of course."

Her heart plunged as he shook his head. "Alex, come on—"

"I'm not saying no." He held both hands up. "I'm just saying not yet. I need to stage a couple of extra tanks in there, so you have an easy extra source of air available. And you need some instruction too." He leaned toward her, meeting her gaze head-on. "I also had to negotiate a tight squeeze. The good news is there was an offshoot leading away from the main passage I want to investigate. There's a chance that might end up at the small cave too and be an easier access."

"What's a squeeze?" Hope's stomach lurched. "That doesn't sound great in an underwater cave."

"It's not. That's why I want to try to find another way in." He described the formation to her.

"Wait. I should be able to do that—I'm a lot smaller than you. If you made it through, I can too."

"Yes, I made it through, but I had to take my rebreather off to do it and push it through ahead of me."

"Huh. You actually took it completely off?"

He nodded.

"I'm not too sure about that."

"You'd have to do the same with your tank and BCD. It's too narrow otherwise. And that's why I'd prefer to find another way in."

Hope groaned, setting the pendant back on the table. "That's probably a good idea, as much as it pains me to admit you're right."

He relaxed in his chair with a smile.

"You enjoyed yourself today, didn't you?"

His face lit up like Fourth of July fireworks. "I did. It makes me feel good to be doing something technical again. I haven't used these skills in a long time. It's been a while since I've felt challenged like that."

Hope picked up a coin, turning it over in her hands. "I think it might be a challenge just to find the time to go back there. The bookings are really picking up. We've got a pretty full dive boat the next few weeks, don't we?"

"Yes. Both Robert and April are working so we can cover it all." Alex picked up his own coin, looking at the embossed image and setting it down with a sigh. "I carved a couple of days off when Katie and her family visit in a few days, but it's packed otherwise."

He reached out and squeezed her hand. "We might have to be a little patient with this. And I don't need to tell you we need to keep this quiet. Even the hint of a treasure hunt could turn that whole area upside down."

"Are you going to say anything to your sister?"

He shook his head. "What would I say? They only have a couple of days and already have a tour booked and want me to take them snorkeling. I'd rather wait until we know if there's more in that cave. Until then, let's keep it just between us."

CHAPTER 14

*A*lex opened his hand and forced his grip to relax on the wheel, taking a deep breath to calm the knot in his gut. Hope was in the passenger seat, peeking at him from the corner of her eye.

"You ok?" she asked.

"Sure." He shifted in his seat before turning into the parking lot of the airport. The impact of their purpose here crashed upon him. He'd been Katie's big brother, and it was his fault that had changed, not hers. Hopefully, she would let him make up for it.

Hope rested her hand on his leg. "It's going to be fine, honey."

He tossed her a grateful smile and tried to relax, exhaling deeply as Hope tightly held his hand.

As they reached the arrivals area, an announcement sounded overhead that Katie's flight had just landed. A few minutes later, his text tone went off. "They're here and should be out soon." A big group of people began pouring out of the secure area of the arrivals hall.

He recognized Katie immediately.

She didn't look that different. Her dark hair was longer now, past her shoulders, and she was a little softer. He straightened and looked her in the eye, surprised when her face went slack, astonishment washing over it.

This transformed into a smile and tears sprang to her eyes as she closed in. "Oh my God, Alex! You look fantastic."

His tension melted completely as he embraced her. "Hey, Halfpint."

Katie stepped back from the embrace and laughed. "Your hair is almost blond! You look like a surfer dude."

Alex ran a hand over his head sheepishly. "Yeah, the sun's bleached it a lot."

The rest of the family stood behind Katie. Dave stared at him, eyes wide. Monica, now a pretty girl with a dark-brown ponytail, smiled politely at him. Next, Alex turned to Jason and found a boy completely transformed from the six-year-old he'd last seen. He still had dark hair and brown eyes, but now he was a long and lean twelve-year-old. Jason wore a guarded expression but returned Alex's handshake.

Alex turned to shake hands with Dave and looked at Monica. "You were really young the last time I saw you—you probably don't even remember me."

"It's nice to see you again," she said with practiced proficiency. Katie was watching closely.

Finally, he turned to Jason. "And I can't believe how much you've grown."

"It's good to see you, Uncle Alex." The boy brushed back a mop of hair as he gave him a small smile.

Alex nodded to him. *Got some work to do there.*

Then he turned to Hope. She was wearing a black floral sundress that contrasted with her tan skin beautifully. Her sleek hair fell to her shoulders, and she wore makeup. He watched her with new eyes—she wanted to make a good impression.

I was so worried about myself I never thought she might be nervous about this!

But Hope met his eyes with her usual smile of calm self-assurance as his heart swelled.

Draping his arm over her shoulders, Alex drew her forward. "And this is Hope."

He introduced her to everyone, his sister last.

"Hi, I'm Kate. It's really nice to meet you." She inspected Hope from head to toe.

"Welcome to St. Croix," Hope said. "I'm so happy to meet you all! We've got a bungalow all ready for you."

The group made their way into the humid afternoon, the family following Alex in their rental car to the resort. Hope had their room key with her, so they went directly to the bungalow.

"This is Frangipani," Hope said. "I chose this one because it's closest to our house. I thought it might be convenient for you to be close to Alex." Hope quickly showed off the updated bungalow as Alex leaned against the wall. Katie swept her gaze over the interior with a professional eye.

Monica had discovered the plate of mango tartlets sitting on the dresser, biting into one. "Oh, yum."

Katie whirled around. "Monica! No one said you could eat those!"

"It's fine," Hope said with a laugh. "I baked them for all of you. And there's more if you want."

Katie looked slightly mollified, but still frowned at Monica. With a sigh, she returned to inspecting the bungalow. Alex bit back a smile.

"This is great! We should have come more often." Dave stood at the front windows, taking in the ocean view as he adjusted his shorts over his paunch. His brown hair still wanted to flop over his forehead.

"Then you might have been disappointed," Alex said. "It hasn't been like this for long. This is all Hope's doing. She did the design herself."

Katie smiled at her. "Nice job. It's really beautiful."

Dave's smiled widened as he turned to Hope. "That's high praise coming from Kate. She's an interior designer."

"Well, I thank you for the compliment." Hope made a small bow to her.

"You've done an excellent job mixing modern with timeless. This design will be relevant for years."

"I'm relieved you said that. It wasn't exactly inexpensive."

Katie trailed a hand over the hand-carved wooden headboard. "I can see that. But you got your money's worth."

"Katie and I took rather different paths in life," Alex said.

"I'm a little confused," Hope said. "Do you prefer Kate or Katie?"

Rolling her eyes, she responded, "I haven't gone by Katie since I was twelve years old. *Someone* just refuses to acknowledge that."

Alex's smile got bigger.

Hope laughed. "Uh-huh. That sounds like him."

"Come on! I wanna hit the pool." Jason had hit his breaking point with adult conversation.

"I'd love to show you around, but I need to go back to work for a couple of hours. I'll let Alex play tour guide." Hope headed back to the lobby office. Katie's visit coincided with some days Patti needed off, so Hope had to work while they were here.

"I'll let you guys get unpacked and meet you at the pool in thirty minutes?" Alex asked.

They already had plans to meet for dinner, then Alex and Katie's family were headed on a jungle adventure tour in the morning. As he headed back to the house to change into swim trunks, Alex breathed a relieved sigh.

Maybe things will be all right after all.

CHAPTER 15

Alex stood next to Katie in a shallow stream, the jungle hot and humid around them. They had to raise their voices over the roar of the waterfall that dropped before them. "It's not that bad," Alex said.

"No way," she said.

"Oh, come on, Mom." Jason had perfected the pre-teen teasing yet whining tone. It was a beautiful morning, which was good—this was the tour Jason had *really* wanted to do.

Dave and Monica stood next to them, looking at each other with wide eyes, and the guide raised both hands in front of the group. "It's ok, guys. We do this all the time. It's perfectly safe."

They had just finished a zipline to the top of the waterfall they were preparing to rappel down. This would be followed by a swim in the pool at the base, and their expedition finished with a jungle hike back to the start.

With her feet grounded to the rocky bottom, Katie craned her neck to look at the roaring drop ahead. "Nope. Not for me. I'm taking the path to the bottom. You guys have fun now." She waved as she stomped through the shallow stream.

"Wait for me!" Monica took off running after her, leaving just the guide, Dave, Jason, and Alex left.

"Ok, Jason," Dave said. "Who do you want to go with?"

"Uncle Alex!"

"Figures." Dave laughed as he stepped into the harness and started down after the guide went over procedures with him.

Next, the guide turned to Alex and Jason, but the boy waved him off. "My uncle has done this a bunch of times. I'll ask him if I need help." Alex gave the guide an apologetic smile but couldn't help the glow forming in his abdomen.

The previous afternoon, Alex had spent two hours in the resort pool with them, mostly with the kids. He hardly knew Monica, but he'd been close to Jason, who had been hurt when Alex moved away. Jason had given him a bit of a cold shoulder when he'd first arrived, but after playing in the water, he'd warmed up again. Alex had brought out some masks and a tank and let the kids breathe off it underwater, which had thrilled both. Even Monica had started treating him like her favorite uncle.

Alex gave Jason an encouraging smile as the guide got them geared up. The waterfall was a good size, close to a hundred feet. "Ok, Jason, just lean straight back and let the rope out as you jump. You'll come back to the wall." Alex demonstrated, the motions coming back quickly. Jason was nervous at first so they took small hops, Alex at his side. Soon he gained confidence, and they were at the bottom before they knew it.

After the swim at the base of the waterfall, the group hiked two miles back to the starting area on a well-marked trail. Alex thought about the rock pool on the hike back, regretting he couldn't tell them about it. *But it'll make a nice surprise for a return trip—even if we don't find anything else.*

By the time they finished the tour, everyone was sweaty, dirty, tired, and thoroughly happy.

. . .

THAT AFTERNOON, Clark buried a selection of beer and soft drinks in an ice-filled steel bucket before pushing it over the bar toward Alex. "That should be enough to please everyone." Clark gave him a broad grin, his silver tooth shining in the afternoon light. Jason and Monica loved him, especially after Clark had shown them how to make one of his inspired mocktails. It was a special recipe just for them.

"Thanks, man," Alex said. "But after your fancy drinks, I think the kids will be disappointed with sodas." He gave Clark a nod as he picked up the bucket and walked barefoot through the sand toward the ocean's edge.

He'd had plenty of one-on-one time with Katie, and she was now fully caught up on his adventures over the past year. He had been more reticent to discuss his relationship with Hope. His feelings for her were intensely personal and not something he wanted to share with his little sister. At least not yet.

Alex sat down on a lounger next to Katie and pulled out two beers, handing her one. Both watched Dave and the kids splash in the ocean. Dave and Jason were throwing a football and Dave overshot, the ball bouncing along the sand. Alex got up and threw it back to Jason.

"Well, you've definitely got your muscle tone back," Katie said. "That was a long throw."

Alex shrugged. "That's a good thing, considering I was a ninety-eight-pound weakling the last time you saw me. When I'd first gotten to Walter Reed, I'd lost almost forty pounds. Don't think I'll ever fully regain my combat form, but I've gotten most of it back now."

Her gaze traveled back to Jason. "This trip has been so good for him. He really misses you, Alex. Dave is a great father, but Jason worships you. He always has."

"I've missed him too." He watched his nephew play in the water before grinning at her. "Send him to me for two weeks and I'll make a diver out of him."

"Back off, jack. I'm not ready for that yet. Hell, I'm not ready for him to be a teenager, and he's damn near there. But we packed a lot into our few days here. The jungle adventure was great."

They sat back for a few minutes. Katie scanned their surroundings. "I can see why you love it here. If we had some extra time, I'd go diving with you just to see the coral project you've started. But I'm looking forward to snorkeling tomorrow."

"It'll be fun. I'm lucky to live here, and this place has done me a lot of good. When I first moved down here, I wasn't sure it would work—me being a dive guide. But it has."

"I know the ocean's always been your greatest love. Though I'm thinking that might be changing." Katie grinned at him and laughed when he shot her a deadpan look. "Ok, ok! I won't pry. I'm sorry we could only come down for a couple of days. It's almost impossible to get Dave out of the office. Had it been anyone but you, I don't think he would have agreed."

"I'm really glad you came. I've missed you. And I'm sorry—for how hard I was to help. You did your best, but I wasn't in a place mentally to listen back then."

"I'm sorry too. About everything you've been through, and that I let you slip away from me." Then a laugh escaped. "Though you haven't managed to evade trouble here, either. Boat sinkings, hurricanes, shootings, trials. It hasn't exactly been a walk in the park."

A wistful smile rose on his face as the sun descended toward the horizon. "Maybe not, but those events brought me to where I am right now. They reminded me of who I once was, and *still* am. Now I'm trying to be someone better, and I'm finally looking forward to the future."

Katie darted her eyes over his face, a small smile appearing. "I was so nervous getting off that plane. I was scared to death about what I'd find. And there you were—tall, strong, *healed*. You looked like the brother I remembered . . . from before." She shook her head. "I'll be honest. I wasn't sure you'd ever find happiness again after you left the SEALs—that was your life. But you have."

"It was a long time coming, believe me. And I haven't completely come to terms with it. Not sure I ever will. You don't get over knowing your best friends are dead because of you."

Katie groaned, pressing both palms against her eyes. "You have to stop that! It wasn't your fault and you know it. At least you can talk about it now—that's an improvement. But you've got to forgive yourself, Alex. Don't be a prisoner to this."

"You sound just like Hope."

"Well, you've got two beautiful, smart, successful women telling you the same thing. Maybe you should listen for once in your life, instead of being all pigheaded and stubborn."

Laughter rose in him, unbidden. "Now you really sound like Hope."

She put an arm around his shoulders and pulled him close. "I'm really happy for you."

"Thanks, Halfpint."

∽

THE NEXT EVENING, Hope watched as Alex sent Jason long down the beach before launching a perfect spiral to him. Jason made a great over-the-shoulder catch. Kate's family had relaxed by the pool and beach in the morning, and Alex had taken them on a private snorkeling trip on *Surface Interval* in the afternoon. Everyone was relaxed and content, which made Hope very happy.

They'd had dinner in a separate, private section of the restaurant. After, she and Alex had built up a bonfire on the sand in front of their house. It was slightly cool after the sun set, but the fire was more for ambience.

Kate sat next to Hope, with Dave on the other side, his arm draped lazily over her shoulders. Hope had gathered several steel buckets from the bar and filled them with ice, sodas, and

Leatherbacks. They sat nestled in the sand now. "You're looking a little low there, Kate. Need a refill?"

Kate's attention drifted to her, her expression still radiant from watching Alex and Jason together. "Oh yeah, bring it on."

Hope couldn't help comparing Alex to his sister. They had the same blue eyes and some similar mannerisms. Both were tall, but Kate didn't have Alex's athletic build.

Jason overthrew and the ball landed between Dave and Monica, who both dove for it. "Come on, sweetie. Let's show them how it's done." They got up and joined a four-way game of catch, leaving Hope and Kate alone.

Hope sighed as her insides melted. "I can't tell you how happy I am that you came down here. Alex needed this so much."

"We've had a really great time—all of us. We tiptoed around a little to start, but now it's like we've never been apart."

"I'm sorry I haven't been around more. It's not because I didn't want to—it's a busy week and I had some co-workers who took time off."

Kate turned a smile to her. "It's fine. We've spent time together in the evenings, haven't we? I feel like we've gotten to know each other a bit." She looked up the beach toward the resort. "Even though this is our first time here, I can tell how much you've improved the place. Alex told me anyone else would have crumbled under the pressure. You should be proud."

A warmth spread through Hope's chest. "I had a lot of really good people around me who prevented that." She paused, then met Kate's eyes. "But thank you. This place helped save me."

Kate gave her a secret smile, as if what Hope said had struck some chord within her, then her gaze wandered back to Alex.

It was time for a change in subject. "Sorry about the power outage last night," Hope said. "At least it didn't last long. They happen from time to time."

"Oh, the kids loved it. We got to light candles—it just added to the adventure. And they devoured that banana bread that mysteriously appeared in our room."

Hope smiled and clasped her hands around her knees. "You have a wonderful family. I love being around them."

Kate's smile faded. "I couldn't believe it when Alex called me out of the blue like that. After he moved here, there was a time when things seemed to get worse for him. We'd talk on the phone, but things were . . . tense. I just quit trying after a while. I feel terrible about that. He needed help so much, but he didn't make it easy, that's for sure."

"I know what you mean. Don't beat yourself up about it. He's like an armadillo sometimes. He just curls up and presents his armor to the outside world."

They both laughed.

Monica made a wild throw, and Hope got up to retrieve the ball, throwing it to Dave. She padded to the ocean, letting the gentle waves wash over her feet as the moon shined on the calm surface. Soon warmth enveloped her as her waist was encircled from behind.

"You look amazing, standing here like this." Alex nuzzled her neck. "What are you thinking about?"

She turned around, looking into those incredible eyes. "How happy I am for you right now. I can't tell you what it means to see you here with your sister and her family."

Alex leaned his forehead against hers, then cupped her face, brushing his lips to hers. "It wouldn't have happened if not for you. You make me a better man, you know."

The football bounced off his shoulder, landing in the sand.

"Come on! Enough of the gross kissy stuff!" Jason laughed as Alex threw the ball, running full speed to catch it as Hope returned to her seat by the fire.

Kate leveled a frank look at her. "I had really mixed feelings about meeting you. It was clear, even talking on the phone, that a lot of the change in Alex was due to you. And now that I've seen you two together, it's even more clear. You helped bring him back from the edge. But you also have the power to destroy him. Just remember that, ok?"

Hope smiled at her as the fire sent a burst of sparks skyward. "Isn't that always the case when you love someone? He's got the power to destroy me too. I love your brother very much, Kate. He's helped me in ways I can't even begin to describe."

"Yeah, he's kind of larger than life, isn't he?"

Hope laughed and threw another log on. "I can't even imagine Alex as an older brother. As protective as he is, being his little sister must've been interesting. I can just see your boyfriends running in horror. I'm amazed you managed to get married!"

"Oh my God! I was still in high school when he became a SEAL. It was ridiculous! He'd come home for a visit and terrify my dates. He'd just *smile* at them, and they'd practically wet their pants. Fortunately, he was deployed overseas when Dave and I were dating—by the time he got back we were engaged, and it was too late."

They were both laughing as Hope turned back to the football match. Alex was staring at them with narrowed eyes.

That only made them laugh harder.

THE NEXT MORNING, Hope needed to fill in at the front desk, so Alex took on the airport drive.

"Anytime you want to come down, we'll make room—please know that." Hope enfolded Kate in an embrace. "You're always welcome."

"Thank you. This is an incredible place." Kate gave her a smile, but her eyes were serious. "Take care of him, ok? I think you've got it covered, though."

Then the family swept out, and the resort was a little quieter and a little less bright.

CHAPTER 16

Hope yawned as she waited for her coffee to brew. She smiled as her gaze fell to the counter and a framed picture of Alex with Kate's family. He planned to display it in his work area. Neither of them was working that morning, and they were joining the dive trip—but off duty. He entered the kitchen, dressed for his morning swim, as Hope studied the new picture.

"So, did Kate's visit accomplish everything you wanted?" she asked.

"And then some. I don't think it could have gone better. I was pretty nervous about it. Other than Katie's reaction, I was most worried about Jason."

"You two were close?"

Alex prepared a travel mug of coffee to drink on the way to his swim. "Yeah, he was only six when I left. He used to love seeing me in uniform. He was too young to understand what happened to me. He just knew I was there, then I wasn't anymore."

"He's a good kid. And you two were getting along great by the end."

"Yeah. I'm glad they came down here." He picked up the framed picture.

"Where are you going to place that?"

"On the shelf above my workbench. Next to my octopus. And the picture of us on the dive boat."

She nodded. Robert had taken the photo of her and Alex. It was a candid, capturing their happiness beautifully. She had a copy on her desk at the lobby office.

Alex encircled her waist. "Sure you don't want to join me?"

"I'll sit this one out. I'm not quite as addicted to it as you are, and I'll have plenty of time in the water in a bit."

A wide smile crossed his face. "It's been a while since we've dived alone. Even if you are a whale-shark magnet, I love diving alone with you."

She stood on her toes to kiss the tip of his nose. "So do I."

"I'll be back up in a while."

Then Alex was out the door, a towel around his neck. She looked forward to their dive that morning but was having a hard time waking up, so she took her mug and curled up on the porch to watch a perfect morning dawn. Alex's distant form dove into the water as she took a deep breath of the bracing air, enjoying the solitude. She sipped her coffee, counting on the caffeine hit to kick in.

As she wrapped both hands around her mug, Hope's head was filled with thoughts of the cave and what it might contain. Despite Alex's proclamations of a treasure hunt, she was doubtful of discovering anything else. Still, it was an exciting adventure to think about, and exploring the cave took on a new urgency. Both were eager for Alex to explore the side passage he'd discovered.

As he neared the pier again, her eyelids grew heavy, and she shook her head forcefully. "You got plenty of sleep! Stop it."

She stood and moved to the master bath. A shower was necessary for a full awakening this morning. She stepped into the large tiled walk-in shower and shampooed her hair into a sudsy froth.

Out of nowhere, the memory of Alex joining her in the shower after their first day as lovers hit her full force. She froze her hands and leaned back into the stream of water, basking in how loved he'd made her feel.

When she'd doubted him.

A frenzy of insecurity had convinced her he wasn't interested. He came to her in the shower, completely unaware of her change of mood. Yet he understood immediately what she needed—comfort and reassurance.

Alex had provided that.

It had been one of the most personal experiences of her life. Not sexual at all, but incredibly intimate.

A completely different woman stood in this shower. One who had finally found what she'd sought. Hope leaned her head back, the water rinsing the lather off her hair as it cascaded down her breasts and over her stomach, then between her legs. She parted her lips and tasted the water beading on them.

She wasn't the slightest bit sleepy anymore.

Hope took a deep breath, arching her back as desire coursed through her from the soft stream of water, thoughts of Alex at the forefront of her mind.

"Do you have any idea how incredibly sexy you look right now?"

A smile slowly spread across Hope's face as she opened her eyes. Alex stood naked before her. As her eyes languidly traveled down his muscular body, it was apparent she wasn't the only one aroused. His ribcage expanded with the force of his breaths.

"You're looking pretty hot yourself." She stepped toward him, stroking both hands over the muscles of his chest. Fresh from his swim, she expected his skin to be cool. It wasn't.

His heat seared through her fingertips everywhere she touched him.

Alex lowered his mouth to hers, beginning with a slow kiss, closing his mouth as he traced over her breasts, feather light. His delicate touch ignited her—he knew her well and would keep things light and slow until she couldn't take it anymore.

Hope upped the ante. She wrapped one leg around his thigh and drew him closer, opening her mouth to brush her tongue across his lips. He smiled as he kept his mouth closed, teasing her.

She moved her mouth over his chin then across his neck, pressing her tongue against his hot, wet skin, still salty from his swim. His dark morning stubble prickled against her tongue and he moaned softly.

Hope grabbed his upper arms and spun him under the showerhead, letting the stream wash his salt away as she pulled his mouth to hers. This time, he welcomed her fully, his tongue demanding and forceful.

She pushed him hard against the tile wall of the shower. The breath exploded from his lungs as he slammed into it and she scraped her mouth across his, drawing her nails down his ribcage.

Alex groaned and pulled her tightly against him, grabbing a fistful of her hair and yanking her head back and her mouth away from his. His eyes blazed into hers. "I want to hear you. Loudly."

"Well, I guess that's up to you, isn't it?"

He tightened his hand in her hair as he gave her a smile that pulsed through her. "Challenge accepted."

He licked his lips before moving them back to hers, stepping away from the wall until they both stood under the showerhead, the water pouring over their faces as they devoured each other.

Alex let go of her hair, brushing his hands down the sides of her breasts to her hips. He ran two fingers across her thigh and up the inside, agonizingly slow and whisper soft. His touch inflamed a drawing sensation deep within her as the waves spread throughout her body. As he continued up her inner thigh, Hope opened that leg wider, and he rushed his hand to her outer hip.

"Oh, no. Not yet. You're barely moaning."

Alex pushed her against the tile wall as the shower streamed over his shoulders. The tile was cool against her back, a complete contrast to the hot skin pressed against her breasts. He crouched in front of her, moving his mouth to the center of one breast and then the other one as he pushed them together.

The sensations rocketed through her.

She tipped her head back with a loud groan as Alex finally moved his hand between her legs.

Lowering to his knees, he nipped the skin of her abdomen and Hope cried out, feeling it down to her toes. She ruffled his short hair as he continued downward, his hands complementing everything he did with his mouth. Hope was panting and couldn't wait anymore. She pressed his head closer, then her voice escalated much more.

Alex got what he wanted.

As her cries diminished to soft gasps, he returned to his feet, sliding his hands under her as he lifted her up to waist-level and entered her with one hard thrust. Hope screamed his name again as she dug her hands into his shoulders. She was so sensitive that another climax built each time they crashed together.

He laughed against her ear. "I guess it's a good thing we live a long way down the beach."

Hope jerked his mouth back to hers as he continued pounding into her, his breaths turning into gasps now. Pulling her head away, she stared into his half-open eyes.

"Now it's my turn," she breathed. "I want to hear you."

She grabbed the back of his head again, yanking him to her mouth. Their lips slammed and raked across each other. Hope swept a wet line to his ear, circling her tongue in it. She bit his earlobe as he cried out.

This time, Hope got what she wanted.

Afterwards, Alex held her gently against the wall, lazily running his tongue around hers. She detached her legs from his hips, one at a time, until she stood on her own two shaky feet again.

"I couldn't wake up this morning," Hope said, kissing his neck. "That certainly did the trick."

When Hope came out to the kitchen fully dressed, Alex was already there, putting toast on his plate. She watched his hands, a jolt shimmering through her at how he made her feel with them. With an effort, she tore her gaze away and prepared her own quick breakfast before joining him.

Alex turned to her. "I want to talk to you about the dive I'd like to do this morning. Believe it or not, that's what I came up here to do."

She flashed him a smug grin and rolled her toe up his shin.

"Behave, Ms. Collins. Tommy's saving us a couple of spots at the stern. I spoke to him down at the pier after my swim."

"Ok, fine. Go ahead."

He leaned across the table to give Hope a fluttery kiss before sitting back down. "My plan is to have Tommy drop us off on the way to the first dive site. We'll do a drift dive and meet them where the boat is moored. The dive I have in mind is one of my favorites, but it's deeper than we usually do."

"How deep?"

"We'll descend and go through a channel in the reef. There's usually a steady current, but it'll disappear once we're in the channel, which is at a hundred feet. You ok with that depth?"

Hope thought for a moment. "I think it will be fine. Is there any reason I should be concerned?"

"Not really. It's considered a more advanced dive because of the depth and the current. After we finish the channel, we'll come back out to the reef and head to shallower water as we drift to the boat."

Hope smiled. "Sounds like fun."

"It's a great dive. Just stay close to me, especially on the descent, so we don't get separated. The current decreases as you approach the reef."

He stilled, regarding her seriously. "And remember, you can call off any dive, for any reason. If you're not enjoying it, let me know and I'll change the plan."

She leaned forward and kissed him. "Thank you, but I'm sure I'll be fine. The current will be a new experience."

CHAPTER 17

Hope kneeled on the fiberglass deck to dig through her box, making sure her fins and mask were there. She wasn't really concerned Alex would leave them behind, but it was her responsibility to double-check, and they were there as expected. The two of them wore board shorts and plain T-shirts —decidedly *not* staff apparel. Alex stood next to her, attaching his regulator to the tank as Tommy walked around the boat, doing a final head count.

"Ok, everybody, I've got some bad news before we leave the dock," Tommy said. That got the six guest divers' attention. "Today is Alex's day off, so he decided to bring Hope along and they're goin' to dive, just the two of them. I recommend stayin' away from them, or you might drown in the pheromones." The sound of laughter filled the air.

Hope shot Tommy a dirty look before turning it on Alex. "The least you could do is defend me."

He grinned back at her as he unscrewed the dust cap from her regulator. "Well, he's not wrong."

Hope pushed him in the chest, making him step back as he laughed.

Robert spoke up. "But there's good news. We're goin' to drop them off on the way to our first dive site, and the two of them are doin' a drift dive. If Alex gets lost like he usually does, we won't see them again. Then we can enjoy the second dive in peace."

"Ouch." Alex had his hands on his hips now. "I never knew I had such a fan club."

Hope sat down to tug on her wetsuit.

Alex joined her. "That was nice of them. They're good to me," he said in a lower voice.

Hope opened her eyes wide. "What? That was nice?"

"Yeah, they basically told the divers to leave us alone so we can enjoy ourselves."

Hope shook her head, sending a dark look at the wheelhouse. "They could have just said that."

∽

Hope performed a giant stride entry off the stern platform, with Alex just behind. As he surfaced after the jump, he signaled Tommy with two bumps of his closed fist on the top of his head, the ok signal when on the surface. Tommy waved at them and throttled away.

And they were alone.

Alex's face was in the water, evaluating the site, and he raised it to reveal a wide smile, his eyes sparkling. "We've got a fifty-foot descent here and there's a decent current today. Stay close, but we'll regroup at the bottom if we get separated. Then we'll swim down to the channel at a hundred feet and go through that. There's usually lots to see in there. I love it. Any questions?"

Hope shook her head. "Nope. Let's go." She had never dived in current before and was both excited and a bit apprehensive.

Alex gave her the thumbs-down signal to descend, and they let the air out of their BCDs, sinking below the surface. Hope stared as the coral reef far below moved rapidly beneath her. She was disoriented and slightly dizzy until she realized the coral was stationary.

She was the one flying past in the moving water.

The brightly colored reef was mesmerizing as it appeared to race beneath her. She shook her head, and her heart sped up as she looked for Alex. He was ten feet below her and up current. He was watching her and signaled her with an ok signal. She responded the same, hoping she wouldn't get any more uneasy.

She continued to descend but her right ear didn't want to clear, so she was stuck at thirty-five feet until it finally popped and she was able to descend further. Breathing a relieved sigh as she finally approached the reef, she added air to her BCD to make herself neutrally buoyant.

Hope was still rushing over the reef, unable to stop, and becoming more anxious every minute. She was much less in control than in previous dives. It was a new sensation for her and not one she enjoyed. Again, she searched out Alex and found him swimming toward her, relaxed as usual.

He pointed to the side, and they swam deeper, drifting with the current. Alex hardly even moved his fins, drifting effortlessly with the current. She felt like she was up, then down, bumping into him.

The current threw her around as her stomach clenched.

The coral reef was vibrant with life, but the bright colors became muted as their depth increased. Her dive computer indicated they were at eighty feet and still descending. She took a deep breath to steady her increasing heart rate, butterflies now a constant presence in her stomach.

Alex dropped over the ledge and drifted along a wall, and she tried to stay close to his fins, but not too close.

Definitely not repeating that experience.

The water was alive, like a hand pushing her into Alex, and making her even more uneasy. She moved to one side to ensure she didn't hit his fins.

A sandy-bottomed channel fifteen feet wide appeared on Alex's right, and he turned into it. Hope didn't begin her turn soon enough, and the current carried her on. She turned around and swam with strong kicks to get into the channel, breathing hard as she worked to avoid being swept away. Now her heart throbbed in her ears, and her dive computer said they were at a hundred feet, much deeper than any of her previous dives.

Stay calm. Just keep it together and breathe slow.

Alex had stayed at the entrance of the channel, and she grabbed his hands when she reached him. Hope wasn't pleased her hands were shaking, and her heart pounded out of her chest.

Alex asked if she was ok, watching her carefully. She returned the ok signal, not wanting to admit her fear, and they moved on. He pointed out a lobster in a deep hole, its long antennae twitching back and forth.

On the opposite side of the channel was a beautiful chain moray eel, dark brown with brilliant, yellow-checkered highlights. Its mouth opened and closed as it breathed, its beady eyes staring at her. She couldn't appreciate the beauty, glancing at the walls of the channel to verify they weren't closing in on her. A constant ache chewed at her gut now.

Deep breaths—you can do this.

As they swam on, Alex spun to her, eyes wide as he spied a bright-yellow leaf scorpionfish. It sat motionless on the coral, its upright dorsal fin waving back and forth. Hope's shoulders slumped, and she swallowed a lump in her throat. He was having so much fun, but all she could think about was the hundred feet of water between her and the surface. She was taking shallow, frequent breaths, so she forced her breathing to slow.

After showing her the leaf scorpionfish, Alex turned and asked her yet again if she was ok, the concern apparent on his face. This time, she held her hand out and waggled it side to side in a so-so gesture.

He stilled, and darted his eyes around her face. He pointed to her ears, asking if she was having an ear problem. She shook her head and shrugged, not knowing how to tell him how nervous she was. There was a volcano of pressure building inside her. Alex removed his magnetic dive slate and handed it to her so she could write what was wrong.

Hope took it and held the stylus for a moment, hating to admit this. Her hands shook and her heart still thrummed. Taking another deep breath, she pressed the stylus to the surface of the slate and wrote, I'm scared. Sorry.

She held it up to him, wanting to cry.

Dragging the slate's erase slider up and down quickly, she continued. Deep + Current = Scary. Then she drew a sad face, admitting defeat.

He softened his eyes and held a hand to her face. Hope leaned into the pressure, taking comfort from it while keeping her eyes glued to his, her tension subsiding a bit at his touch.

He raised his eyebrows and gave her the thumbs-up, asking if she wanted to quit the dive. She shook her head several times and gave him the thumbs-up, plus her thumb and index finger an inch apart. *Go up a little?*

Alex nodded, taking his slate back and writing. He turned it back around. We'll go a little shallower but will be back in current. He waited for her to acknowledge before wiping the slate clean and writing some more. I'll keep you next to me. You'll be fine. She smiled and nodded at him, already more relaxed.

He clasped her hand, keeping her close as they swam up to the top of the reef channel, which was about ten feet tall. As the current swept them up again, Alex angled them up the reef until they were at about fifty feet. With him at her side, her breathing slowed and her tight muscles relaxed as they swam with their hands clasped together, though that frustrated her.

I should be able to handle this. I've been diving for a while now.

They came to a bend in the shallow wall they were following, and Alex led them around the corner. The current stopped and

Hope's body unclenched, now back in the type of dive she was familiar with. More confident now, she removed her hand from his.

They swam on and Hope started investigating in the nooks and crannies they passed to see what lurked within, finally enjoying herself. She reached out and touched his arm.

Alex whipped his head around, checking if she was ok. She smiled and leaned into him, enfolding his hand again. He squeezed it and their eyes locked for a long moment before she let go to look at a sea fan. *Why was I so scared before? I feel fine now.*

They continued, slowly rising as the reef sloped upwards, now at thirty feet. She spied two stunning three-inch-tall black-and-white striped fish with tiny bodies and greatly elongated top and bottom fins. They flitted back and forth in their crevice, never still.

She got Alex's attention and pointed to them. He shouted through his regulator, then applauded her and whipped out his slate. Juvenile spotted drums. Great find, baby!

She had to smile at that. Her watch showed their dive time getting close to an hour, and she had less than 1000 psi of air left.

How are we going to get back to the boat?

Of course, Robert had been joking about Alex getting lost, but Hope couldn't help wondering about it. He gave her the signal to start their three-minute safety stop, and they moved up to fifteen feet. *The boat must be coming to get us.*

Hope held her hands out to him, angled with her palms up and the lower edges pressed together. She shrugged, asking where the boat was. Alex smiled back at her and pointed right above her head. She craned her neck at the boat moored directly overhead as Alex's laughter sounded through the water. She smiled and shrugged at him, feeling silly. At least the dive ended on a happy note.

∽

THE OTHER GROUP had just gotten on the boat when Hope and Alex surfaced, and once aboard, Alex made sure everyone knew Hope had found the two spotted drum fish. She was surprised when several jealous moans came from the group—apparently they were a much-coveted fish to see.

Hope and Alex relaxed as the boat slowly motored to the second dive site. The other divers were on the sundeck, and Robert had joined Tommy in the elevated wheelhouse, leaving the two of them alone.

They had their wetsuits pulled down to their waists and were sitting on the side bench in front of their tanks. Alex leaned against his tank and pulled Hope back against his chest as he wrapped his arms around her. She melted into him with a happy sigh.

Alex stroked her hair and kissed her temple. "This is great," he murmured in her ear. "Sitting here with you in my arms right now. Good thing that shower happened this morning or you might be in big trouble right now."

She rubbed her foot against his, smiling at the deep rumble in his chest. "Calm down, sailor. We still have to set an example of professionalism, you know."

"Screw the professionalism. It's my day off. I can do whatever I want to."

"Oh? And do you usually speak to your bosses like this, Mr. Monroe?"

"I have a special arrangement with my current supervisor." He was kissing her ear, making her squirm. "Are you getting flustered, Ms. Collins?"

"Oh, stop it or I'll move to the other side of the boat." His mouth retreated as he laughed quietly. Alex shifted position and leaned his head against hers as they watched the wake behind the boat.

Hope had mixed feelings about the dive. Now back on the

surface and basking in the sun, she couldn't understand why she'd been so frightened.

"Thank you for telling me you were uneasy down there. I'm proud of you for not wanting to quit the dive, but remember that's always an option." He stroked her hair, and she closed her eyes, leaning further back into him. "You looked like you enjoyed the rest of it—I did too. Except the last part where you thought I was lost, of course."

Hope laughed without opening her eyes. "I'm sorry. I had no idea the boat was right above my head. I'd been wondering for the last ten minutes of the dive how we were going to get back to it."

He kissed her temple before leaning his cheek against the side of her head. "You know, you're a real challenge for me as an instructor."

"Oh? How so?" It was wonderful being wrapped up in his arms. Right now, she'd be happy to skip the second dive and stay where they were.

"Well, we should do some more deep and current dives so you can get more experience, which will lead to more confidence in the water. Especially with current, there are some techniques I can teach to help you negotiate the reef."

He tightened his arms around her for a moment. "But as a man who loves you, the last thing I want is to see you scared. I want to protect you from anything that might cause you fear or harm. That's why I don't like the idea of you in that cave."

She put her hands over his. "You can't protect me from everything, you know. I am a fairly capable person."

"I know you are. Believe me, I do. That current was a little stronger than usual. I'm sorry—I probably should have picked another dive."

"Don't apologize. I'm the one who feels dumb now." She heaved a big sigh. "If anyone should be sorry, it's me. I could see how excited you were during that dive, and I'm pretty sure I ruined it for you."

Without warning, Alex leaned forward and sat upright with Hope slightly bent forward in front of him, his arms still around her. His chest moved behind her with the force of his deep inhalations, and his eyes were closed behind his sunglasses.

"Hope, I have spent a lot of years now guiding people on dives. Leading a lot of couples. I make a point of watching them underwater." A faint smile crossed his face. "It's usually similar to how they act above the water. Some bicker and fight, and some pay no attention to each other—if one got into trouble, the other wouldn't even know."

The smile faded, and he rested his chin on her shoulder, tightening his arms around her with his eyes still closed. "And there are the couples who stay near each other. They make sure the other is ok and show each other the stuff they find. I'd watch them touch each other during the dive, hold hands sometimes, and just enjoying being together. I've always thought that was so cool, so *special*—to have someone you can love and trust so much. To be excited with."

Taking a deep breath, he spoke next to her ear, barely above a whisper. "And now I've got that. I have been alone for so long."

Alex's arms gripped her, his chest moving with emotion. "You never have to apologize to me about ruining a dive. You can't imagine what it means to me to be down there with you. Every day you make my dreams come true."

CHAPTER 18

May...

ALEX FINNED DOWN the dark tunnel, his beam of light bouncing around the walls as he reached the squeeze. His body thrummed and he was practically humming a tune. *Finally! Back in the cave.* Detaching the scuba tank he carried along his side, he secured it on the floor, just inside the stricture. This was the final of three tanks along the primary passage.

Turning around, he swam back to the slender offshoot, eager to investigate another possible way into the room ahead. He tied off a new line, today using bright green, and turned into the smaller entrance of the side tunnel.

This passageway sloped down at a twenty-degree angle and was much narrower top to bottom than the main channel. It was a smooth gray rock passage with minimal silt. He continued, performing slow frog kicks.

After thirty feet, the passage evened out but took a sharp left turn. He carefully angled around the turn, wincing as the case on his back scraped against one wall.

Shortly after, another stricture appeared, and he unclipped his large handheld light. This squeeze was roughly hourglass shaped, with openings on the left and right as the center narrowed to only a foot. Immediately, Alex determined the left side was a no-go. It was much too tight, but the right side looked promising.

It was considerably narrower than the squeeze in the main passage, but also much shorter. He shined his powerful light in but couldn't see any walls on the far end, making it worth investigating further.

He'd rather take Hope through a squeeze that was much shorter than the one in the main channel, even if it was tighter.

If he could get through this, she could too.

Alex considered the obstacle in front of him. It was essentially the right side of the hourglass, with the widest portion to the far-right edge. The restriction was about eight feet long and made of the same ominous dull-gray rock.

But it was very tight.

If he had only himself to worry about, he'd just use the main channel. But this squeeze looked short enough that he could go through first, then turn around and grab Hope's tank and help pull it through as she followed behind. Assuming, of course, he could make it.

Only one way to find out . . .

Unbuckling his rebreather, he placed it in the stricture and pushed it ahead of him, clambering in afterwards. The rebreather slid through easily—his shoulders were a tighter fit. Alex pushed the rebreather forward with his right arm and angled his left backwards along his side to make himself less broad. Continuing to inch on, the passage got tighter with each inch but still allowed movement. The walls constricted all four sides of his chest and shoulders now. The beam of his headlight bounced around like a hopped-up strobe light, adding to the eeriness.

Still making slow progress, Alex continued, inching forward on his stomach with his legs straight behind. But the squeeze was getting tighter, and he needed to be extra cautious since he was alone. He was considering stopping when his forward progress halted, his shoulders stuck tight.

Great.

He moved each shoulder separately, testing how bad it was. They were both wedged, but the right was tighter. The constriction was like a band around his shoulder blades and chest, tightening with every inhalation.

Letting go of the rebreather, Alex wiggled his right hand up to brace it against the wall.

He pushed back hard. No movement at all.

Yep, pretty stuck here. Good one, Monroe . . .

There was no panic. Any vestiges Alex had ever possessed were trained out of him years ago—but this was still a bad situation to be in. He rested, bubbles circulating back into the rebreather in front of him as he assessed his options, the fingers of his right hand drumming on the floor before him.

After weighing several choices, he decided.

Both legs were free, though his left arm was wrenched at an uncomfortable angle behind him. But at least that made his shoulders narrower. Alex bent his knees and wedged his neoprene-covered heels against the ceiling of the squeeze, giving himself some purchase as his fins pointed back and down. He moved his right hand along the wall until he found a small rock outcropping to push against, then did the same with his left hand behind him, lower to the floor.

Next, he began taking deep breaths, flooding his blood with oxygen. With his final, longest inhale, the rocky constriction pressed around his ribs like a steel band encircling him. One sharp edge dug into his shoulder blade.

Exhaling as hard as he could to decrease the size of his ribcage, he contracted every muscle in his body and propelled himself backwards, pushing against his hands with everything he had.

Alex shot a foot backwards like a cork out of a bottle.

There was a scrape of pain on the back of his right shoulder as his wetsuit ripped, but he ignored it. Instead, he took a wonderful deep breath. Now he could move both shoulders.

Ok, this passage is definitely off the table.

Returning his right hand to grab the rebreather, he shimmied backwards until he was completely out of the squeeze and floating in the water. Glaring at the constriction, he moved his right shoulder around but there was only minor pain. With a growl, he replaced the rebreather on his back and reeled in the extra line before turning around and heading back to the primary channel.

Alex exhaled an angry breath.

That was a real dumbass thing to do. You know better.

Even if he'd been with a qualified partner, he could have gotten stuck—permanently.

I'm letting my worry about Hope cloud my judgement.

Which didn't give her enough credit. She was a great diver. With some instruction on cave procedures, she could get through the other squeeze. Though her uneasiness during their deep dive gave him pause. And Syria had taught him you could be fully prepared and still have things go horribly wrong.

The mere thought of her having an accident in this cave chilled him to the bone.

Once back at the junction, he untied the green line and clipped his reel back onto the rebreather. Then he turned left and headed toward the squeeze in the bigger channel, shimmying an extra scuba tank further into it. Now that the squeeze was the only path forward, he needed to ensure a nearby source of air for Hope. He carried his own in the pony bottle.

One task left.

Alex made his way back down the passage once again to the offshoot, tying off a length of his green line in a vertical slash across the opening, a standard signal to all divers of a No Entry Zone.

After climbing out of the pool, he made his way to the hidden small cave and took off the rebreather with a sigh. The tear in his wetsuit was easily reparable. He picked up his phone and texted Hope that he was done diving. With one final look at the black cave, he turned toward the path.

He had plenty to occupy his mind on the hike back.

∽

Alex checked his phone periodically on the way back to the resort, but there was no answer from Hope. She was probably knee-deep in some invoices or guest emergencies. He was in awe of her focus on the minutiae of running the thriving resort. He sure couldn't do it.

Wanting to check in with her in person, he climbed the lobby steps and entered. There was a small crowd checking in, and Alex sharpened his gaze. Hope was working the front desk, probably filling in for Martine.

Focused on the six guests in front of her, she hadn't seen him. A happy, polite smile graced her face, but it was strained. Concerned she hadn't seen his text, he stepped out of the shadows. She turned her attention to him immediately, pleased but not surprised to see him. *Ok, she's just been really busy*.

He had a group of six divers starting tomorrow, and the odds were good this was them. Alex joined her behind the front desk, clasping her hand behind the counter.

"Well, you're in luck. Here's the guy you'll be diving with tomorrow." Hope squeezed his hand tightly.

The older gray-haired man shook Alex's hand. "We just wanted to make sure we didn't need to check in today at the dive shop."

"No, don't worry about it. Just show up at the dive shop about

8:30 and I'll get you checked in and ready to go. Today, just enjoy a beer and dig your toes into the sand."

The guy grinned. "I like you already! You talk my language."

Hope turned her professional smile to him and said, "Go on ahead, Alex. I'll get these folks squared away."

He watched her closely, and she squeezed his hand again. Relenting, he left and stopped by his mailbox before walking toward the house, pleased to see the latest issue of *Scuba Today*.

He stopped by the kitchen and filled two containers with pasta before heading down the beach. Cruz was on the porch, wagging and ready to go in for the night. The two of them entered, and Alex dove into his dinner, starving. Guilt rippled through him at not waiting for Hope, but he didn't know how long she'd be.

Finally, he couldn't resist the rich cinnamon scent permeating the house and moved to the kitchen. Multiple containers of freshly baked cookies lay on the counter, ready for several days of dive trips. He couldn't resist lifting two—Hope's cookies were every bit as good as Gerold's. He settled in the great room with his magazine. There was a feature article on different methods for nursing coral fragments, and he was soon absorbed.

Eventually, Hope entered, not seeing him. With pain and weariness etched on her face, she made a beeline for the kitchen, filling a glass with water. She opened a cabinet and took out a bottle of ibuprofen, shaking out several and swallowing them with a deep sigh, her brows lowered.

Alex understood the problem immediately. "You ok?"

She snapped her head up and the pain disappeared behind her mask.

And she calls me stubborn.

"Yes, I'll be all right." She smiled tightly and joined him on the couch, settling into the hollow of his shoulder.

"I grabbed some pasta for dinner. Yours is in the fridge."

"Thanks. I'm not very hungry, though." She sat up, the lines etched in her forehead. "I think I'll just head to bed. I'm pretty tired."

He studied her. *This isn't the time to press the issue.* "I'll be along after a while."

"Don't be too disappointed if I'm asleep. It's been a long day." She kissed him and headed toward the bedroom.

With a sigh, he padded into the guest room and did his usual weight routine. Cruz had been sitting outside the bedroom door as he passed but joined Alex in the guest room while he worked out, lying down next to Hope's new treadmill. "I know, boy. I'm worried about her too."

After, he took a quick shower in the guest bath so he wouldn't disturb her, then crawled into bed, wanting nothing more than to curl himself around her and give her comfort, but afraid to intrude on her private misery when she'd finally found relief in sleep.

CHAPTER 19

Hope opened her eyes to morning light streaming into the bedroom. She glanced at the clock and flinched. It was past 6:30, yet she was still groggy. Unsurprisingly, Alex's side of the bed was empty. Pulling on leggings and one of his sweatshirts, she made herself a cup of coffee with the mug he had set out for her. She smiled at the simple, thoughtful gesture. She rarely beat him out of bed, but always made his coffee when she did.

After taking her morning dose of ibuprofen, Hope opened the sliding glass door, widening her eyes. Alex sat on the porch couch, staring at the ocean.

"You're still here," Hope said, snuggling up to him. "No swim this morning?"

"No. I was planning to but decided on an extra cup of coffee and watching the ocean instead."

"I'm glad you did." She yawned, taking another sip. Even an extra cup of coffee wasn't waking her up anymore.

Alex's coffee remained untouched on the table as he stared with unfocused eyes at the beach. Despite what he'd said, skipping his morning swim wasn't something he did without reason—it was integral to keeping his injured hip healthy.

"Everything ok this morning?" she asked.

He didn't answer right away, tapping two fingers on his thigh. "I've been out here thinking about the cave. I need to tell you something about my trip yesterday."

She sat up straighter. "Go ahead."

Alex dropped his eyes to the floor. "I got stuck. Trying to get through that alternate passage."

Hope's blood ran cold. "Stuck?"

"There was a really tight squeeze in that offshoot, but it was short. I thought I could get through . . . I was wrong."

"But you made it out."

He nodded. "Without too much trouble. But it wasn't one of my smarter moves."

It didn't sound like Alex at all. "Why did you try it?"

He gave her a faint smile before rubbing his hands over his face. "Because it was short. I thought it might be safer for you."

Ok, that sounds like Alex...

Hope kept a rein on her temper, not at all sleepy anymore. "I'm glad you told me, but this is a perfect example of you just deciding what's safe for me. You know damn well I never would have wanted you to do that."

"I know. I'm being honest here." He met her gaze steadily, not backing down. "My natural instinct—my *very strong* natural instinct—is to protect you. I just found out that can be rather counterproductive."

Hope tried to bite back a smile, unable to resist him. "Well, it's about time something got through that thick skull of yours."

"It's not easy." Alex cracked his knuckles on his head. "Pretty much solid cement in here."

Their eyes locked, and they broke out into smiles. "So, having learned an important lesson, what's the next move, Jughead?"

Alex laughed. "The next step is a night dive, so you get a feel for how to dive in the dark. And I need to give you some instruction on cave techniques."

Hope's smile faded. "Be honest with me. Is it safe for me to go through that squeeze?"

He matched her serious expression. "Caves are never completely safe. All you can do is mitigate the danger. But, yes. With some additional training, you could get through it with minimal danger." His eyes softened. "And I'm always honest with you."

She brushed her lips over his. "Then let's go ahead. I've got the manager's reception tonight, so how about tomorrow for the night dive?"

"Deal. We'll do it here on the house reef." He glanced at his watch. "I need to get going. We've got a full boat today."

Alex left a short time later as Hope finished her coffee, contemplating the cave. Of course cave diving was dangerous, but Alex would make sure she was prepared. She sighed, trying not to chafe at his overprotectiveness.

If there is more treasure in that cave, I have every right to be there alongside him!

"Time to work off some of this negative energy," she murmured, then strode into the house. After changing into running clothes, she hopped on her treadmill in the guest room. Planning a forty-five-minute run, she started easy, but her legs were like lead this morning. She slowed the belt to walking speed. *Just a little breather, then I'll pick up the pace again.*

After ten minutes, she gave up. Slamming a frustrated fist on the stop button, Hope climbed off, having barely broken a sweat. She marched to the bathroom and appraised her reflection.

No doubt about it. She was paler than she used to be. "Make the call, Hope."

With a frustrated moan, she picked up her phone from the

kitchen table and dialed. She'd selected a gynecologist here on St. Croix months ago, but just hadn't gotten around to making an appointment. The time had come, but she couldn't secure an appointment until next month.

Putting the phone down, Hope headed to the shower to prepare for her day. First on the list was heading into Frederiksted to pick up some of Robert's photos to hang in the lobby. She still had a resort to run, no matter how tired she was.

∽

LATER THAT EVENING, Hope sipped a glass of white wine as the manager's reception wound down. She'd asked Alex to come, but he'd declined, saying he had a project he needed to work on. *More scuba equipment, no doubt.*

Clark approached with the bottle of wine, but her glass was over half full. "Oh, no you don't. I've had plenty. Thanks."

He grinned, silver tooth shining. "Ah, you're no fun."

"Sounds like Half Moon Hope has been a success?"

"Our number-one cocktail."

"Well, I know you won't rest on your laurels. How's the new one coming along?"

"Good! It's a variation of a mudslide. Not quite ready to debut it, though."

"You've still got several months before the next mixology contest. I'm sure you'll have it dialed in."

With a nod, Clark continued circulating, doing one final fill before the reception ended. Hope glanced around, making sure she'd made conversation with all the guests present. The resort was fully booked, and most of them had come. By this time, the majority had headed into the restaurant for dinner, so she made her exit.

Flipping her hair back, she walked down the beach toward the house as wispy clouds raced past the moon. She climbed the stairs, opening the slider.

And stopped dead.

Alex sat at the kitchen table with a partially disassembled light-tan rifle spread out before him. He was screwing a long metal tube onto the end of the barrel when she entered.

"What're you doing there?" Heart pounding, she kept her voice even as she approached the table, resting her hands on the back of the chair opposite Alex.

He shrugged, shifting in his chair. "I've been thinking of going to the shooting range. Thought I'd see if I still remember how to put the rifle together. Not much point in shooting if I can't remember how to put her together."

Hope wasn't sure how to respond to that. "Very true." Alex had mentioned before that he'd never even taken the rifle out of its case since he'd been discharged.

He observed her closely, pausing his movements. "Going to the shooting range is kind of a big deal for me. I was a diver before I joined the Navy—going back to that felt natural to me. But this was all about me being a SEAL."

He continued assembling the rifle, watching it as he went through the practiced motions. "I was in denial for a time when I was at Walter Reed, thinking I could go back to active duty. I'd go to the range all the time and shoot, preparing for the day. Then it became apparent that wasn't going to happen. Of course, they offered me a different position—light duty or a desk job. No way. It just hurt too much. I had to get out."

He paused, looking at the rifle, his posture stiff and tense. "When my CO gave me this rifle, I didn't want anything to do with it. It was just a reminder of everything I'd lost. He told me a day would come when I'd want to shoot again. And that would be when I was ready to start living again." He gave her a tiny, crooked smile. "I'm not quite there yet. I still need to work on this a little more. But I'm a lot closer than I used to be."

~

THE FOLLOWING EVENING, Hope soaked in the beauty as the sky glowed with a vestige of red near the horizon, a canopy of glittering stars overhead. She and Alex sat under the palapa, discussing the plan for Hope's first night dive.

"One of the biggest differences is hand signals," Alex said. "Remember, if you don't shine your light on your hand, I can't see it. And Rule Number One of night diving—never shine your light in someone's face, *especially* your guide. It destroys my night vision, ok?"

"Aye, aye, Commander."

He stared at her before breaking into a grin. "I used to get pretty worked up over this subject. SEALs tend to work at night, you know."

The pair geared up and jumped off the dock into the black ocean. It was strange diving in the dark and having her world reduced to a beam of light. Alex pointed to a blue tang. It was a common solid-blue fish that developed vertical bars only at night. It hardly looked like the same fish! Tucked into crevices, several iridescent blue parrot fish produced sacs of protective mucus around themselves so predators couldn't smell them as they slept.

It was fascinating.

Hope spied a lobster scrabbling from its lair when it froze in her light. Moving the beam back and forth like Alex had taught, she caught his attention, and he turned around, seeing the lobster. He instantly toggled his powerful dive light to a red beam and gently tilted her light down. The lobster continued scampering across the reef, illuminated by Alex's red light but not afraid of it. It disappeared into a hole and Alex changed his light back to normal as they continued.

AFTER THE DIVE, they walked up the pier, hands clasped.

"That was fun," Hope said. "A little eerie, but not scary. It was so different from a day dive. So, am I ready for the cave now?"

"Yeah." He turned to her with a smile, but his eyes were serious. "We need to practice in the rock pool first. There are a couple of skills you need to be comfortable with. First, I want you to be able to take your kit on and off without any help from me—that's important. You have to take it off to get through the squeeze and I want you confident in your ability. And the second is practicing your frog kick. That's the only type of kick you do in a cave—no flutter kicking."

"Right. So you don't kick up silt?"

He nodded.

"I remember you talking about it in my class, but I don't think I've actually seen it."

"Sure you have. Remember the infamous dive with Marcus? I did a frog kick drawing away Oscar. It was just backwards."

"Oh." She laughed. "I didn't even realize backwards was possible until I saw you do it."

"We'll just stick to a forward frog kick for now. Back kicking takes a little more practice."

"I'm excited. This will be a new adventure for us, especially for me."

CHAPTER 20

A week later, Hope worked in the lobby office, anxiously awaiting her afternoon trip to the cave with Alex. The previous week, they had spent several hours in the rock pool, where she had practiced getting into and out of her scuba kit in the water and without help. Then Alex demonstrated a frog kick, which Hope quickly got the hang of, zipping around the pool with ease.

Finally, Hope entered the dark passage of the cave. After experiencing the night dive, the black environment wasn't as unnerving. Alex was adamant they go no further than the entrance of the squeeze, since they were both tired from practicing in the rock pool. They hovered side-by-side before the narrow opening, so Hope could study it fully. It was narrow, but it looked very passable to her.

Now she couldn't wait to get back. Her morning had passed at a snail's pace. Then, just after 11 a.m., a proposal appeared in her inbox from the laundry service she was considering. She carefully compared it to their current vendor, whose quality had slipped lately.

"I knew I'd find you here working. I thought we had a date

this afternoon?" She snapped her head up as Alex leaned against her door frame. Glancing at the wall clock, she was astonished it was 12:30.

"I'm so sorry! Believe it or not, I'm lost in a laundry proposal."

Alex grinned at her, impossibly handsome as he rested against her doorway. He walked into the room, leaning close behind her to look at the document in question.

"You are the only person I've ever met who can get lost in something like that."

Hope sat up with a snort. "You should see yourself when new scuba equipment comes out." His breath was hot on the back of her neck as Hope locked her computer. "Let's get going. If you stay this close to me, we'll never get there."

He laughed, then brushed her neck with his lips before standing straight. "Wait—I bet you haven't eaten anything."

"I don't need to. Come on, let's go."

"No way. I don't want you all hangry on me."

He grabbed her hand and led her out of the office. Entering the kitchen and still clutching her hand tight, he bellowed, "Gerold! What do you have ready that's suitable for hungry, cranky bosses?"

"I'm not cranky!" Hope kicked him in the shin, and he sent her a sly look.

Trying to stay serious, she sent it back since he'd obviously recognized their conversation on the Frederiksted pier about this very topic.

Gerold was putting the finishing touches on some fish tacos and glanced up. "Well, I was just makin' these for Clark, but this sounds like an emergency—he'll have to wait. And you're in luck. He wanted an extra-large order, so there's probably enough for both of you. Well, you might have to add somethin' else. Alex eats like a horse."

Gerold grabbed a to-go container, transferring the tacos before glancing at Alex. "We still on for my divin' refresher?"

"Sure. Just let me know what works for you. I've already got one set up for Tommy. I'll go over the coral-restoration procedures then too." Alex turned to Hope with a wide smile. "Even Boss Lady is getting involved. The four of us will get the transplants going together."

"I can't wait," Hope said with a grin.

Alex sent a dirty look Gerold's way as he grabbed a bag of chips. "And enough comments about my eating habits. Diving burns a lot of calories, you know. And I only have the lady's best interests at heart—I'll even give her a chip or two. Sorry, Gerold, but we've got to run."

With that, Alex picked up the box and grabbed her hand again, rushing her out onto the beach.

"Alex, would you slow down? Your legs are twice as long as mine!"

"Gotta keep the tacos warm. We're in a hurry here. Come on, let's move!"

"Oh my God, you are so bossy! This is what you were like as Commander Monroe, isn't it?"

He laughed. "Not even close."

~

BY MID-AFTERNOON, Hope hovered in front of the squeeze, breathing slowly and evaluating it. She was glad Alex had given her the chance to look at it before she had to tackle it, but it didn't look that scary. It was probably just him being his usual overprotective self. Still, she knew enough to take this seriously. Alex touched her arm and gave her an ok, and she returned it. Hope removed her tank as they had discussed, resting it on the lip of the squeeze.

She nodded to Alex that she was ready, and he removed his rebreather before scrambling into the squeeze. She waited until his fins were well inside before pushing in her tank and following behind it.

It was more difficult than she had anticipated. The aluminum tank kept getting hung up on seemingly minor protrusions. Continuing to push, tug, lift, shimmy, grunt, and swear, Hope made slow progress as she took care not to overexert herself and breathe too heavily. Hyperventilating would be a quick path to disaster in the tight confines. Finally, the staged tank appeared on her left, marking halfway.

It seemed so much shorter from the outside.

Groaning, she gave a huge push, and the kit rewarded her by sliding forward quite a bit. Hope rested for a moment, breathing steadily from the regulator before finally sighing. She belly-crawled after it and grunted it forward again, repeating this several more times. Her arms now ached with fatigue.

Then the tank magically began moving, slowly making progress as she followed.

I love you, Alex.

The BCD and tank disappeared into the void in front of her, and she exited the squeeze as Alex waited in the water.

They exchanged high fives, Alex smiling around his reg. He helped her back into her BCD, but prevented her from closing the buckles, giving the thumbs-up. They ascended together and Hope broke the surface, gazing around a much smaller cave with a domed, tan ceiling.

"You did so great." Alex cupped her face and kissed her, as if making sure she was really ok.

"I'm fine—you worry too much."

"You're welcome to tell me that as soon as we're out of here, looking up at the sky, ok?"

"All right then. Thanks for your help. That was harder than I thought it would be." She examined the area. "Where to now?"

Alex pointed to a rock ledge. "That's where I found the gold."

He climbed out and helped her up after him. After removing their tanks, the pair scrambled along the back wall to the tunnel opening. Brush marks from Alex's hands were scattered on the dirt floor.

"It seems like forever since I was here. I really want to see where this goes." Alex practically vibrated, his gaze fixed on the void before them.

Hope turned on her headlamp, making a mental note not to blind him, then stepped forward to enter the tunnel.

He stopped her. "Let me go first."

Hope sighed, gritting her teeth. "Fine. Lead on, then."

The passage was well over eight feet tall and quite wide at the entrance but narrowed once inside. After thirty feet, Alex turned sideways, scraping through a short narrowing.

Hope also turned aside, but made her way through with ease as the passage opened out again. She was able to walk normally, and finally, the tunnel opened into a third arched cavern, much smaller than the second. A shallow rock ledge led down to more water, ten feet away. This smaller room was a deep gray, and shadows flitted about as the walls absorbed the light from their handlamps. The vaulted ceiling rose high above, and it smelled staler than the last cavern.

Hope proceeded to the water's edge, observing the small room. The walls were sheer as they descended into the water, and she couldn't see any fissures or tunnels.

Hope sighed, disappointment rising. "Looks like the end of the line."

As she turned back toward the tunnel, her headlamp beam illuminated the floor where a small cloth bundle was wedged against the rock wall near the entrance. She knelt and unwrapped the fabric. It mostly disintegrated in her hands, revealing a leatherbound book with gold-leaf edges.

"Alex, come here."

He approached and added his light to the scene. Hope opened the book, which was printed in English. Thumbing through it, she found archaic spellings of words and vibrant, multicolored illustrations. It was an old Bible.

She stopped when several folded pieces of paper were revealed in the middle of the book. Hope opened them to find a letter, the handwriting choppy and hard to read. She glanced through the aged pages, but the scrawled lines were too difficult to make out in the dim confines.

"This looks really old," Hope said. "We need to get this back to the house where we have better light. I can barely read this, but maybe I can transcribe it. This might explain where the gold came from."

Alex inspected the small area. "This shelf is solid rock, so there's no place to bury anything. Though if the water level has fluctuated over the years, it could be submerged now. I can look around underwater."

Hope put the letter back inside and held up the Bible. "Do you have a way of keeping this dry?"

Alex nodded. "I've got a dry pocket. I'll put it in there. How much air do you have left?"

She checked her wrist computer and sighed. "1950 psi."

Alex shot her a sad smile. "Time to head back. But now we've got something more to work with."

∽

After showering, Hope stood in the closet as she pulled on a T-shirt and shorts. The cave exploration was bringing out more of Alex's protective side. And her impatience was growing.

"He's not condescending on purpose, you know," she murmured to herself. "And you aren't exactly perfect, either."

Her gaze drifted to the locked metal box on the floor, which she could look at without any qualms. Alex had moved her deeply with what he'd told her the night he'd assembled his rifle. It also made her more comfortable having such a deadly weapon in the house.

Alex wasn't violent, but walking in on him at the table had shocked her. Her own history with a violent man saw to that. His explanation, and even more, his calmness, with no hint of aggression, eased her own misgivings.

But her thoughts quickly turned back to their discovery. She spun around, eager to start deciphering the mysterious letter.

CHAPTER 21

*D*ressed in a long-sleeved shirt and jeans, Alex entered the stifling, humid garage, and climbed into his classic Land Cruiser. He pulled onto the highway with his jaw set tight. His cave exploration with Hope had been a week ago.

A week he'd spent building up to this decision.

Thirty minutes later, he was bumping down a dirt track in the middle of nowhere—or more specifically—central St. Croix. He parked in the dirt lot and drummed his fingers on the steering wheel, pensive now that he was actually doing this. Studying the sign in front of him, he was full of equal measures of anticipation and dread. Buccaneer Shooting Range.

Alex had started thinking about shooting again when it became obvious he'd have to take Hope into that cave. A constant ball of anxiety had throbbed in his stomach the entire time she'd been in the squeeze, and a five-thousand-pound weight had come off his shoulders at the sight of her exiting it safely.

She had every right to be there, and he couldn't protect her from everything. But exposing her to the dangers of an underwater cave unsettled him deeply, and he started thinking about a healthy outlet for his tension.

"You can only swim and lift weights so much," he muttered to the empty car.

And this was about much more than tension relief.

Shooting again was a huge step for him, and he was glad this tropical-island range was so different from those he'd used before. It was time to make new memories and stop defining himself by his past. But that was harder now that his past was a known commodity. He'd never gone after accolades, and his minor celebrity status didn't please him.

I don't go looking for trouble, but it seems to find me.

With a final bump of his fist on the wheel, he opened the door and entered the office of the gun range. A portly bald man stood behind the counter, his nametag reading Earl. "Howdy. Here to shoot?"

"Yeah. It's been a while. What do you have here?"

"We got several hundred-yard lanes and a few two hundred. And skeet and clay pigeon too."

"Any long range?"

Earl sent his brows skyward. "We got one with targets to a thousand yards. You gotta qualify for that, though. You like to pretend you're a sniper or something?"

"Nope, I don't pretend to be anything." Alex clamped down on his irritation, keeping his voice even. "Just asking some questions is all."

Earl cocked his head, studying him. "You been in before? You look familiar."

"Nope. First time here." Alex avoided eye contact.

"You must have one of those faces—you look familiar. What're you shooting?"

"Handgun and rifle."

"I'll give you Lane 6. It's got short-range targets for handguns, then you can knock 'em over to use the ones downrange for rifle practice."

"That'll work. Thanks."

"Sure. I'll check you in and get you a waiver to sign. Can I see your ID?"

Alex dug his wallet out and handed him his Navy ID.

"Navy man, huh? I imagine you've shot before then." Earl frowned for a moment, inspecting the ID and mouthing "Alex Monroe" before handing it back with a polite smile.

"Like I said, it's been a while."

Wonder if I can even hit the target.

"Got everything you need?"

Alex nodded, looking down as he replaced his wallet.

"Ok, you're set. We've already got targets out there. Bill is the range boss—ask him any questions you might have." Earl glanced at the clock. "The range is hot for another thirty minutes, so you can get going."

Alex went back to the car and opened the back, pulling out a duffel range bag with his pistol and Betsy's padlocked case. It was a short walk to Lane 6, and he passed a bull of a man on the way, nodding at him. Alex confirmed this was the range boss when his nametag read Bill. The two men walked side by side, nearly the same height except Bill had the physique of a muscular man who had added a layer of flab over time.

"Haven't seen you before. First time?" Bill studied him closely, and Alex suppressed a sigh.

"At this range. But I haven't shot in a while."

Alex got to his lane and set his things down on the concrete table. There was a pad down for prone shooting, and plenty of room to stand next to it. There were only two other shooters, both at the other end in hundred-yard lanes.

"What're you shooting today?" Bill stared at the padlocked case.

"A rifle and handgun."

Bill whipped his head up to meet Alex's eyes. "You don't know the models?"

"Yes. MK13 and Sig P226." Alex spoke evenly, waiting for Bill's reaction.

His face went slack. "Don't see those every day. All right then. I'm here if you have any questions. We're hot right now so go ahead." He gave Alex another hard look before moving away.

Alex opened his bag, putting on ear protection and safety glasses. He removed the pistol and quickly loaded it. There were a variety of near targets, and farther downrange were four more spaced between twenty-five and two hundred yards. Bill was now on his cell phone, no doubt getting the scoop from Earl.

Alex stood at the line and assumed a firing stance, taking a deep breath and trying to ignore the nerves in his gut.

I'm probably about to make a fool of myself.

Alex sighted the three-yard target, both eyes open. Breathing out, he shot three times. All three hit center target, and he twitched the corner of his mouth. He repeated it with seven and ten yards and then again until he emptied the magazine.

After reloading, he aimed at the twenty-five-yard target and fired two shots. These ended up slightly left of center. He adjusted and the next rounds entered the center of the bullseye.

A rush replaced the nervousness, and the first glimmerings of hope appeared.

But fifty yards would be the real challenge. Alex stood back and forced his shoulders to relax. Resetting, he watched the wind as he shot at the end of his inhale. He overcompensated and the first shots went slightly right, but the third entered the center. He fired several more at the end of an exhale or inhale. They all hit dead-on, and a slow smile crept across his face.

Alex moved back to the table and unloaded his weapon, quickly putting it back in the bag, and unlocked the metal case. The nerves came back just looking at Betsy, but he ignored them, rapidly assembling the rifle and screwing the suppressor on the end of the barrel. At least his movements were comfortable and assured once again.

He'd loved the challenge of long-range shooting—the mental aspects of it. It wasn't about being a badass with a fancy gun. Alex had been a professional who calculated precise trajectories and angles in an instant. And he'd been good at it.

Really good at it—making shots from thousands of yards.

Everything was set up and ready to go when Bill announced cold range and Alex could enter the field and push over the near targets onto the ground, making the farther targets easier to see.

Two hundred yards. Seven years ago, I wouldn't have even bothered.

Stopping the thought in its tracks, he picked up his casings and other debris.

Once the range was hot again, Alex stood at the line, an extra magazine in each back pocket. After some indecision, he started small with the one-hundred-yard target and took another deep breath, settling himself. Though the handgun had given him confidence, the rifle was a very different animal. Fortunately, his nerves had never manifested in shaking hands.

Standing, he brought the rifle up to his right shoulder. With his cheek against the guard, he sighted down the scope, astonished at how natural it felt. Like he'd just done it yesterday. With both eyes open, he breathed normally, and after exhaling, pulled the trigger.

And missed the target completely.

"Shit."

Alex didn't move, just closed his eyes and calmed himself.

You can do this—you've done it a thousand times. Concentrate!

Reopening his eyes, he gauged the wind and terrain and focused on his breathing. Concentrated on the familiar feel of the stock against his shoulder. He was an expert at this.

Alex shot again.

This time, he hit the target dead center, and his heart soared. He shot four more rounds with the same result, as the rifle recoiled hard against his shoulder. *Guess it's a good thing I got shot in the left shoulder, not the right.*

He swapped out magazines and aimed for the two-hundred-yard target, now standing tall and confident. Same procedure—watching the wind and calculating the angles. Alex softly squeezed the trigger three times, using the bolt action to chamber each new round. All hit the center, and he shot twice more with the same result.

Raising his head, he stared at the target for several moments. His smile returned as a rush of strong emotion rose inside him.

After retrieving two more magazines, he lay down on the mat in prone position. Bill was openly watching him now, his eyes wide. Alex refocused himself and pushed the memories away—memories of many operations where he'd been in this same position.

Stop it. You're starting again.

With the loaded weapon and two spare magazines, he now had fifteen bullets for the bolt-action rifle. Alex set up, rifle in its rest, and aimed at the two-hundred-yard target, confident now. He shot all three magazines in quick succession, making all fifteen shots to his satisfaction. Not all dead center, but everything hit the target. He returned to his feet with a satisfied sigh, feeling lighter now.

Definitely rusty. But yeah—it's still there.

Alex ran his left hand over the barrel as he closed his eyes. Relief washed over him, along with the same emotion as a few minutes before. It took him a moment to define.

It was pride.

He moved to the table and disassembled the rifle, replacing it into the case and padlocking it shut. Bill called cold range, walking toward Alex's lane as he picked up the shell casings and made sure the area was clean. "You want me to get the targets?"

"No, don't bother. We do that when we clean between shooters." He approached Alex. "How long has it been since you shot?"

"About seven years."

"You must've been hell on wheels. Nice shooting." He held out his hand. "Bill Jenkins."

"Alex Monroe."

Bill nodded as they shook. "That's what I thought. You've been in the news a fair bit."

"Not by choice."

"No, I can't imagine getting shot is anyone's choice. Sounds like you did a lot to put that asshole away, though."

Alex shrugged, ready to change the subject. "I'd be interested in your long range. What do I need to do to qualify?"

Bill laughed, lifting his baseball hat to scratch his head. "You just did. It goes to a thousand yards, but I'm guessing you've got some experience with that."

"Some, yes." Excitement built at the prospect—returning to a familiar challenge.

"So, you're a dive guide these days?"

"Yeah," Alex said with a smile.

Bill started laughing. "That was some fine shooting. I think you might be a little overqualified for your job."

Alex's smile widened into a full grin. "What can I say? Diving's always been my first love." He nodded his head toward the range. "Shooting was just my job."

He picked up his things and headed back to his car, his smile lingering. That final bit of conversation with Bill was something he never would have shared even a few months ago.

~

As Alex drove into the garage, the final conversation he'd had with his commanding officer was at the forefront of his mind. That someday he'd be ready to live again. Hope's face filled his mind, and warmth radiated through his chest.

Someday had officially arrived.

A grin cracked his face as he looked around Steve's old garage, then opened the front door to his old house. It was Hope's now, but Alex was at home there and secure enough not to be threatened by living there or that she was his boss.

In fact, he rather enjoyed the role reversal, especially in contrast to his former life. He might have gone years here in St. Croix without an intimate relationship, but he was making up for lost time now.

The grin grew wider as he became aroused.

He closed the front door against the late-afternoon heat and inhaled the incredible scent permeating the house. Hope stood at the dishwasher, cleaning up as several loaves of freshly baked bread cooled on the counter. She had always worked too hard, and he was relieved she was finally confident enough to turn over much of the day-to-day operations to Patti—which was the general manager's job, after all. Now she could be productive and explore a favorite hobby too.

And he certainly wasn't going to complain that her newly rediscovered passion had such delicious results. Passion was at the forefront of his mind as he stared at her low-cut top as she bent over the dishwasher, forgetting about the bread.

Standing straight, she cocked her head at him as a warm smile appeared. "You certainly are happy about something. Things went well at the shooting range, I take it?"

He tried to pay attention. "Yes, and I didn't embarrass myself too badly."

She removed her apron to reveal a black and yellow sundress, the one he loved because it matched her eyes in the sunlight. Now he was hard as a rock and marched over to her, lifting her against his stomach so he could kiss her face-to-face. She gave a squeak that quickly turned to a soft moan as she ran her hands through his hair.

Hope pressed against him before breaking their kiss. "You are happy to see me, aren't you?"

The evidence was obvious, so he didn't deny it. "I was

thinking about you on the drive home and wanted to greet you properly." He kissed her again and set her back on her feet as he looked at the three neat loaves. "Your bread smells amazing."

"Is that supposed to be a double entendre?" She rubbed her hand against the front of his jeans, and he whipped his eyes back to hers.

He pressed against her hand and gave a soft laugh. "It can be whatever you want it to be."

An electric jolt ran through him as their mouths met again, and their tongues brushed. He lifted her skirt, placing his hands on her hips and discovering nothing but Hope.

"Oh my God," he breathed against her mouth. "You haven't worn panties all day?"

She responded with a throaty laugh that made him jerk. "No, I took them off as soon as I got home. Apparently, we were having similar thoughts."

"Oh? And what did you have in mind, Boss Lady?"

She had his shorts open now. "I think you already have a very good idea."

Alex pulled the dress off over her head, then he traced his hands up the skin of her back and unhooked her bra, sliding them around to her breasts and circling them. "I have no clue what you're talking about."

His breathing was getting faster by the second.

He broke off the contact to quickly undress, tossing his clothes aside without a care, and moaned as their hot skin came together and he kissed her again.

Alex lifted her as she wrapped her legs around his waist, setting her down on the kitchen table. He leaned forward, pressing her down on her back. As he settled between her legs, Hope pulled his mouth to hers again, hungry for more.

He did his best to give it to her.

. . .

AFTERWARDS, he rested his head on her chest as his rapid exhalations raised goosebumps on her sweaty skin. Both his arms were out sideways, gripping the edge of the table, and his left shoulder was sore. He must have been gripping hard. He let go of the edge, taking the strain off his left arm as he brought it closer.

Alex relaxed, snuggling his head into her neck. "I could stay like this forever."

"Easy for you to say. You're not the one lying on the kitchen table."

He laughed against her chest, kissed her breast one last time, then stood and pulled her upright. He couldn't think of a better way to end a very satisfying afternoon.

CHAPTER 22

Hope spent her afternoon at the front desk, taking over when Martine needed time off for a prenatal appointment. Most of the guests had already checked in, leaving her time to fully investigate the two recipes Patti had given her that morning. They were native Cruzan baked goods, and Hope couldn't wait to get started.

Though awaiting her doctor's appointment and the news it might bring, she had a renewed surge of energy at reconciling two of her new passions—the resort and baking.

A smirk rose on her face. *Other than Alex, of course.*

She had always loved cooking, even taking culinary classes, but quickly discovered Gerold didn't need her help. Baking goodies to provide the divers on their surface interval had been warmly received by all.

Patti had given her a recipe for a local shortbread cookie and a quick bread, and Hope loved the idea of providing a local touch for their guests. Patti had been in a wonderful mood when she shared her family recipes, but it had faded by the end of the day. Hope followed her progress as she stormed off to give her latest reprimand to the errant dishwasher, though so far she'd stopped short of firing him outright.

The next time she looked at the wall clock, it was past quitting time, so she shut down the front-desk computer. At last, she was able to give her full attention to her other project—even more exciting than Patti's recipes. Her attention fell to the scrawled note former owner Steve had left, reminding the front-desk agent to shut off the computer before leaving. With a frown, she ripped it off. Though meant as a friendly reminder, it had always irritated her. Martine didn't need any reminders, and neither did she.

And Steve is a reminder of the past. The resort is in a new era now.

As Hope made her way to the house, the expectancy built further. Cruz met her inside the slider, a clear indication Alex had beaten her home even if she hadn't heard the shower in the master suite. After a quick hello, Hope rushed to her office, then returned to the kitchen with her laptop and the precious file folder.

At last.

She sat at the table and opened the folder, rubbing her hands together. Staring at the yellowed paper before her, she studied it for several minutes before typing on the computer.

"Are you ever going to finish that and show me what you figured out?" Alex asked, retrieving a beer from the fridge.

"Yes! I'm so close. I should finish tonight."

Alex came over for a kiss, running a light finger over her tattoo.

Hope slammed her laptop closed and turned over the paper as he laughed.

"Don't worry. I wouldn't dream of trying to breach your defenses."

She crossed her arms. "Well, you did tell me not long ago that no secret was safe from you."

"I'm betting I'll find this one out soon enough."

She went back to work as he settled on the couch with his own laptop. An hour later, she was done. Typing the last word in triumph, Hope sat back in her chair.

Is this real?

After printing the results of her project, Hope returned to the great room, a smirk forming as she noted Alex's laptop was open to some review of a new BCD just released.

The energy bubbled up as she sat next to him. "Alex, it's done."

"Oh, are you finally going to let me see it? You ripped that Bible out of my hands as soon as we got back from the cave and spirited away the letter." He leaned forward, wagging his eyebrows. "I thought maybe you were trying to cut me out."

She shot him a dirty look. "I hope you know me better than that." But her excitement couldn't be denied. "I think I've figured most of it out. Well, really all of it—I was able to piece together the parts that were the hardest to make out."

She broke into an awestruck smile. "Here. Read."

O*CTOBER (?), 1671*
Dearest Brother Henry,

I HOPE *this letter finds you well. I want to make you aware of my endeavors, for they are significant indeed. There must remain a record of my adventures and resulting peril.*

How did I come to be here on this wretched island? Even now, I am not sure. It began in that deplorable town of Cartagena, in Colombia. Yes, I can see you reaching for the decanter. You know well my avarice for gold. I came to be there courtesy of a British merchantman on which I was serving, which put into port for repairs after one of the infernal storms that plague this sea.

I wandered the dirt animal tracks that serve as roads here, carrying my venerable King James Bible as ever—and with these very sheets of blank vellum contained within—to protect against misdeeds on my part. I shall let you be the judge of its effectiveness.

I was amazed watching the mule trains come in from points further inland, which are even more horrible than this town, I have been informed. The mules go on for miles, Henry, each one loaded down with gold, silver, and precious works. It is an astonishing sight.

I watched the mule train for quite some time, then followed—discreetly!—to the quay, where the panniers were transferred to sturdy boxes and loaded onto the Spanish galleons. I studied this for a long while and eventually found myself quite thirsty indeed.

Fortunately, there were many drinking establishments nearby. I entered one and enjoyed a glass of ale. The next thing I recalled, I was at sea, inside a barrel onboard the Senora de Margarita. I am afraid rum might have been involved as well as ale. My experience as a seaman came in handy, as I was able to explore the ship without detection during the night watch.

I located where the treasure boxes were stored, but they were under heavy guard, as you might imagine. Several days continued like this, spending days inside my barrel and nights exploring and stealing food from the hold and twice from the galley! Trying to find a way to pinch one of the tantalizing boxes.

Then one of the horrible storms worked in my favor for once.

It sank the ship!

Once it became clear the ship was foundering, I alighted from my barrel and took advantage of the chaos, rushing down to the hold. I was able to liberate a single box, place it on a door that had broken free in the tempest, and push myself into the raging ocean. I clung to my door for dear life—completely alone in the world.

I drifted for a full day and night before I came ashore here on this jungle Hades of an island. I have no idea where I am, only that I overheard the Spanish sailors talking about Santa Cruz, which would be a sign of Providence, as I know you were stationed there (here?) over a *decade ago. I am marooned on the western expanse of this island, no habitation nearby that I can deduce.*

I made my way inland a mile or so and found an ample supply of fresh water in the form of a large pool with a cave to provide a shelter of sorts. I spent an indescribably terrible day dragging my precious, but very heavy, box through the jungle and into the cave—a very perilous venture as the entrance is just a narrow shelf above the waterline.

But I succeeded!

And I am determined to hide my great secret and return to it later. Though in the event I am unable, I wanted to describe its location to you, as a sort of earthly bequest to leave behind. With help from Providence, I shall deliver this letter to you in person, if only to see your astonished face upon reading it.

There are two passages that must be traversed. The first is no issue except a narrow section at one point. However, the second passage is partially filled with water and thick mud. I retrieved my faithful door and was able to float my box to the final, enormous cavern! I can see you smiling at my cleverness.

Here I decided I had gone quite far enough indeed. I thought of burying the box in true pirate fashion, but the floors of these caverns are solid rock. Alas, I had to leave it pressed into a corner. The larger question remains, however. What am I to do now?

Fate seems to have intervened, sending me a message—I have lost my talismans. Shortly after arriving, I took to carrying around in my pocket some trinkets from the box, including a stupendous pendant. Now they are gone. There is a rend in my pocket, and I am bereft.

I must seek rescue. I cannot carry this letter on my person in case I am attacked. My plan is to hide it inside my Bible well inside the cave and make my way overland. After I am rescued and safe, I will return to the bay near here. After all this time, I am all too familiar with the area and will recognize it instantly.

I shall leave this awful island with my box in hand, to head home to Mother and Father and prove to them that the younger Morgan son is capable of great feats also, and thus, deliver this letter to you in person. But first I must determine that there are indeed people on this island.

Alas, my quill from some wretched local bird is nearly destroyed and my crushed berries used for ink are waning, so I must end my missive for now. I will update this letter as soon as I return.

Your very best brother and servant,
   Barnaby Morgan

Alex turned his attention from the typed pages in his hand to the stained and yellowed vellum she held. "You got all this from that chicken scratch?"

"That's what took me so long. I wanted to make sure I got it right. At least it was in English." As he had read the letter, she retrieved the coins and necklace from the wall safe in her office before sitting next to him.

Hope inspected the pendant, saying, "It looks like this came from Colombia. I've read up on it, and Columbia was the primary source of emeralds for the Spanish Empire, so I guess that explains the size of this thing." The oval pendant itself was the size of her hand, with the emerald nearly as big as her palm. "Barnaby says his plan was to return and take the box home with him. He carried that Bible all the way across the Atlantic Ocean —it meant a lot to him. I don't think he would just grab the box and abandon the Bible."

Alex nodded as he turned a coin over in his fingers. "He took off overland and probably got killed somewhere on the island." He shook his head, but an excited smile escaped as he turned to Hope. "This letter means there's a good chance the box is still there."

She laughed, swinging the pendant back and forth on its golden chain. "I know!"

"The letter says there's a second passage that leads to another big cavern. I'll try to get in there sometime in the next week and see what it's like. Though we can be pretty sure it ends up on dry land, or at least it did several hundred years ago. The whole place could be submerged now. And Barnaby describes the entrance to the main cave as being a narrow shelf. I saw that on my first dive—it's about ten feet underwater now."

"You're just going to explore the passage, right? Don't you dare go treasure hunting without me."

His face became serious as he brushed the hair away from her face. "I'm sorry I can be an ass sometimes. I don't mean to coddle you—I can't help wanting to protect you. This is your find. I promise I'll turn around as soon as I find enough dry land to be worth exploring."

"I'm sorry too. I get too impatient. You never call attention to yourself—" she touched his left shoulder— "and your protectiveness has come in pretty handy."

A ghost of a smile crept across his face. "If there's any treasure in that cave, we'll find it together. Of course, we're assuming the tunnel is passable. Only one way to find out."

CHAPTER 23

The late-afternoon sun cast a golden glow over the ocean. Hope breathed in the bracing air and wriggled her bare feet over the wooden planks of the pier. Laughter erupted behind her, and she turned to see Tommy and Gerold walking down the pier. "Here they come."

Alex glanced up from the last of the four scuba kits he was assembling. "Right on time."

"You've got everythin' ready to go," Gerold said. "I thought for sure you'd make us set up our own gear."

"I did that when I gave you two your refreshers. Besides, Boss Lady is watching. I need her to think I know what I'm doing."

"Too late for that," Tommy added.

Hope smacked him in the belly with his wetsuit. "Here. This is yours." She handed over a second wetsuit to Gerold more gently.

Alex straightened and pointed offshore to the north. "The roof is over there in forty feet of water. I've got several different species of coral growing there, but today we'll just transplant some of the staghorn to the house reef."

"I'm excited you guys want to help with this," Hope said. "Especially since you both worked today."

"Are you kidding?" Gerold said with a laugh. "We love the idea! I've been wantin' to do more divin', and we can help with something important while we do it."

Tommy regarded Alex, his usual joking nature gone. "When you make your livin' from the ocean, keepin' it healthy is important."

"Thanks. The extra pair of hands will be a help," Alex added. "This is a labor-intensive process, so the more the merrier."

He turned to the wooden bench behind him and picked up several small plastic bags filled with white putty. "Here's the cement. Just keep it in the pocket of your BCD. When we get down there, I'll demonstrate how to transplant the coral. Then we'll work in buddy teams until we're done or low on air." He pointed at Tommy. "That means you."

"Yeah, yeah." Tommy patted his belly. "You're just jealous of my manly physique."

A wave of happiness rolled through Hope as the four of them zipped up their wetsuits. Alex had spent time with both Tommy and Gerold alone over the previous several weeks to tune up their diving skills, and Hope was excited to dive with her three favorite guys.

Soon, the four divers were finning toward the new coral nursery. Alex led them to the PVC staghorn-coral trees, indicating the one with the largest fragments of the spiky brown growths. He cut the most promising prospects, and the group proceeded across the sand to the house reef.

Hope's dive computer indicated they were still at forty feet. Alex wrote on his dive slate, turning it around for them to read. Transplant 35-45 feet. They need the same sunlight and water temp as the nursery. After getting their confirmations, Alex withdrew a baggie of cement, snipped off a corner of it, and squeezed a small portion onto a smooth surface of rock. He attached the coral fragment, pressing it onto the reef.

Next, Alex pointed to Tommy and squeezed out another measure of glue as he instructed him on how to anchor the coral to its new home. Gerold and Hope followed. After everyone had a good idea of the procedure, they split up into their teams.

Hope had a wonderful time working beside Alex, and it was good dive training for her. Hovering still above the reef while transplanting the corals gave her a new appreciation for how much harder it was to maintain neutral buoyancy without forward movement.

An hour later, there were numerous spiky brown and tan fragments of staghorn coral firmly attached to bare portions of the reef. Curious fish flitted around them, investigating even as they brought nutrients, helping the corals adjust to their new homes.

Alex floated a short distance away from Hope, scanning the reef. He caught her glance, and a satisfied smile crossed his face. Tommy and Gerold attached their last pieces of coral and the quartet joined together once again.

As they were turning from the reef, Alex grabbed Hope's arm, jabbing his finger at a very pretty foot-long black-and-white fish she'd never seen before. He unclipped his slate and wrote on it. When he turned it around, Hope discovered it was an adult version of the tiny spotted drum fish she'd found on their deep dive in the current.

It looked so different!

Now the elongated dorsal fin was much smaller than its body. Its vertical bars were limited to the front half of its body, while the back was covered in white spots. They shared a smile, then moved away so Tommy and Gerold got a good look. With a nod, Alex led the group back to the pier.

The restoration had truly been launched now.

. . .

Tommy and Gerold left after Alex and Hope insisted on cleaning the gear. As the couple walked along the wooden planks toward the resort, a vision sprang to Hope's mind of when she had manhandled Sara up this same pier after her sister had seen Alex for the first time. She couldn't help grinning, but it faded when her thoughts turned to their treasure hunt. "It feels kind of weird to be keeping the cave from Sara, or anyone else here."

"I know what you mean. But we have to—we can't risk word getting out, especially locally. If someone decided to explore that cave by themselves, they could die."

"Yeah, I know. And it's not like we really have anything to report to our sisters. How's Kate doing?"

"Busy," Alex said, then turned to her with a grin. "She told me the kids are already asking when they can come back here. That made me feel pretty good. Speaking of sisters, is Sara up to date on everything that's happened?"

"Yes." Hope turned a smug smile on him. "She wants to meet Kate sometime, so she can get new ammunition to use against you."

"Great. I was hoping I wouldn't face a cross-examination on her next visit. I'd rather face the defense attorney again."

Hope laughed at him, sliding her arm around his waist. "I'm just giving you a hard time. I think she's more on your side than mine at this point."

"I highly doubt that."

∿

That night, Hope woke from a sound sleep as dull pain radiated through her gut. It was 3 a.m. Sighing, she crept out of bed, trying not to wake Alex as she padded out to the kitchen and gulped some ibuprofen. As she crossed to the slider, Cruz yawned at her from his bed in the corner but wasn't inclined to follow her outside. "Well, you've gone soft, haven't you?"

She sat down in one of the two glider chairs she'd bought, finding the rocking motion soothing as another cramp hit. Fortunately, the ibuprofen knocked down the pain. She just needed to wait for it to kick in.

It was a beautiful night. The moon was nearing the western horizon and throwing a shimmering white stripe along the ocean. The water was gentle tonight, softly shushing as it swept along the beach.

As she watched the area in front of her, a movement caught her attention. Something large was exiting the ocean. Hope stood and crossed to the railing. It was a big turtle wandering around on the beach, and she experienced a stab of alarm.

"Is it sick?"

She spun around and hurried into the bedroom, shaking Alex gently on the shoulder. As usual, he was sound asleep one second and ready for anything the next. "What's wrong?"

"Get some clothes on. I was sitting on the back porch, and there's a huge turtle on the beach. I'm afraid there's something wrong with it."

He quickly rolled out of bed and threw on a T-shirt and shorts before following her out to the porch. Alex would know what to do if it was sick.

By this time, the turtle had settled in one spot about twenty feet in front of the porch and was waving two flippers back and forth, spraying sand everywhere. Forehead lined, she turned to Alex and was surprised at the smile spreading across his face. "What's wrong with it?"

He wrapped an arm around her. "Nothing's wrong. She's digging a nest, baby. This is fantastic! She's getting ready to lay eggs."

"Oh! That's pretty neat."

"Very. Several years ago, we had a hawksbill turtle lay eggs on the north end of the beach, but that's the only one in the time I've been here."

"Is that what she is? A hawksbill?"

His smile grew. "Oh, no. That's a leatherback. She's a big one too—probably five feet long. When I first got here, I heard about a leatherback that nested nearby. This must be her. They don't nest every year, but they always come back to the same general area. Come on, let's watch."

He turned around and carried their two gliders to the porch rail, so they had a good view without disturbing the turtle. The large reptile was nearly black in the moonlight. Long parallel ridges reminiscent of the material she was named for formed the substance of her shell. After digging a deep hole, she settled at the edge of it and became still.

"Now she's laying her eggs," Alex whispered without looking away.

She stayed like this for over an hour, then pushed the sand back over the nest with her flippers, smoothing the surface to hide the nest. Finally finishing, she trundled back into the ocean and was gone.

"How long until the eggs hatch?"

"About two months. She's likely to come back in ten to fourteen days and make another nest. I'm going to mark this one, so we know where it is." He turned to her. "What were you doing out here, anyway?"

"I got my period and came out here until the ibuprofen kicked in."

"You feeling better now?" He reached out a hand, and they relaxed, hands clasped between them as they sat in the gliders watching the black sky fade to indigo.

"Yes, it's kicked in now. I made an appointment to see a new doctor here. We'll see what she says. I'm not eager to have surgery, but I'm coming around to the idea."

"No, it's never fun to think about, but if it ends this, I'm all for it. I hate seeing you so miserable every month."

"One step at a time. Besides, it came in handy this time—I

never would have seen the turtle otherwise." Hope checked her watch. "It's nearly six o'clock now. No point in going back to bed. You want some coffee?"

He nodded. "I'll come in too. I need to figure out something to mark the nest."

As she brewed the coffee, Alex stood in the kitchen, tapping his jaw. Then he brightened, opening the silverware drawer and removing four teaspoons. When she returned to the porch with the two coffee mugs, he was climbing the stairs and the four spoon handles stuck straight up from the sand in a square pattern.

"Well, aren't you Mr. Clever?" She handed him his coffee.

"It'll do for now. I'll put some flags down later, but I want to keep this quiet and give the hatchlings every chance. We need to keep Cruz away too. He might dig up the nest and eat the eggs."

Hope frowned. "That wouldn't be good. I'm rooting for them now."

He smiled at her, his eyes wide as his face broadcast wonder. "Thank you so much for waking me up. Leatherbacks are rare now—we have a real opportunity here. You have no idea what this means to me."

"I think I know."

CHAPTER 24

Hope ate a piece of freshly picked mango before pushing the rest toward Alex as they sat at the edge of the rock pool. They were finishing an informal picnic lunch before Alex investigated the second passage. "I think I might explore the dry part of the big cave while you're diving."

He took the container of mango from her and turned toward the cave. "Be careful in there, ok? Don't go off into any side passages. If you find any, we can look at them together and I'll string some line so we don't get lost."

"Honestly, I'm not ten, you know. I plan to stay in the main area to the right of the entrance."

He winced. "Sorry. I'm doing again, aren't I?"

"Yes. Moving on, Barnaby's letter said he lived in that cave—it would be interesting to see if there's any sign of his camp."

"Poor guy. Living in that thing all alone for months." Then he laughed, shaking his head. "I'm sure you figured out who his brother was that he wrote the letter to?"

Hope grinned and a laugh escaped. "Amazing, isn't it? I can just picture him standing there with one leg propped up on a rum barrel. Captain Henry Morgan. Too bad we can't tell anyone about this—it's kind of an incredible story."

"Maybe after we're done. Though if we find a box of treasure, the last thing we want to do is advertise the fact." Alex's eyes wandered over the sandy beach and rock pool as the trees waved in the breeze around them. "This place would be crawling with people who think they're experts." He started cleaning up. "You ready?"

She nodded. "And I'll make sure I'm back over here long before you get back. No more feet tickling, thank you."

He glanced at her, a big smile spreading across his face. "Sorry about that."

"No, you're not! The only reason you're not thinking about doing it again is because I'm on to you now. Besides, I won't be too long. I'm probably going to get cold in that cave in wet clothes."

"I've got a small dry bag in the little cave. You can put your clothes in that."

She rolled her eyes. "You are such a Boy Scout."

He smiled, but it didn't reach his eyes. "Preparation has saved my life more than once."

˷

An hour later, Alex was inside the cave, and Hope was shrugging into the dry backpack. She wore her headlamp, and Alex had insisted she carry a second light source.

Once inside the mouth of the cave, she turned on her headlamp and swam toward the right where a shallow, dark-gray rock shelf led back from the water's edge. She followed a series of ledges that formed a staircase of sorts before flattening into a broad expanse of rock. It was very dark up there, and she couldn't imagine staying in here for long periods.

She toweled off before dressing in a long-sleeve shirt and

board shorts. She pulled on running shoes last and began exploring, her light beam waving on the ground in front of her before illuminating the towering gray ceiling above her.

After forty-five minutes, she had scoured the plateau with nothing to show for it, so she investigated the back wall. There were some pockets and recesses, but nothing large until she came to a vertical opening, six feet tall and about the same wide.

From the entrance, her beam illuminated an opening a short way down the passage and she set off toward it. A considerable room with a tall ceiling opened up on her right. Upon entering, her light illuminated a pile of cloth debris mounded up in one corner.

Kneeling, Hope sifted through it, finding the remnants of fabric and small pieces of wood. It looked like an animal had shredded them, creating a nest from the materials. She smiled sadly as a glint of gold sparkled at the bottom of the pile and she picked up another doubloon. Her stomach twisted as her headlamp cast a beam around the dark area.

This is it, where Barnaby made his home. After more than three hundred years, there's just nothing left of it.

She pocketed the coin and stood. "The question is, what else did you leave behind?" Her voice echoed around the chamber.

Hope left the room and made her way back out to the cave, continuing her search but not turning up anything else of interest. Looking at her watch, she was surprised nearly two hours had passed. She placed her shoes back in the bag, but kept her clothing on, which would dry quickly in the sun. After an easy swim across the pool, she returned the dry bag to the small cave.

Hope was just turning around when Alex rose like a silent wraith from the pool. Her heart raced for a moment as she stared at him. Dressed in a black wetsuit with the rebreather on, he looked like the man in the Night Photo. But his gaze was filled with warmth and satisfaction.

This was *her* Alex.

He spit out the regulator and pulled off his mask as he made his way to the sandy beach and kissed her hello, his lips cool from being submerged for so long.

"Hi there, handsome—you're back sooner than I thought. I just got here myself."

"It was a smooth trip." He walked to the small cave and deposited his rebreather, retrieving the small tanks to refill back at the resort. "Did you find anything interesting in the big cave?"

"Sort of." Hope gave him a recap of her explorations, holding the coin out to him, but he shook his head, still taking off his wetsuit.

"I'm more interested in what you found."

Alex opened the small cooler they had brought and downed a bottle of water, nodding his head back toward the pool. "Let's sit down and I'll tell you about it."

They sat on one of the flat boulders, both facing the cave. "I've got good news and bad news. The good news is the second passage isn't as long as the first and there's no squeeze. That's why I made good time. It widens into a small room about halfway through. It's kind of cool. There was an opening off to one side, but I didn't investigate it. The passage continues before ending in a big cavern. Really big—it's similar size to that cave there." He turned to her with a smile. "And yes, that's where I turned around after tying off my line."

"I know. I didn't really think you'd explore without me. That sounds promising—I can't wait to see it. What's the bad news?"

"The passage leading to that cavern must have been exposed to the elements at some point in the past." He pierced her with his gaze, all traces of humor gone. "The floor is covered in silty mud. It's a good-sized passage, with several feet of clearance above the silt layer. But good buoyancy control will be imperative in there. One careless fin kick is all it would take to turn that passage into a complete silt-out—I'm talking about not being able to see a thing."

"Well, that still sounds doable. Even if I couldn't see, there's air available at both ends. I'd just continue on until I got out."

Alex smiled faintly, but his eyes remained serious. "That's the idea. Unfortunately, it's not as easy as it sounds. You can get disoriented very easily in situations like that. People have died inside shipwrecks where a small room got silted up and they couldn't find their way out. I'll stage a couple of extra tanks in that tunnel, and you've got great buoyancy skills. But we're gonna practice procedures of what to do in zero-vis situations."

He paused, making sure he had her full attention. "We'll go over it until you're sick of hearing about it. And then some more."

"Preparation, huh?"

"You got it."

CHAPTER 25

June...

Alex shut off the compressor and began removing the air whips from the filled scuba tanks. Lifting one tank with each hand, he carried them to the full-tanks area of the compressor room before returning for another pair. As he wiped the sweat from his brow, he double-checked to make sure the single window in the room was open.

It was. There just wasn't much breeze this afternoon. He didn't bother turning on the modular air-conditioning unit. It couldn't overcome the heat put off by the air compressor or the tanks themselves as they filled.

Finally finished, he returned to his workbench to ensure everything was put away. He was straightening the desktop when his gaze was drawn to the bottom left drawer. Alex opened it and rooted to the bottom, pulling out the item he'd secreted away during his first trip to the cave when he'd found the pendant.

Examining it closely, he murmured to himself, "You need to figure out what to do with this."

He had been disappointed when he first inspected it in the clear daylight—it was totally unsuitable. But Alex didn't give up easily. An idea had been percolating for a while now, but he needed help. This was out of his wheelhouse, for sure. Smiling, he looked at the calendar, checking his next day off. Then he buried the item back in the bottom of the drawer.

Alex crossed the room, shut the window, and escaped out the door, locking it behind him. Basking in the cooler air, he turned toward the end of the pier and his breath caught. Hope stood under the palapa, her head leaning back as the breeze blew through her hair. As he neared, Alex covered his approach with a cough so he didn't startle her.

Hope smiled as he slid up behind her, drawing her close in front of him.

"You're a nice surprise," he said.

"I finished up and wanted to wait for you. I need my Alex fix." She squeezed his hands. "Are you done for the day?"

"Yes. I was just locking up when I saw you here. Let's go home." As they turned and started walking, Alex kept his hand on the small of Hope's back, just so he could touch her.

A man stood on the wooden decking, facing away from them. He rested his hands on his hips as he looked at the spa. Alex noted the familiar gray hair and stocky build, and his stomach dropped as disbelief warred with certainty.

Alex stopped some distance away as the older man turned to face them. He widened his eyes, clearly recognizing Alex before they tightened in wariness.

I don't believe it!

Alex had gone rigid with tension, glaring at him when Hope grasped his forearm.

"That man looks familiar," she said. "Who is he?"

Alex's breath exploded in a hiss. "That's Steve."

Hope lifted her head and stepped back. "Steve Jackson? As in the former owner?"

Alex's shock was being replaced by fury. "Yes. I have no idea why he'd just show up out of the blue like this."

He detached Hope's hand from his arm and marched up the pier, both fists clenched at his sides. Steve straightened, like he was stiffening his spine and trying not to step backwards. Alex stopped a foot in front of Steve, who didn't look any different—he had the same craggy face and brown eyes. Alex was much taller and no doubt intimidated him, but he couldn't care less at the moment.

"Give me one reason why I shouldn't throw you off this pier right now."

"Take it easy, Alex," Steve said, holding out both hands. "I can see you're not real happy to see me."

"Did you think I would be?"

"It's been over a year. I was hoping the dust had settled a little."

"No. It hasn't. Who the hell do you think you are, waltzing back like this? You just bolted like a coward in the middle of the night! And I guess you've just been hiding for the last year because you couldn't face what you did?"

"I've been hiding?" Steve barked out sarcastic laughter. "What do you call what you've been doing the past six years?"

Alex reared back, Steve's words knifing through his gut. He forced his breaths to deepen and reined in his temper. "I call it healing, you son of a bitch."

"Stop it," Hope said, her lips a thin line. "Both of you."

She stepped between the two men, placing both hands on Alex's chest and forcing him back two steps. His tension relaxed a little until he moved his gaze to the tightness in Hope's face. Her hands against his chest shook, as if she needed the contact for reassurance.

He whipped his head back to Steve. "Do you have any idea

what you did to Hope? The colossal shitstorm you just dumped on her?" He put an arm around Hope's shoulders, pulling her closer to him.

Steve turned to Hope while keeping a wary distance from Alex. "Yes, I do. That's why I came back. To apologize. I've never actually met you before, Hope."

She gave a wild trill of laughter. "No, you certainly haven't." She moved one of her hands to encircle Alex's waist. Tension radiated from her body, further increasing his.

Steve darted his eyes back and forth between them, his lined brow even more wrinkled, then his face slackened as he understood. "Wait. Are you two . . . together?"

"Yes," Alex said.

A small smile cracked Steve's face. "I'm happy for you."

But Alex wasn't ready to let him off the hook that easily. Steve squinted at the complex of buildings behind him before turning back to Alex and Hope. "I was looking at that when I walked down here. A spa? Where are you living, Alex?"

Alex grinned savagely. "In your old house, Steve."

And I'm sleeping in your old bed.

"I can see there's been a lot of changes around here." Steve continued to bounce his eyes between Hope and Alex.

"Yes," Hope said calmly. "We've had some tough times since you've been gone." She turned a warm smile to Alex and some of his strain drained out as she held his gaze. "But some really wonderful things have happened too."

"Why didn't you call and let us know you were coming?" Alex's tone was a little more even now, but Steve's hiding comment had cut to the bone.

Steve rubbed the back of his neck. "Uh, I was afraid you would refuse to see me. Though if I'd known you wanted to throw me off the pier, I might have gone that route instead."

"I'm still taking it under consideration."

Steve raised his hands again. "Let's head up to the bar and have a drink."

"I've got nothing to say to you. Go to hell."

Hope's hand was back on his chest, pressing firmly. "Alex, why don't you go back to the house? You need some time to mull this over."

He moved his eyes to hers and she stared back with a steel gaze, her message coming through clearly.

"All right." He sent a message back to her. *Steve and I aren't done yet.*

With one last glare at Steve, Alex headed up the pier. When he got a short way down the beach, he turned around and stopped, his arms crossed over his chest. Steve wasn't dangerous, but Alex wasn't about to leave Hope and just open a beer and hang out on the porch. She clearly wanted to handle Steve herself, and there was no denying she was a hell of a lot more diplomatic than he was.

Alex stepped into the shallows, calming further as the warm waves splashed over his feet. Hope talked to Steve on the pier, and after several minutes, they began walking, heading around the pool toward the lobby.

He shifted from foot to foot, mulling over whether to follow. "If you go storming after them, you'll be doing exactly what she hates. Managing people is what she does. Let her do her thing."

Finished muttering to himself, he trudged home.

∽

ALEX TOOK a cold shower and was just entering the great room when Hope opened the slider, carrying a bottle of wine. She promptly opened it and poured two healthy glasses. He'd calmed down and accepted the offered glass, taking a long drink.

"Well, that was unexpected," she said, then glanced at him from under her brows. "You ok?"

"Yeah. He and I had kind of a father-son dynamic. Or oil-water if you prefer. We cared a lot about each other, but that didn't stop us from butting heads."

"I know you were hurt when he left."

"So was everyone else, including you."

"He's staying at a resort in Christiansted. I agreed to meet him for coffee in a couple of days. I presume that's all right with you?"

Alex took another drink and set his glass on the granite island, taking Hope into his arms. "You don't need my permission for anything. I'm sure you've got plenty of questions for him." He gave her a rueful smile. "And it'll probably go better if I'm not there."

She snorted, acknowledging his comment.

He tilted her head up, watching closely. "You ok? That was a major shock for you too."

"It was, but he seemed sincere about wanting to see everyone. And yes, I want to ask him a few things. It might do you some good to see him too."

"We'll see." Alex picked up his glass and went to the wall of windows, shaking his head.

Every time he was back on solid footing, the rug got pulled from underneath him again.

CHAPTER 26

Hope sat in a hard plastic chair in the corner of the exam room, her eyes watering at the smell of disinfectant in the air. *At least I know they take cleanliness seriously.* It was the morning following Steve's arrival, and she was finally at the appointment with her new gynecologist. Dr. Susan Grainger was a warm, middle-aged blonde woman who gave Hope a frank expression after taking a history and examining her.

"Based on your exam and what you've told me about your cycles, I'd like to draw some blood and schedule you for a pelvic ultrasound. That will give us a better idea of what we're looking at."

Hope jumped at a last-minute cancellation at the imaging clinic and barely had time to get her blood drawn before her ultrasound appointment, which was rather uncomfortable.

It was late afternoon before she drove her Jeep into the garage and greeted Cruz at the front door. Alex was leading a night dive, so she flopped on the couch with a big sigh, trying to stay awake as the exhaustion washed over her. *What a day!*

Just before 5 p.m., Dr. Grainger called. "I just got your bloodwork back and wanted to give you a call. You're anemic—really anemic. I'd like you to come into the clinic for three days of iron infusions."

Hope closed her eyes. "Ok, I can do that. I guess this explains why I'm feeling so tired?"

"Definitely. Looking at your labs, I'm surprised you could even run a half marathon."

"Well, that was several months ago, and I've never felt like I fully recovered from it."

"You haven't. And I hate to pile on, but your ultrasound report just came back and it shows that your fibroids are extensive."

The doctor sighed. "I know you already discussed a hysterectomy with your previous physician, but you might want to think about surgery. There's no emergency, but this is definitely affecting your health now."

Hope leaned her head in her hand. "Ok, I will. Let's start with the iron and go from there."

"That sounds like a good place to start. The infusions should give you some energy."

"I'll call the infusion clinic tomorrow and get scheduled." Hope tossed her phone on the coffee table and rubbed her face with both hands. The news wasn't unexpected, but she wanted to delay any surgery as long as possible.

Hope prepared a salad for dinner and sat down on the couch with her laptop, researching cities on the Spanish Main and the New World treasure routes while trying to wrap her head around her health news.

∽

AFTER FINISHING THE NIGHT DIVE, Alex sat alone behind the counter in the dive shop, taking in all the changes and imagining them through Steve's eyes. He and Hope had expanded the retail offerings and there was now a professional, white display wall of scuba masks and fins, while several cubbies held resort dive-themed T-shirts and rash guards.

It was a far cry from the humble, cobbled-together dive shop/classroom of Steve's time.

Masks and fins were fairly low-cost items that guests might want to replace while there. They'd held off on more expensive equipment for now, such as BCDs and regulators, figuring guests could rent them if needed. Alex had been more skeptical about the T-shirts and rash guards, but they had proven so popular he had to continually reorder them, which was his current task. He shook his head with a smile.

You should know better than to question her judgment regarding anything business-related.

But having more inventory meant having someone available to sell it—that was the problem. For years, his procedure had been to open the dive shop in the morning to check in all the divers, then lock it up when they left for the dive. After returning, he'd reopen if necessary until he was done for the day. He was thinking about hiring a high school kid to work in the dive shop and fill tanks in the afternoon, freeing up time Alex could spend on more productive things.

Like treasure hunting.

Alex's phone buzzed again, and he looked down, verifying it was Steve. He tapped *ignore* and set it down again. His visit had thrown a major wrench into their cave plans. Alex was adamant about not saying anything about the cave to him, so their adventure was officially on hold until his visit was over. But they'd accomplished a lot recently.

Over the past two weeks, Alex had spent many afternoons with Hope in the ocean just off the pier, practicing buoyancy skills and procedures for finding a guideline in low-visibility situations. As usual, she was an excellent student and mastered the skills quickly. He made her do them again and again until he was satisfied and she felt confident.

The last time they practiced had been just prior to Steve's arrival. Alex made her continue searching for the line, just so he could enjoy her steadily escalating irritation with him. Her mercurial temper was one of his favorite things about her. They had been off the beach in thirty feet of water, and he'd laid a guideline and stirred up the sand, making her find the line.

Over and over.

He should have done it at night so it would be a better simulation of actual conditions she might face in the cave, but he had led several night dives and she had the manager's reception, so they did the best they could.

She found the line for approximately the thousandth time, and Alex was amazed she hadn't blown up at him yet.

Maybe I emphasized the preparation too much.

He signaled that they were going to repeat it yet again when she reared up on her knees in the sand and crossed her arms over her BCD. She glared at him, and her shouted "NO!" came through loud and clear.

It took all his control to put on a stern face and shake his head at her, twirling a finger to repeat it. She narrowed her eyes and launched herself off the sand, barreling into him and knocking him over onto his back.

That was when he lost it and started laughing, water leaking into his mouth around his regulator. She gripped his shoulder straps with both hands, her eyes furious as she realized she'd been had.

Hope didn't have much of a poker face, and he could practically see the wheels turning as she contemplated how to get back at him. She darted her eyes to the regulator in his mouth, then to his mask. She was probably thinking about turning off his air too.

Oh, baby—there's nothing you can do to me down here that someone a whole lot bigger and uglier hasn't done a thousand times already.

So he flipped her on her back, resting on top as she struggled. Then she became still and fully relaxed. Her eyes softened and she reached up and stroked his cheek while her other arm rested on his right shoulder. She just lay there, staring at him with tender eyes and a slight smile.

Then, in one motion, her face went fierce as she grabbed his shoulder strap, her other hand busily cranking his air off.

Of course, Alex had seen it coming a mile away. She pushed against him and he held firm, not letting either of them move as she narrowed her eyes again.

He spit his regulator out with a grin and murmured in her ear, "Love you." Alex grabbed her arms, lifting them both upright, and started ascending, breathing out a steady stream of bubbles. Her furious struggle prevented her from holding her breath, keeping her safe.

They surfaced, and he backed away to a safe distance as he inflated his BCD, then started laughing again. He ducked as she sent a huge splash at him.

"I should have known that wouldn't do any good!"

"That wasn't the first time I've had my air shut off. But it was the first time I've enjoyed it that much."

Smoke was about to come out of her ears, which only made him laugh harder.

"How long were you going to make me keep doing that down there?"

"Oh hell. I thought you'd have killed me half an hour ago." Another wall of water hit him.

"I suppose having my air turned off is my next adventure, huh? Maybe try that in the cave?"

With that, things had gone far enough. His smile dropped, and he swam up to her still-furiously thrashing body.

"Stop kicking and inflate your BCD, silly." He filled it for her, and Hope quieted. "You can do anything you want to me underwater—I don't mind. But I promise I'll never turn your air off. Ever." He cupped her cheeks and her face relaxed. "When we're in that cave, I won't ever mess around, ok? You don't need to worry about that."

"I know."

He leaned in and kissed her.

She returned it very nicely, then gave him a slight smile. "One of your most annoying qualities is that I can never stay angry at you. I swear you make me mad on purpose."

He grinned and another laugh burst through. "I can't help it. You're kind of adorable when you're irritated."

"So, are we finally ready to tackle the second passage?"

Alex admitted they were, though he was still uneasy about Hope in that cave. But the exploration was on hold for a few days until Steve left.

Now, he finished the order for more T-shirts and stretched his sore shoulders. After yesterday's turmoil at meeting Steve again, Alex had worked off some of his frustration by attaching double scuba tanks to his backplate and hiking them into the cave. He dove them as far as the small room after the dry passage, then returned outside using an extra tank he had carried. It had been fully dark when he'd returned to the house, and Hope had made a fuss over him, bringing him a beer and giving him a shoulder rub.

He'd eaten it up, fully relaxing at last.

A smile crept across his face at how domesticated he'd become since moving in with her last September. They'd been pretty inseparable before that, but he hadn't hesitated when she'd asked him to move in after the hurricane destroyed his apartment.

This was a new experience for him, and for Hope as well. He hardly counted his matrimonial error at age eighteen. When he was a SEAL, he'd avoided deep emotional attachments and the complications they could bring to his unpredictable life, going long periods between relationships. But he couldn't imagine anyone else now.

As he shut down the dive shop, his thoughts turned back to the cave. He couldn't wait to explore that big cavern with Hope beside him. He was having a great time planning and diving this cave, though he could have done without getting stuck.

He was curious if there was treasure in the big cavern, but its historical value interested him more than its monetary value—not to mention the thrill of discovery. Overall, they were as ready as they were ever going to be.

He checked his watch, and it was after 8 p.m. Alex walked up the silent pier, making his way toward home and Hope, curious if she'd had any results from her appointment.

She was sitting on the great-room couch when he entered, greeting him with a tired smile but not rising.

"Did you eat dinner?" she asked.

"Yeah, I got something in the kitchen before the dive, so I'm good." His eyes took in her bruised inner elbow, a hollow stab sliding through his gut as he sat next to her. "How did it go this morning?"

She gave him a recap of her day and the plan for three days of iron infusions.

He drew her close and kissed the top of her head. "You could stand to take a few days off, anyway. I'm sure Patti would be happy to hold down the fort."

"We'll see. There's plenty I can do from my home office, anyway. I'll get the infusions set up as soon as possible—they should help. I'm meeting Steve tomorrow morning, and it would be nice if I could schedule one for right after." She melted against him. "I'm sick of being so tired all the time."

CHAPTER 27

The morning loomed still and cloudy, though the rain held off. Hope exhaled forcefully, trying to breathe out her nerves as she crossed the tile patio of Tropical Bean. Steve was already seated, smiling broadly at the server. Hope took a seat at the table, not wanting to interrupt their conversation.

"It's so great to see you again," the woman said in her lilting accent. She had close cropped black hair and incredible cheekbones.

"Nice to be on the island again, Sasha." Steve had a warm smile. He'd seemed like a nice man when Hope had done some internet snooping prior to moving, though she had revised that opinion upon her arrival.

"What can I get you, Hope?" Sasha turned her brilliant smile to her. She knew Hope from the weekly coffee meetup she had with Cindy.

"Large, iced coffee, thanks."

She nodded and left to place their orders.

Steve leaned forward, folding his arms on the table. "Thanks for meeting me. Does Alex know you're here?"

Hope bit back a retort, determined to be civil. "Of course. We don't keep secrets from each other."

"I'm sure you don't. How long have you two been together, anyway?"

"Since last summer."

Steve raised his bushy brows and couldn't hide a smile. "You two hit it off right away then. I'm glad—Alex isn't the easiest guy to get to know."

"And he has his reasons for that."

Sasha came back with their drinks. Hope wasn't surprised Steve had ordered a plain black coffee. He twirled the mug before glancing at Hope from under his brows. "I'm really sorry for leaving you in the lurch. But you obviously landed on your feet. The resort looks like it's doing great."

"It was very difficult, but we're doing fine now. After the boat sank and a hurricane nearly destroyed the resort." Perhaps a slight exaggeration about the hurricane, but it hadn't been an easy road.

"I'd say you're a force to be reckoned with."

A slight smile cracked Hope's face. "Or too stubborn to know when to quit."

Steve laughed, a warm, friendly sound that widened Hope's smile. "I can see why you and Alex are together."

There was a break in the conversation as they nursed their coffees, and Hope worked up to the question that had brought her there. "Why did you leave like that? I would have understood if you'd said you couldn't stay."

Steve heaved a long sigh. "To be honest, I panicked. The night before you arrived, I sat in my house with my heart pounding. I had to get out. So I scrawled out a letter to you and a second one to Alex and Patti. A friend drove me to the airport with one packed suitcase. And I sat there until the terminal opened and bought a ticket on the first plane off the island. Didn't even care where I was going."

Steve shook his head and stared at the ocean, a faraway look in his eyes. "I landed in Atlanta with no idea what to do next. So I called my daughter, who lives a couple of hours from there." He gave Hope an embarrassed shrug. "That part seemed like fate. I moved in with her and the two grandkids until I got my own place a few weeks later. And I've been there ever since.

"But that last week before I left, the walls were closing in. The employees weren't exactly happy with me. Especially Alex. I never really thought about how the raffle would impact their lives. That was pretty selfish, in retrospect. He wasn't pleased with the raffle idea and thought it was a big risk."

Steve grinned, and his face was transformed. "I think he's singing a different tune now, though."

Hope couldn't help smiling back. "In a strange way, I think your sudden departure helped cement us all as a new team. Patti especially saw how shell-shocked I was, and everyone rallied around me. They're an incredible group of people."

She paused, searching for how to phrase her next question. "I recently got another surprise—a pleasant one this time. I had no idea the resort property was so large, and that most of it is on the east side of the highway."

"Yeah, Susan and I never did anything with that big parcel, just the oceanfront one. There was an old rumor about a spring somewhere over there, but I never thought it was worth following up. The resort kept us plenty busy, especially in the early years, and I was never keen to go hacking through the jungle."

I guess that answers that question. Alex will be happy we're the only ones who know about the cave. "The oceanfront parcel is spectacular. I can't really be upset with you in the long run, can I? Moving here has been the best thing that's ever happened to me. And it wouldn't have been possible without the lottery."

"Maybe you can get some of that attitude to rub off on Alex." A shadow crossed his face. "Before you arrived, Sasha told me he was involved in some sort of shooting. He looked healthy enough to me. What was she talking about?"

Hope hesitated, shifting in her chair. "I'm sure the stories are still online at the *St. Croix Chronicle*. But if you're after the specific effects it had on Alex, I suggest you ask him yourself."

Steve ran a hand over his chin. "I'd love to, but he won't return my calls or texts. I've only got a couple more days here, and I really want to talk to him. Maybe you can help?"

Alex should set things right with Steve, for his own sake. "I'll mention it to him."

"Thank you. Alex is a very loyal man. He's also one who thinks loyalty trumps personal feelings, which doesn't make him the forgiving type. I've got my work cut out for me."

Hope drilled him with her gaze. "Yes, you do. You hurt him a lot."

~

AFTER HER MEETING WITH STEVE, Hope arrived at the clinic for her iron infusion. A plump, extremely efficient nurse got the IV going on her first attempt and hung a bag of sinister-looking dark fluid which ran down a clear tube into Hope's vein. She didn't have any reactions from it, though, and drove home without any problem, scheduled to return the next two afternoons.

She spent the rest of the day in the office with Patti and gave her a quick update on the meeting with Steve, including how Hope couldn't hold a grudge against him. "But how do you feel about all this, Patti? You worked side by side with him for years."

"It was a right shock to see him appear at the office door there. But I forgave him a long time ago." She gave Hope a mischievous grin. "I didn't let him off too easy at the start. It was just a *little* nice to see him squirm some."

Then Patti became serious. "How is Alex? I had a close workin' relationship with Steve, but Alex was different. Until you came here, Steve might have been the only person who could get him to open up."

Hope sighed. "Alex is mad. So far, he doesn't want anything to do with Steve, but I'll try to talk him around. Steve's trying to make amends, but he's fighting an uphill battle."

When Hope walked home along the beach, Alex was at the shoreline, throwing a stick into the ocean for Cruz to retrieve. He saw her coming and greeted her with a smile. She wore a blue and white sundress, and he let his eyes take a slow trip up and down her body. "You look beautiful. All that just for Steve?"

"No. All that just for you." She drew him down for a kiss as their arms came around each other.

"Your iron infusion go ok?"

"Yes, no problems." Alex took her hand, and Hope tossed her sandals near the porch to let the waves wash over her feet as they walked along the shoreline.

"And how was coffee with Steve?"

"Good. I got what I wanted out of it, which was knowing why he left like he did." She turned to Alex. "You two were close, weren't you?"

"Yes. Sometimes he was a friend and other times he fell into a father figure-type role. I didn't seek that out. Since my folks were killed in a car crash years ago, I never thought I needed another father. But it helped because Steve was the only one who knew my background."

"You've never told me the full story on how you came to be here."

Alex laughed as the warm sea swished around their feet. "My physical therapist at Walter Reed vacationed here at Half Moon Bay, believe it or not. He didn't even dive. One afternoon he had a beer with Steve and they got to talking. Steve was having a hard time finding a reliable dive guide, and James, my PT, thought about me. I contacted Steve about it, and when I got discharged, I moved down here and stayed."

Hope squeezed his hand. "Lucky for me. So Steve was someone you confided in?"

Cruz dropped the stick at Alex's feet, who threw it into the shallows. The dog bounded after it, water flying. "Not really. Steve was in the Navy too, so he was more perceptive than most about what I was going through. We talked about Navy life some, but mostly danced around Syria."

"It sounds like he honored your feelings about keeping it quiet."

"He did."

Hope took a deep breath. "Don't you think you'd feel better if you had lunch with him? Or at least a beer or something?"

Alex gave her a crooked smile. "Is that your tactful way of telling me to get off my stubborn ass and forgive him?"

"Maybe."

"If it were just me he hurt, it would be easier. But his leaving affected everyone who works at this resort." He stopped walking and drew Hope against him. "And he hurt you. That makes it damn hard to forgive him."

"You hardly knew me then."

Alex's face went slack. "That doesn't matter. That asshole you dated hurt you years ago. Doesn't stop me from wanting to pound him into the ground."

"He's ancient history, so we don't have to worry about it."

Alex stared at her, piercing his eyes into hers. "I know I can be overprotective and stubborn. I'm trying to ease up on that a little. But I need you to understand that if someone threatens you, I'll do whatever's necessary to protect you. I can't change that, Hope."

"I know that. It's one of the many things I love about you." She brushed her lips over his. "Let Steve make amends. For both your sakes."

CHAPTER 28

The open-air restaurant sat like a tacky eyesore on the main street in Christiansted, one of a chain of tasteless vacation restaurants located in exotic destinations. Fake palm trees and plastic parrots abounded. Alex walked in, flinching as he looked around.

What am I doing here? In more than one sense...

He'd finally relented and texted Steve back, agreeing to meet for lunch. For some reason, Steve had chosen this monstrosity for their get-together.

He was already there, and Alex sat across from him, swiping a fluorescent-green plastic crab off the table onto the fake wood floor. "Ok, I gotta ask. Why the hell are we here? We're the only locals in this place." Alex furtively glanced around before ducking his head.

Steve gave him a satisfied smirk. "Believe it or not, that's the reason I chose this place. You seem to have become something of a celebrity around here, so I thought you might appreciate a little anonymity."

Alex paused, meeting Steve's eyes as the heat crept up his neck. "I would. Thanks."

"You're welcome. After I arrived earlier this week, everyone who knew me kept mentioning the resort—and you. I asked Hope about it, but she told me to look it up or ask you. So here we are."

Alex tried to hide a grin. "She told you to look it up? Like—go to the library or something?"

"More or less. She wouldn't tell me anything. That woman's got your back." Steve softened his eyes. "She's a good match for you."

"She is." Alex leveled a stare at him. "But are we really here to discuss my love life?"

Steve gave a hearty laugh. "Why not? The last real conversation we had, I said you needed to find someone. I'm really glad you did."

Alex considered a smartass comment about being tired of celibacy, but that would be disrespectful to Hope. And what they had was much more than physical—for both of them. Instead, he just said, "I'm a lucky man."

Steve raised a brow. "I've never heard those words come out of your mouth before."

"A lot has changed since you left."

"I noticed. I hardly recognized the resort. Your Hope knows what she's doing." Steve paused for a long pull from his Leatherback. "I'm sorry, Alex. For how I left and for what I said on the pier the other day. I was prepared for you to be cool toward me, but you threatening to throw an old man off the pier caught me a little off guard."

Alex let a smile slip out. "If you're an old man, I'm Tinkerbell."

Their server, a young blonde woman wearing short shorts, came by to take their orders. She widened her eyes as she recognized him, and Alex kept his face expressionless. "You're that dive guide, aren't you? The SEAL."

Alex hated this question and never knew how to answer it. So he simply nodded. She shot him a flirty smile, holding one long leg out so he could get a good look, and asked what he was interested in. Alex refrained from rolling his eyes, ordering a burger and fries and handing her back the menu with a cool stare. She got the message and turned to Steve with a small frown.

"Still enjoying the spotlight, I see," Steve said after she left.

"I've never been after attention. Even . . . before. That's not why I did it."

"I took Hope's advice and looked up the articles in the *Chronicle*. You've had a hell of a time since I've been gone. Especially for a guy who likes his privacy."

"There's been some rough parts, but I've rediscovered what it's like to be part of a team. And not just with Hope. Everyone at the resort rallied around me."

"Until I read that article, I didn't know the full story behind your injury."

Alex stiffened. "You still don't. No one does. No one can—except those of us who were there." He wasn't about to tell Steve he had no memory of the ambush.

Steve met his gaze steadily. "Navy Cross, huh?"

Alex shrugged. "The Navy awarded it. I didn't go looking for it."

"That's the thing about you, Alex. You don't ever go looking for it. But you can't help being a hero. It's part of your makeup."

"That's a crock of steaming horseshit."

"It must be your sparkling personality that keeps Hope hooked."

That made Alex laugh. "I told you I was a lucky guy."

Steve shook his head, picking at the label on his beer. "I wish I could take that night back. I really regret leaving the way I did."

"That's the problem, isn't it?" Alex sobered. "We all have to live with things we wish hadn't happened. Sometimes a line gets drawn in your life—*before* and *after*. And you have to figure out a way to make the *after* work."

"That's what I'm trying to do here."

"That makes two of us." *It's time to give a little.* Alex cracked a smile. "You want to come diving? I can put an extra tank on. It would give you a chance to be jealous over our fancy new boat. Since the one you left us with sank. Like I told you it would."

"There's that sparkling personality again! How could I say no when you put it so persuasively?"

Alex's smile broadened. "Guess I've given you a hard time long enough, you cheap bastard. I'm sure you expect me to pay for lunch too."

A half dozen employees walked by dressed as pirates, the lead one carrying a scoop of ice cream in a plastic boot. They set the appendage in front of a nearby diner, who winced as they promptly belted out "Happy Birthday."

Both men burst out laughing and Steve said, "After inflicting this place on you, I'll definitely pick up the tab."

"How about diving tomorrow morning? I'll see if I can get Hope to dive—you can buddy up with her."

Steve grinned. "So you did end up certifying her, huh?"

"She couldn't resist me. All that sparkling personality."

∽

THE SLEEK DIVE boat sliced through the water, moving at top speed back to the resort. Even over all the noise, Tommy's and Steve's laughter drifted toward Alex. They stood side by side on the elevated bridge, one of Tommy's arms thrown casually over Steve's shoulder. Tommy was incapable of holding a grudge and had welcomed the older man back with open arms. Alex smiled, shaking his head as he removed a regulator from its tank.

The water was flat calm, the only breeze created by their movement. It had been a wonderful morning with perfect diving conditions and a good group. The guests relaxed on the bow, the sound of their voices occasionally drifting back.

Still wearing his wetsuit pulled down to his waist, Alex caught movement. Hope headed toward him, carrying a staff polo shirt in each hand.

She handed him his shirt after replacing her own. "You should put this on. You're distracting the guests. Not to mention me."

Alex leaned close. "Me? What about you? It's about time you got dressed again."

"This is a perfectly respectable one-piece suit. I'm not the one walking around half naked."

He sat down on the bench and held out the arms of his wetsuit to her. "You want to strip me?"

She folded her arms and stood straighter. "You have no idea."

Alex's grin widened, and he pulled off his wetsuit in one practiced motion, tightening the drawstring on his board shorts before pulling on the proffered shirt. He glanced up at the wheelhouse. Steve stood facing them and wearing a big, smug smile.

He descended the ladder and joined them. "Looks like maybe I did you guys a favor by not repairing the old boat. This is great."

Alex's smile fell off his face as Hope pressed her hand against his lower back.

"I wouldn't go quite that far," she said, deftly stepping in before he could act. "But Alex found us an even better replacement. And thank you for being an excellent dive buddy this morning."

"Likewise. I can tell you had great instruction."

"I did. It's—"

"She's hardly a beginner," Alex interrupted, not happy with Steve's joke about the boat sinking.

"She's also fully capable of speaking for herself," Hope snapped at him, her eyes flashing.

He raised both hands and stepped back, trying not to bristle as Steve's smile grew. He went back to unhooking the equipment as Steve and Hope discussed the two dives. The next time he checked, Hope had moved on to chat with two guests and Steve was walking toward him.

"Ok, that boat comment was out of line," he said.

"For a guy who's trying to make amends, you sure keep putting your foot in your mouth."

"Fair enough." Then Steve laughed. "At least I've got company. You're still the same prickly bastard, but you've managed to find a woman who's not afraid to stand up to you, that's for sure."

Alex's gaze was drawn to Hope, who stood laughing with the two guests, and all his irritation melted away as a smile grew. Glancing over, Hope saw it and gave him a slight nod before turning back to the couple.

"You don't have to say it. I know I don't deserve her."

Steve cocked his head. "I wasn't going to say that. Seems like you two are well suited for each other." He paused, looking at the turquoise water before turning back. "Can I give you a piece of advice? As a man who was married to a strong woman for many years?"

Alex sighed. "Ok, Dad."

"Be careful stepping on her toes." Steve was serious now. "You're the kind of man who's going to want to protect her and keep her safe at all costs, even if that's not what she wants. You might want to watch that."

A hot flush crept across Alex's face. That had hit home, more than Steve could know. "I will. Thanks, Steve."

He nodded with a small smile and went to the bow to get some sun. Hope returned to Alex, who drew her in for a quick kiss.

"I was thinking about inviting Steve to have lunch with all of us," she said. "What do you think?"

I think I'm incredibly lucky to have you in my life.

"That's a great idea."

"You think you can refrain from harming the man?"

Alex thought of all kinds of comebacks to that but restrained himself to say, "Because you asked, yes."

But it wasn't easy. He'd had another nightmare the previous night, not a terrible one, but the first in a couple of months. Fortunately, Hope had slept through it. They tended to come back when he thought about Syria—or had a lunch that involved a discussion about it. Still, Alex had enough perspective to recognize that allowing Steve a farewell meal with everyone was a good idea—Hope's idea, of course.

CHAPTER 29

*A*lex and Steve pushed two tables together in a closed-off section of the dining room. Soon Hope and Clark returned from the bar, each carrying a bucket of Leatherbacks brimming with ice. Alex was quiet, standing back to enjoy the interactions before him.

"I stopped by the office," Hope said. "Patti's on her way, but Martine's got guests due to arrive any minute so she'll have to pass." She handed Steve and Alex each a beer. "You two sit down. I'll see if I can get Gerold out of the kitchen to join us, at least for a few minutes."

Alex tamped down a grin after glancing at Steve, who stood holding his beer with a wide-eyed expression. Hope knew how to take charge.

She returned a few minutes later with two large bowls of chips in one hand and smaller ones of salsa in the other, setting them on each table. "We're going to do tacos since that's quick and easy. Gerold will bring them out in a few minutes."

. . .

Thirty minutes later, Alex stared at the people surrounding the two tables as his old and new lives collided in the most incredible way. Patti sat next to Steve and their heads were together as they caught up and Clark interjected occasionally from Steve's other side.

In some ways, it was like nothing had ever changed.

Then Alex ran a hand down Hope's thigh. That was all he needed to know that everything was different now—better.

Steve laughed at Gerold, who had been pushed out of the kitchen by Pauline. "You have a *sous chef*? I don't even know what the hell that is."

"It means Gerold can take time off and the kitchen doesn't fall to pieces," Hope answered.

"And the dive op is obviously going strong," Steve said. "I'm glad you're a regular now, Robert."

"Me too," the divemaster said.

"Robert's photography is really takin' off," Tommy said. "Hope hung a bunch of his prints in the remodeled bungalows and around the resort too."

Steve gave Robert an impressed smile. "I saw those in the lobby! Great job."

"Ah, it's nothin'," Robert dropped his eyes to the table, then shot a shy glance at Alex and Hope. "I'm lucky. This is a great place to work."

"We're lucky to have you, man." Tommy turned to Steve. "We do everythin' we can to keep Alex off the boat. But somehow we keep gettin' busier, anyway."

"Ask Hope," Alex said. "I'm hard to get rid of. She's been trying since she met me."

"Count your blessings, Tommy," Hope said. "At least you don't have to live with him."

She squeezed Alex's knee under the table. He reached down and took her hand in his, pressing their shoulders together. She turned her smile to him, and her love showed so clearly in her eyes Alex's breath hitched as their eyes held. But Hope saved him from something truly embarrassing by winking and turning away.

He glanced across the table, trying to get it together again, and made eye contact with Steve, who looked at him with an expression of happiness and . . . pride?

With a sigh, Steve tossed his napkin on his plate and pushed back. "I'd better get going. I know you all have jobs to go back to." He swept his gaze around the table. "Thank you. I'm sorry for how I left, but I'm grateful you let me start making up for it." His last words were directed at Alex.

Steve and Patti rose, embracing. "I'm glad you came," she said. "It wasn't right that we never got to give you a proper send-off."

One by one, they all embraced Steve and said goodbye, though Hope held back. When it was Alex's turn, they embraced stiffly as Steve spoke softly. "I'm really happy for you. It's good to see you finally living."

Alex nodded and stepped back, more emotional than he thought he'd be. After Tommy and Robert said their goodbyes, he turned to them. "Let's get back to the boat. With the three of us, we can get it wrapped up in no time."

"I'll walk you out to your car," Hope said to Steve before turning to Alex. "See you later."

The three men made their way down to the boat, with Alex in the middle.

"How 'bout that," Tommy said. "Steve arrived *and* left, and you didn't kill him." He shoved Alex in the shoulder, making him stagger sideways as everyone laughed.

"It was a near thing to start."

Tommy threw back his head and laughed. "Yeah, Steve told me about that."

"A cooler head than mine prevailed." Alex got momentarily distracted by a stingray feeding in the sandy shallows, then turned back to the conversation. "But it was good to see him again. Eventually."

Tommy gave him a sly smile. "You still haven't forgiven him, have you?"

"Not completely. I know he was hurting, but that's no excuse. You don't leave people behind with no explanation."

He tossed an arm around Alex's shoulder. "Not everybody's got that kind of courage, you know."

"He caused a lot of heartache and trouble that could have been avoided. We were never afraid to go at one another when we needed to—it was kind of a weird relationship. I guess it was sort of like father and son," Alex said with a laugh. "I'm not as forgiving as you, Tommy. But it was a start."

∽

Hope walked with Steve out of the restaurant and into the balmy afternoon. "I hope you got what you came back to St. Croix for," she said with a slight smile.

"I think I did. Thank you for being so welcoming. You didn't have to be." He smiled, then his rugged face turned to wide-eyed bewilderment as he viewed the remodeled bungalows in the distance. "I can't believe the changes around here."

"I'd show you one of the new bungalows, but they're all booked." She might sound smug, but Hope didn't care.

"I checked out the website the other night, so I saw some of the pictures. Even the website is different. You've got a page on it describing a new coral restoration on the house reef."

"Yes, all of us have gotten involved, and by focusing on environmental concerns, it's a good way to differentiate Half Moon Bay."

He paused, studying Hope. "I'll be honest. It's a strange feeling. I'm really glad the resort is doing well and so is everyone who works here. I can see they're thriving. But it also leaves me feeling empty. Knowing you guys are doing just fine without me. Better even."

Sympathy tugged at her heart. "I imagine it's similar to the feeling when a child moves out on their own."

Steve laughed. "Yeah, that is kind of what I'm feeling." He reached his rental car and turned to her. "You have my cell number and email. Please don't hesitate to ask me any questions you might have."

"Thanks. I will."

A bit late for that, Steve.

She couldn't imagine needing to call him at this point. The resort was fully hers now. And Alex's. "If you plan a return visit and want to stay here, just let me know."

He nodded. "I'd like to return. I wasn't expecting Alex to fall over with forgiveness, but I guess I was hoping for a bit more from him. I need to work on that some more."

"Well, you got wet voluntarily this morning, so I'd say that was progress."

Steve's smile lingered as he regarded Hope. "Since you didn't know Alex before you got here, I'm not sure you really understand the change in him. I watched you two this morning and at lunch. You've done more to help him in a year than I did in over five."

Her smile broadened. "I might've had a few advantages you didn't."

"It's more than that, I think."

"Yes. Much more."

"It's funny how you can sense someone's character right off the bat. Alex is one of those guys you notice as soon as he walks into a room. From the very start, I was determined to help him. Over time, he let me in a little. Never all the way, though. I didn't know the story behind Syria until that article. That must have been terrible for him."

She raised a brow. "He's a very strong man. He got through it."

Steve laughed, causing Hope to look sharply at him. He raised a hand and took a step back. "Take it easy. My laugh is a compliment—I like that you don't give anything away. I told him the two of you were a good match. Alex is fun to be around, but he can be intimidating as hell when he wants to be. The last thing he needs is a woman who's a pushover. Seems like you're pretty good at putting him in his place when he needs it, and that's a good thing."

Hope smiled, accepting the compliment, and Steve dug his keys out of his pocket. "Safe travels." She embraced him, sensing his awkwardness at initiating the contact.

"Thank you." He took one last look around the resort. "And congratulations. I can't imagine this resort being in better hands. Including mine."

HOPE SPENT the afternoon working in her home office in between making several sheets of mango tartlets. Gerold had sourced an abundance of frozen miniature pie crusts that worked perfectly. They were the number one request of the divers—and the crew. The second mango tree in her yard was just coming into season, so she would have plenty of raw material available.

She was placing tartlets in a container when Alex came home and headed for the master bath after saying hello. He was soon back, carrying the metal case housing his rifle to the kitchen table. "I need to clean her. Not sure when I'll get back to the range, but I want to keep up on things now."

He stood, watching Hope carefully. "I've been a little worried about how you'd react to me shooting again. Do you understand I would never hurt you? Never."

"I know. I was a little uneasy at first. But after you explained what it meant to you, it put me at ease. And your face was positively glowing when you came back from the shooting range." She pressed close to him, running an index finger over his raspy chin. "But I refuse to call your rifle Betsy. I'm not thrilled about another woman in your life, you know."

His chest moved with laughter. "You don't have to worry about that." His smile lingered as his eyes washed over her face. "You're the only woman I'll ever need."

"You're the only man I've ever needed. I just didn't know it."

Hope threw together dinner and they ate outside. "Today was a great day, wasn't it? Steve was a good dive buddy."

"It's been a weird week," Alex said. "But it's always a great day when I can spend most of it with you."

"We had a nice talk on the way to his car. He said he was happy to see us doing so well, but a little sad to know we did it without him."

Alex snorted and dropped his fork on the plate. "And whose fault is that? Look, I'm more sympathetic toward him now than I was a couple of weeks ago, but . . . Steve is the past. You and me, this resort, we're all moving toward the future. He gave up his part in that—willingly. I wish him the best, but he's not a part of our lives anymore."

Hope studied him, but this was something Alex would have to work out on his own. Or not.

He straightened a bit and pointed at her. "You know, we have some exciting things going on without Steve. There's a certain cave I'm rather interested to get back to investigating, you know."

"I know! I tiptoed around the subject with Steve, and you were right. He doesn't know anything about the pool or cave. That big cavern Barnaby talked about sounds pretty exciting."

"Our next day off, it's priority number one."

She fist-bumped him, more than eager to return to the cave. Alex's overprotectiveness irritated her sometimes. Even though she understood his reasons for it, she'd been comfortable in that cave—now she was ready for anything. Even if Alex didn't understand that.

CHAPTER 30

Oh, come on! Move, dammit.

Hope gave one last hard push, and the tank finally slid several inches through the squeeze. Then Alex grabbed it from the other side and she scrabbled after it, finally leaving the stricture behind.

Steve had left a few days previously, and they were back in the cave at the earliest opportunity. Hope especially was excited. Alex had spent so much time training her, she couldn't imagine being more prepared.

As before, Alex was holding her BCD open for her, and she put her arms through the straps but didn't clip the buckles. Together, they climbed out of the water and up onto the shelf leading to the dry passage.

"The tanks I carried in here are on the other side of the dry passage." Alex pointed to it. "Go ahead and remove your reg and BCD from the tank and we'll leave that one here." She nodded, replacing the empty BCD on her back and carrying the regulator in her hand as he led the way through the narrow passage.

On the other side, two tanks stood side by side against the dark-gray wall. She attached her BCD and regulator to one, smiling to herself. Alex had gone to a lot of trouble to stage her extra tanks, and in a way that prevented her from having to carry the heavy tank through the passage they had just traversed on foot. Instead, he had carried two at once.

She stood to watch him at the edge of the water, his mask around his neck and his rebreather on, just staring at the black surface. Turning off her headlamp, she slid up to him and closed her eyes, giving him a long, deep kiss. It still amazed her how well they fit together.

As they pulled apart, he tipped his headlamp up. "What was that for?"

"For taking such good care of me."

"Well, it's only fair. You take pretty good care of me too. Let's go over the plan one last time."

Hope sighed and tried to listen as he described the passage for the umpteenth time. Despite their ridiculous encounter off the beach before Steve's visit, Alex was very serious right now. Still, she was ready to push him in the water herself if it would hurry him up—she couldn't wait to get to that cavern!

Finally, they sank beneath the black surface.

The room continued in a similar fashion underwater with sheer walls. As she looked ahead, a triangular-shaped opening loomed in front of Alex. Beneath her was an expansive, featureless surface—the nearly black silt he had warned about. Her gaze followed the mud forward in the direction they traveled. The flat surface continued into the passage.

Alex swam into the black tunnel, performing a perfect frog kick with his fins straight out sideways behind him, pushing the water backwards as he propelled himself into the tunnel. Hope wasn't that elegant, but her kick was still efficient. She made sure to stay a good distance from the silty surface, and the bright-green line he had lain on his previous trip was easily visible.

Hope followed his slow, controlled pace, and the channel closed around her. It wasn't as big as the primary tunnel, but much larger than the squeeze—she was well above the mud and her tank hadn't hit the ceiling.

This tunnel was an ominous black-gray color, with the darker mud underneath. It was more claustrophobic than the other passage, and a prickle of unease ran down her spine.

She was already looking forward to the far end and concentrated on Alex in front of her. They soon passed an extra tank he'd staged, and he continued at his measured pace. As her focus narrowed, she became more aware of how slowly they were moving.

Come on, Alex. Let's go!

But Alex was nothing if not deliberate, so she sighed through her regulator and tried to ignore the black tube creeping in on her. The passage turned sharply to the right and dipped. Hope winced as her tank scraped the side as she negotiated the turn, but it continued straight from there. After fifty feet, the walls of the tunnel started to widen.

Soon she was in the middle feature of the tunnel. It couldn't really be called a room like the one they'd just left, more like a massive closet. It widened out, an opening to her right leading off to parts unknown. She tilted her light up, eager to see the ceiling.

When Alex had described this mid-tunnel room, he'd smiled and told her to pay attention to the ceiling. "But watch your fins!"

She'd rolled her eyes and nodded.

Now Hope stared at the ceiling, her heart pounding. She drifted her gaze to Alex. He had turned around and was looking at her with soft eyes, smiling around his regulator.

The entire ceiling of the—Closet maybe?—was a mass of stalactites, colored medium brown to a light tan, all much different from the dark-gray rock surrounding them. Thick ones and thin ones, each about two feet long as they tapered to sharp points.

It was stunning.

The formations appeared out of the darkness as she broadcast her handheld light across the ceiling. The water was so clear she could have been looking at features in air. Alex moved to the side, leaving the line for a closer look at the ceiling. Hope stayed where she was—he'd given her strict instructions never to leave the line. And she had plenty to occupy her, totally forgetting her unease as she concentrated on the beauty above.

Hope tilted her light up. Some of the stalactites were multicolored—red, gray, and tan, all in one spire. She moved closer, hovering vertically and craning her neck as she counted six layers in the stalactite she inspected. The one next to it was even more intricate.

Then the ceiling started moving away as she tipped over backwards. Reacting instinctively, she flailed her arms and kicked hard to reorient herself.

In an instant, Hope was lost inside a cloud of impenetrable blackness.

A rush of emotions raced through her at once. Embarrassment—this was exactly what Alex had tried so hard to prevent. Anger at herself for screwing up. She hadn't been paying any attention to her position in the water.

Finally, a deep, primordial terror rose inside her.

She was underwater, deep inside a cave, and *completely blind*.

Her light worked fine. It just didn't illuminate anything. The effect was like shining high beams at dense fog. The narrow shaft of light only reflected back the coal-black silt.

She began taking great, gasping breaths and her heart raced—she needed to get a grip on herself, now.

Stop, breathe, and think, Hope.

Forcing her flailing body to stop, she concentrated on deep breaths and kept her eyes closed while maintaining a death grip on her flashlight. Hope consciously forced her clenched muscles to relax and her breathing slowed further.

Think. You were right over the line. It should be below you.

She reached down a hand until she felt the more solid surface of the mud layer, but couldn't locate a line anywhere, and her heart took off again.

Stop it! You can think your way out of this. Alex might as well be in another world right now.

It's up to you.

She must have gotten turned during her loss of balance—the line could be anywhere. Alex had taught her how to perform a search grid, so she began, waving one hand slowly back and forth under her body, continuing in what she hoped was a straight line. There was no way to tell in the inky silt. Hope held the hand with the flashlight out in front and eventually it hit the wall with a solid thump. The rock was sharp and cool beneath her searching hand.

Ok, all you need to do is follow this around and you'll come to one of the two entrances and be able to find the line again.

Hope brushed her hand along the jagged wall as she slowly finned her way forward, the other hand with the flashlight only illuminating the impenetrable silt all around her.

There was no sign of Alex.

It wasn't long before her trailing hand encountered only water—she had found an opening and wanted to yell a joyful shout. Hope turned into it and eagerly began swimming. She had ventured well down the black passage when dread washed over her, its icy fingers tickling down her spine.

I haven't looked for the line!

The silt wasn't as bad here, but the visibility still wasn't great. She sank down and ran her hand over the mud but found no guideline.

How can the line not be here? I must be missing it!

Once again, her breathing and heart rate rocketed, and she stopped to calm herself. Closing her eyes, Hope felt around again.

Still no line.

Frustrated now, tears threatened as she stopped to think it through. Alex had laid the green line a solid foot over the surface of the mud so it could easily be found. So why couldn't she feel it? She swept her hand back and forth in broad strokes, but encountered nothing but water.

The answer came over her like freezing water pouring into her stomach.

Alex had told her about it repeatedly. She had seen it with her own eyes when she entered The Closet.

There was a third, *unexplored* passage off to one side—it could lead to her death by drowning if she got lost in it.

Turn around now!

Hope forced herself to calm once more and to slow her racing heart as she touched the cool rock wall with one hand to ground herself. She turned around in a tight ball, kicking up more silt in the tight passage, her eyes useless.

Hope swam forward, keeping one hand on the wall for orientation, and soon she was back in The Closet. She closed her eyes to the blackness and concentrated on slow, deep breaths. Before entering the unknown tunnel, she had traveled clockwise with her left arm tracing the wall, so she continued in the same direction. Hope slowly finned on, keeping a tight hold on her fear and dread.

Panic could mean the difference between life and death.

The small room was still awash in black particles—she was completely blind. Again, there was no sign of Alex.

Eventually, her hand once again lost contact with the cool, jagged surface, finding only water as an opening appeared on her left. She turned toward it and exhaled, lowering herself toward the muddy bottom.

Oh please, oh please.

CHAPTER 31

After taking several more deep, calming breaths to center herself, Hope swept her light down and the bright green line appeared below her, swirling in and out of the black silt like a beacon.

She heaved a relieved moan.

With her left hand, Hope looped her thumb and index finger around the line, maintaining a loose hold as she swam down the tunnel. This had been part of the drill she had practiced with Alex. If she got lost in silt, she would follow the line until it reached air and they would regroup there.

She had no idea if she was headed away from the entrance to the cave or back toward it and didn't care. She just wanted to get to open air again.

But what if Alex goes the other direction?

Then you'll deal with that when you get there. Alex is fine—he's been in zero-visibility conditions multiple times.

Hope continued down the passage, focusing intently on the task at hand with her hand looped around the line. She could see around her again. The silt continued to thin and soon the passage was crystal clear again. She negotiated a tight turn, and after several minutes more, the walls opened out into a big room.

Hope surfaced. She was back in the small room where they had started. She inflated her BCD and took her regulator out, tipping her head back as she took a massive inhalation of the stale air—she'd never smelled more wonderful air.

She closed her eyes and finally relaxed, safe. She had followed all the procedures necessary to save herself.

Next, a tremendous upwelling of pride surged and Hope shouted, "Yes!" The echo returned to her.

Alex will be so proud of me!

"But he's still in there. What if he's in The Closet looking around for me? What if he goes in that side passage and gets lost?" Her voice was shrill in the small room. "He wouldn't do that."

He might if he thought I was in danger . . .

Hope made her decision. Deflating her BCD, she sank beneath the surface and headed back into the tunnel. She hadn't gone far when Alex's powerful handheld flashlight lit up the tunnel as he came around the tight turn. She sagged as some of her tight muscles began to relax.

He swam powerfully, closing the distance between them in nothing flat. They faced each other and his eyes were enormous as he made contact with her, grabbing her arms in a tight hold and propelling her backwards as he kicked.

They flew out of the tunnel and Alex angled them up to the surface, wrapping his arms tightly around her. Once they were on top, he ripped his mask down around his neck and established positive buoyancy for them both.

"Hope! Oh my God! Are you ok?"

"Yes! I'm fine. I was coming back to find you."

"Oh my God." He was panting as he pulled her toward him, holding her so tightly she could hardly breathe. "What was I thinking, bringing you in here? I thought you were gone—I wasn't sure I'd ever see you again." He grabbed her wet, tangled hair and crushed her mouth to his, then said, "I'm so sorry. This was a huge mistake."

He was almost unhinged with worry about her. She hardly recognized the man in front of her.

"Alex, I'm fine. I followed all the training you gave me and found my way out. It's ok. There's nothing wrong."

He was shaking his head back and forth, barely listening. "We're getting out of here right now. This was a horrible idea—how could I have risked you like this? We need to go. Now."

Alex took her hand and swam hard toward the rocky shoreline, pulling her along in his wake. He led her up onto dry land, his hand like steel on hers, and unbuckled her BCD. "Let's get this tank off and get through the dry tunnel."

Alex met her eyes, widening his own as he rested both hands on her shoulders. His chest visibly moved up and down with the force of his emotion. "You're going to have to swim back through the first passage to get out. I know that's got to be awful for you, but I'll be there every step of the way. You can do this."

She backed away, irritated now. "I'm fine to swim through the passage. Yes, that was a very scary situation, but I handled it and found my way out—just as you taught me. Calm down! I dealt with the situation just fine."

"You did. But I've made too many mistakes in this cave. It stops now." He turned toward the water, staring at it like he could make it do his bidding as his face hardened.

"Your mistakes? It was my fault. I wasn't paying attention to my position, and I screwed up." She dropped her gaze with a frustrated sigh. "But you're right, we have to go back. I'm sure it's going to take some time for all that mud to settle again—we can continue then."

Alex whipped his head around, fully facing her. "No."

His demeanor was changing before her eyes. His fear was being replaced by iron resolve.

"What do you mean, no?" Her mouth settled in a grim line.

Alex snapped to his full height, legs square and jaw tight, and Hope's stomach sank like a rock as she recognized his stubbornness setting in.

His voice was like steel. "Absolutely not. You're never going back in there. No way."

"Oh, stop it. I've learned my lesson. It won't happen again."

Alex stepped in front of her, his body rigid and his eyes blazing—this wasn't his usual stubbornness. He spoke with absolute authority. "Hope, this isn't a conversation. You're not going back in this cave, and that's final. You're done here." She ground her teeth as he loomed over her, his face hard and eyes glinting like iron. "We're going. Now."

Hope stared at Commander Monroe, a man who expected to be obeyed without question.

Furious now, she consciously unclenched her jaw, taking a deep breath as she spoke evenly. "This isn't the place to have this little chat. You are much too wound up. Let's just get out of here."

She turned around, removed her BCD and reg from the tank, and began walking down the passage with them. After a few moments, his footsteps echoed behind her.

Hope emerged out of the tunnel and reattached her scuba kit together with the tank she had used on the way in, verifying it still had plenty of air. She started dragging it toward a nearby rock to get it on when Alex picked it up for her.

"Let me help you. I need to do a double check on it, anyway."

She glowered at him.

"It's standard procedure! A buddy check. We're still in a goddamn cave here, with a tight squeeze just ahead. Stop being so defensive!"

She choked down her fury and nodded, letting him inspect the gear, both of them tense and quick to anger.

Alex's mood had changed drastically, from ragged fear for her safety to this cold, iron anger. He wasn't issuing orders at the moment, but tension radiated off him.

She put the tank on and they continued, swimming through the rest of the cave without mishap, the underwater environment preventing either of them from saying anything else they might regret.

They were still quiet as they put away their gear in the small cave and redressed. She continued to fume, hurt that he wasn't giving her any credit for getting out of the situation on her own—using the training he'd provided. In addition, she was furious he'd seen fit to give her a direct order like that.

And he was still seething. There was a huge gulf between them now, and neither knew how to cross it.

Finally, Alex turned toward her. "I'm looking out for your safety. I'm not letting you back in there."

Hope's anger boiled over and she stomped up to him, jabbing her finger in his face. "Knock it off! I'm not one of your goddamn troops to order around. Do you understand that? How dare you!"

"I dare because I know a hell of a lot more about this! Diving in caves can be deadly—you just showed how. I'm not discussing this anymore—your cave-diving days are over."

"You overreact and see danger in everything! Like all of this." She flung an arm wildly, encompassing the jungle they stood in. "You bit my head off for coming out here alone, but guess what? It was FINE!"

He stood with his arms crossed and his mouth a grim slash. "You didn't know that! I didn't know that until I reconned the area. I'm not the one being irrational here, Hope."

"Oh, give me a break. Come on, let's go back to the house. I'm not fighting about this in the middle of the damn jungle." Hope stormed off, not caring if he followed.

· · ·

It was early afternoon when they got back, but neither felt like eating lunch. She took a shower while he stood on the porch, then they changed places. They needed to talk, but Hope didn't know how to start. Somewhat calmer now, she wasn't sure she'd stay that way.

Alex came back out carrying two bottles of beer and handed her one, sitting on the couch next to her.

"Thanks," she said quietly.

"Hope, you are more important to me than anything in this world." His whole face was still tense. "Your life isn't worth a few more gold coins."

"But yours is?"

He hissed a frustrated sigh. "It's not nearly as dangerous for me. Look, I have been trained in ways you can't begin to imagine."

"Oh, I know." Hope spat the words. "You're the big, bad Navy SEAL. You know what else you told me? That there were several times when you were with other SEALs who kicked up silt. You trained me ad nauseam for just this circumstance. And it worked! I found my way out."

He rounded on her, his eyes implacable as he enunciated each word clearly. "You could have died in there today."

"But I didn't! I didn't panic. I didn't lose it. I used my training and a level head and found my way back to the line, then out. Without any help from you, I might add."

His head whipped toward her and he widened his eyes, clearly hurt. Hope's anger ratcheted up further. "Is that what this is all about? You can't stand the idea that I saved myself this time, instead of you! Your precious male ego can't handle that?"

His wounded look disappeared and was replaced with tightly controlled fury. "Don't accuse me of that. Stop acting like I'm some chauvinist pig—you know better." He took a deep breath. "You have no idea how proud I am of you. You did everything exactly right."

She stood up with a groan. "Then why are we going on about this? Look, I know you're protective, but I'm not some china doll for you to keep on a shelf to admire but never risk anything bad happening to."

"Dammit, you know how capable I think you are!"

"Then act like it! We're just going around in circles right now." She set the beer on the coffee table. "We both need to calm down. I'm going for a walk on the beach."

∼

Hope woke the next morning tired and worn out. Alex had already left the house. He'd set out a mug and coffee pod for her as usual and had included a note next to it.

I need to get an early start. I want a swim, and I have to prepare for the group starting today. Then, at the bottom, *I love you. Always.*

"I love you too, you mule-headed, overprotective man."

She took her coffee cup out to the porch and settled in. She was feeling more stable this morning. It hadn't been her best night's sleep, but it was good enough to put some emotional distance from yesterday. And from the tossing and turning next to her, Alex hadn't slept well either.

She pressed her palms against both eyes, hoping he was all right. She could easily work from home, and a bad night's sleep wouldn't affect her performance much. But Alex was another story. Ninety-five percent of the time, his job was a walk in the park compared to what he used to do. But he took the other five percent very seriously and was always ready for an emergency. His plan had been to spend yesterday afternoon preparing for the new group, but that had been derailed.

"I didn't exactly behave with grace and composure yesterday, did I, Cruz?" The dog came up and set his head on her knee, whining.

She and Alex had never gone to bed angry with each other

before. Alex shut down and got stubborn when upset, and she tended to fly off the handle at him. Which was rather astonishing considering how many years she had spent being afraid of men and what they could do to her. Hope shook her head, remembering how she'd jabbed her finger in his face and yelled at him. He'd even raised his voice in return, yet she'd never been afraid during any of it.

Just another example of how much you love and trust him.

They had danced around each other yesterday after she'd come back from her walk, neither willing to make the wound worse. As they prepared the dinner she'd brought back from the kitchen, he'd brushed against her several times, but she'd still been too upset to return the contact. They'd sat on opposite ends of the couch watching a movie, and she was sure he hadn't paid any more attention than she had. Finally, they went to bed, both still far apart.

Still, she was mystified by how different he'd reacted compared to her accident shortly after becoming certified. Then, he had insisted on her completing the dive immediately and nagged her for the next week to dive with him again.

Yesterday had been the exact opposite, and she couldn't understand why.

"We need to talk this out. Today."

The windows in her home office faced north, providing a view of the pier and ocean. Hope spent her morning working, trying to concentrate, but mostly running over the fight with Alex instead. Finally, the dive boat came back just before noon, and she stood up with a flutter in her stomach. After squaring her shoulders, she headed toward the pier.

CHAPTER 32

Alex busied himself gathering the wetsuits into a pile as his group left the boat.

"See you tomorrow, Alex," said the curvy blonde as she threw him a suggestive smile.

"Enjoy your afternoon," he said as she tried to keep eye contact, but he turned back to the wetsuits.

You're not the one I want to see smiling at me.

After a terrible night's sleep, Alex had gone for a hard swim, hoping it would make him feel better. It hadn't. Fortunately, his dive group hadn't presented any real challenges, but he wasn't in the mood today for his usual easy humor.

His anger had dissipated by the time he and Hope went to bed, and by morning it had been replaced with a hollow ache. Yesterday, every time he'd tried to explain why he didn't want her in that cave, he'd just made things worse, finally realizing he needed to shut up until he had a chance to figure out his tumult of emotions.

With a dejected sigh, Alex tossed the pile of wetsuits onto the dock and glanced up with a jolt as Hope walked down the wooden pier toward him.

He flashed back to their Chapel dive, when she'd also approached him like this, but the emotion was so different that time. Instead of the tight rash guard, Hope was dressed in a staff uniform today, but she was still beautiful. The hollow ache intensified to a twisting pain, and he clamped down on all the swirling emotions, schooling his face as she approached.

She stopped beside the boat. "Guys, I need to borrow Alex. Could you finish without him today?"

Of course, Tommy and Robert said yes, and he soon joined her, walking back toward the resort. He wanted to reach out but hesitated, remembering yesterday when he'd been rebuffed, and was still concerned about saying the wrong thing. Hope took his hand and relief poured through him as he squeezed back tightly.

She started with a safe topic. "How was the big group? I just passed them—they were all smiles."

"Mixed. Some good divers, some not so good. All pleasant to be around, though. It was an easy morning."

They made small talk until they got to the house, where Alex headed for the shower, still trying to calm the uneasiness clawing through his gut—the fear that he'd really screwed things up. And he was still hurt by what she'd said to him.

When he returned to the kitchen, Hope had prepared lunch for them, setting it on the island. They ate quietly, Hope picking at her meal, the strain clear in her shoulders. He searched for a way to bridge the gulf between them but came up empty.

Finally, she took a deep breath. "I'm sorry I got so mad at you yesterday. I was really upset and said some things I regret."

The tension drained out of him like a plug being opened. "I'm sorry too. And there's a lot I regret about yesterday."

"I should never have accused you of being upset that I saved myself, which was stupid, not to mention unfair. And you're right—I know you better than that. I was thinking this morning about how amazing it is that I feel safe blowing up at you like that." She gave him a wry glance. "Not much of a compliment, huh? Your protective streak rubs up against my independence. But you know that."

She turned fully toward him. "Alex, I still don't understand. I handled the silt-out yesterday completely opposite from my other accident. Instead of panicking, I kept my head. I did everything I was supposed to, and I'm damn proud of myself. You said you were too. But you're sure not acting like it." Her voice was calm, but her eyes were wounded and imploring.

Hope's words stabbed straight into his heart. Alex pushed his plate away and looked into her hazel eyes. "I'm proud of you every minute of every day." Then he paused, turning his stare to the kitchen wall. "I've been thinking nonstop about yesterday. I just don't know how to put this into words."

He spoke slowly, wanting more than anything to make her understand. "When you found that picture of me on the dive op, you said your reaction to it—your panic attack—was about you. That it had nothing to do with me. Yesterday it was my turn. It was your experience, but I'm the one who needs to work through the aftermath."

Hope wrinkled her brow as her eyes broadcast confusion, but she didn't interrupt.

"When you go through the dive-training portion of BUD/S, they do everything possible to rattle your cage. To make you panic. You've got two choices. Day after day, and week after week. You either get over your fear and become unflappable underwater, or you quit. I got over it."

"I can't imagine there's much quit in you."

"Or you." He gave her a quick smile before returning his gaze to the wall. "When I'm diving alone or leading a group, nothing phases me. I can handle anything. I hadn't felt anything close to fear while diving in close to two decades—until that day your face hit my fins. I already told you how that shook me up. My reaction made it very clear my feelings for you were deeper than I'd been willing to acknowledge. But I still had no problem keeping it together. I could still act like I was your instructor and you were my student."

He stopped to gather himself, moving his eyes over her face. "I reacted differently yesterday because the situation was completely different for me."

Say it.

"Hope, I've waited forty years to find you. When I lost those eight men in Syria, it almost destroyed me. I'm pretty sure if anything happened to you, that would finish the job. I can't stand the thought of losing you."

She got up and stood between his knees as he sat on the stool. He drew her close, pulling her tightly to him and speaking against her temple, his words rushing out now. "I was so scared yesterday when I saw that black cloud of silt. I searched that chamber—it seemed like forever—and couldn't find you. So I headed down the passage, and I can't even describe what it felt like to see you there. Unharmed. All I could think of was getting you out of there as fast as possible. I'm sorry I ordered you around, but I'm not sure I can live with the idea of you back in that cave."

Alex paused, fighting back tears now as his gut roiled with turmoil.

"Sometimes I feel like I'm still drowning," he whispered.

Hope pulled back and brushed her fingers down the side of his face. "No, you're not. You're proving that right now by talking this out and not shutting down or getting defensive."

She gave him a small smile, her face smoothing out as she relaxed. Reaching up the other hand, Hope held his face between both hands. "We're a team—you and I. We make each other better. You told me how much you loved exploring that cave. You would have never been in there if I hadn't found it. And neither would I if it weren't for your experience. It's been good for me too. We need each other."

He watched her intently, riveted to her eyes.

"You were afraid yesterday," she continued. "Well, I'm an

expert on fear. I spent nearly two *decades* terrified of repeating my experience with Caleb. It never happened. I was so afraid I wasn't even really living. *You* helped me see what a waste of a life that was.

"Let me show you the same thing. You can't just keep me in a glass house and protect me from all harm. You gave me the training and skills to handle that situation, and I did."

She studied him closely, rubbing her thumbs over his cheeks. "And this isn't just about fear. It's about faith too. You've got to have faith in what *you've* taught me. After my accident, I didn't have any faith in myself. All of it was in you. And what you're doing now isn't that different. I know you have faith in me—you just don't believe what you've taught me is enough. But it is. Yesterday I finally had faith in myself, which I'm really proud of." Her voice thickened on the last sentence.

Alex was a confused jumble of emotions as he took her in his arms. Pride, fear, immense relief—and above all—deep love. He flashed back to Steve's advice, now understanding it perfectly. "You were incredible yesterday. And you're so much smarter than I am."

"Of course I'm not. But I know a lot about overcoming fear. You've taught me about having faith. I can't describe what it meant to me. What it still means to me. To put all my trust in you, and actually *believe* it's going to be ok."

They held each other for a long moment before Hope broke the embrace. Her eyes pierced into his. "We have to go back in that cave. You've got to dive it with me and understand that it's going to be all right. Remember, you weren't happy about me going through that squeeze, either. And I got through it just fine —multiple times. Though I will say I'm damn grateful for your help. Pushing that tank through kind of sucks."

She brushed a feathery kiss over his lips and Alex turned it into something deeper, needing the contact.

Finally, she broke away. "I've waited my whole life for you too, you know."

Alex sighed deeply and pulled her against his chest. He still hated the idea of her back in that cave, but her words rang of truth. "Ok, I'll think about it."

She tensed in his arms before relaxing. "That's all I ask."

A small smile crept across his face, knowing she had bitten back a retort to meet him halfway.

Then she closed the rest of the distance. "And you're not drowning anymore—you're rising. You've got hope now, and that's a very important thing."

He smiled at her play on words. "It absolutely is. I never need anything else but you." Alex closed his eyes and held her in his arms.

After a long moment, Hope locked gazes with him. "One more thing, Alex, and I mean it. If you *ever* order me around like that again, you're going to be singing in the Vienna Boys' Choir after all. Compliments of me this time, not the shrapnel." She raised a brow at him, a humorous spark in her eyes now.

She wasn't kidding, but Alex couldn't help the small smile that escaped. "Well, there's one thing I've learned. Even when you're a commander, there's always somebody around who outranks you. Don't worry, I know who my commanding officer is." He brushed her face with his hand. "But it just comes out sometimes. I'll do my best to prevent that, and I have the feeling you'll let me know if I slip up."

"Damn straight, sailor." She smiled back and snuggled closer into his chest.

He wrapped her up tightly, gratitude seeping into his bones. "Why do you put up with me?"

Hope's shoulders shook with laughter, then she met him eye to eye, her love clear to see. "I don't think you will ever understand what a miracle you are to me. Sara and I talked once about who my perfect man was before I came down here.

"I said he was a man strong enough that I always felt safe, yet had no fear of physically. A man I could trust down to my soul—who would stand firm if things got tough, not cut and run. And a man who set me free to be myself without trying to control me. Maybe we're still working on that last one, but you tick an impressive number of those boxes, you know. And yes, I realize there's a huge difference between protective and controlling."

She shook her head, and tears filled her eyes. "You don't even hesitate to protect me from my dumb moves. Like running into hurricanes. And yesterday too—I was impatient when we started, then got distracted looking at the ceiling. I didn't even try to understand your point of view. You've had every reason to run from me. Yet here you are. I meant it when I said you're the very image of a hero, you know."

Alex stiffened. Even before Syria, he'd never liked that word. "We might have to agree to disagree on that last one, but I've never been one to turn and run when things get tough. And I'm not about to start now. I love you."

"I love you too." Hope slid against his chest again and stroked his back. It felt wonderful. She kissed the center of his chest before snuggling closer. "This is my favorite place in the world."

"The kitchen?"

She laughed, and he knew everything was going to be ok.

"I was referring to being in your arms, but now that you mention it, we've had some very good times here in the kitchen." She pulled his head down to hers in case he missed her meaning.

Alex let the feelings roll over him as his desire built, finally breaking the kiss to murmur against her mouth. "And how do you feel about the bedroom?"

"Mmm. Much more comfortable than the table. Let's go."

They'd just started to move when the power went out, silencing the air conditioning. Hope turned back to Alex with a grin. "Mr. Monroe, I think we're about to get hot and sweaty."

Alex drew her in and kissed her. "Ms. Collins, I promise we are."

He picked her up in his arms and carried her to their bedroom, determined to show her exactly how much he loved her.

∼

HOPE STIFLED a groan as she woke up later that night with a stabbing pain in her abdomen. She got up and padded to the bathroom, shaking out several ibuprofen tablets and swallowing them. She met her gaze in the mirror. "Maybe it'll kick in before the cramps get too bad and you can get some sleep."

The eyes staring back at her were skeptical, and she returned to bed, pulling the covers tight around her. Soon, another cramp hit, and she inhaled, breathing through the pain.

"Everything ok?"

She turned to Alex. "Sorry, I didn't mean to wake you. I just got my period."

He softened his eyes, but the worry was clear in them. "I've noticed you're starting to look pale again."

"Yeah, I know. The infusions didn't last as long as I thought."

"Come here, baby."

He pulled her into his arms and she settled in, drawing comfort from his presence, and even more reassured now that things were ok between them again. Alex's breath deepened immediately, and secure within his arms, Hope was able to doze off into a fitful sleep.

CHAPTER 33

The next morning, Alex woke just after 5:30, pulled on board shorts and a staff shirt, and headed out to the kitchen and coffee. Cruz yawned and came over for a scratch, then Alex let him out. He was in a *much* better frame of mind than yesterday morning, though still not thrilled with the idea of Hope going back in that cave. He needed more time to process it all.

Alex sat down on the couch in the great room and picked up his teaching binder. Yesterday, one of his divers had approached him about adding an advanced scuba course during the remainder of her trip. He picked up his laptop to order more course materials and naturally ended up looking at scuba gear instead. Three new regulators had just come out, so he investigated their specs thoroughly. "Yep, still lipstick on a pig."

Quiet movements in the bedroom indicated Hope was awake, so he got up to fix her coffee, surprised it was already past 6:30 and time for his swim. He was waiting for her cup to finish brewing when she dragged herself into the kitchen, dressed in sleep shorts and a T-shirt, her face exhausted and pinched. "Coffee?"

"Thanks." She took the mug with a tired smile and shuffled over to the couch, slumping onto it.

He swiveled his head, watching her with alarm. "Are you ok?"

"I'll be all right. Just need to get through the next couple of days. I'm thinking about calling in sick today."

"Looks like you should." He hated seeing her like this. He'd much rather be in pain himself than watch her suffer. Alex picked his laptop up again, this time checking on the course materials like he was supposed to.

"I'll be right back." Hope set her untouched coffee mug on the table and headed back toward their bedroom.

Alex watched her go, frowning, then turned back to the website. His frown deepened as he read about potential curriculum changes the scuba-certifying agency was implementing. *Looks like the instructor has some new learning to do. I really need to investigate hiring a high school kid to work in the dive shop.*

Then Hope's scream tore apart the morning.

"*Alex!*"

The desperate fear of it stabbed through the depths of him as he sprinted to the bedroom. Not seeing her, he ran toward the bathroom, where his heart nearly stopped.

Hope lay crumpled on the tile floor, a pool of blood spreading beneath her.

"Call 911. Something's. Really. Wrong." She panted the words, hardly able to speak.

"Oh my God! I'm calling."

She clutched her abdomen, shrieking another agonized cry. Alex ran back to the great room and retrieved his phone, dialing on the way back as a frigid sweat broke out all over his body. After the dispatcher answered, he told her the situation and gave the address, pacing back and forth in front of the open bathroom door.

Hope watched him dully from the floor. "No sirens or lights. No noise."

"Hope!"

"Dammit, Alex."

Gritting his teeth, he repeated her request. "We're in the owner's house, not the resort. Take the sand road to your left once you hit the roundabout in front of the lobby."

He hung up and knelt next to her, grasping the hand that wasn't holding her abdomen. His pulse raced even more at its cold and clammy feel. He tore his gaze away from the blood to meet her glassy eyes. "They're on their way. Stay with me."

She was getting paler by the second and closed her eyes.

"Hope? What can I do to help?" His voice cracked as the blood pool expanded, its crimson tendrils snaking across the tile.

"Stay with me. I think something. Ruptured inside." She whispered the last words.

After what felt like hours but was likely just a few minutes, doors slammed outside and Alex ran to the front door as the paramedics climbed the stairs, carrying a stretcher between them. He led them back to the bathroom and stood in the doorway as they bent down to work on Hope. He swallowed, trying to soothe his parched throat.

One paramedic was a woman with an American accent who immediately noticed where the pool of blood was coming from. "Is she pregnant?"

Alex shook his head. "No, she got her period last night. They've been getting worse, and she was planning on a hysterectomy in a few months."

The other paramedic took her vitals, his dark hands steady and calm. "Blood pressure is 80/50, pulse 140 and thready. We need to get her out of here." They got to work with the stretcher, moving Alex out of the way. They tried to talk to Hope, but she only responded with vague moans.

The woman glanced at Alex as they wheeled her to the front door. "You can meet us in the emergency room. Follow us and use GPS if we get separated."

"Yeah, I know where the hospital is."

He glanced at Hope's nightstand and grabbed her phone on impulse. Pocketing his wallet, he ran out the front door and followed the ambulance to the hospital.

As Alex entered through the sliding doors of the emergency room, a voice paged a trauma-team activation through the overhead speakers. The receptionist made him wait in the lobby—he wanted to punch something but took deep breaths instead. A few minutes later, a blonde woman in green scrubs bent over the receptionist, who pointed to Alex. He stood as the woman approached.

"I'm Dr. Grainger. I happened to be doing surgeries today, and I'm Hope's usual doctor."

He nodded and introduced himself.

"Ok, Alex, I'm taking her to the OR immediately for an emergency hysterectomy—she's already on her way. I anticipate being able to perform the procedure laparoscopically, which would result in minimal scarring. But if the bleeding is too bad, I may have to open up her abdomen . . ." She droned on and her words ran together in Alex's mind. "Hope listed you as her decision maker. Do I have your consent?"

"Yes, of course. Do whatever you have to."

She gave him a reassuring smile. "I've done this procedure many times. She's in good hands. Normally this takes about an hour, but this isn't normal, so don't worry too much if it takes longer, ok? We'll have someone escort you to the surgical waiting room and I'll inform you as soon as I'm done." With that, she rushed away.

Soon, a tiny man who looked a hundred years old led him to a cavernous waiting room painted a depressing blue color. Alex checked in with the attendant and gave her his cell phone number just in case, but she told him not to leave. He turned around and found a secluded chair in the corner of the room next to a hideous fake plant. Alex exhaled a sigh and closed his eyes for a moment, his stomach knotting even more as he imagined the worst.

He checked his watch and groaned, shocked it was well after eight. Swiping a hand over his eyes, he dialed Robert.

"'Bout time you called. Where you at, man?"

"The hospital. Hope's having emergency surgery."

"Oh shit! I'm sorry."

"It's ok. But needless to say, I won't be there today."

"No problem. I got it covered. Hope's gonna be ok, right?"

"She will." *She has to be.* "I need to go. I'll update you guys later."

He hung up and dialed Patti to inform her.

"Jesus, Mary, and Joseph! What's wrong?"

Alex hesitated, but Patti knew about Hope's problems. "She's having an emergency hysterectomy. She started hemorrhaging this morning in our bathroom. It looked like a war zone in there."

"Now you listen, Alex Monroe—Hope is a very strong woman. She'll come through this just fine. You keep me updated, now."

"Will do, Patti. Thanks." He hung up and leaned his head against the wall behind him, eyes closed.

Oh, shit. Sara! How am I going to get a hold of her?

He remembered grabbing Hope's phone as he rushed out of the house. After entering her passcode, he dialed Sara, but the phone went to voicemail. "Sara, it's Alex. Call me as soon as you get this."

Then he sent a text: Call ASAP. 911

He'd just hit send when the phone vibrated, and he swiped to answer. "Sara, it's Alex."

"What's wrong?" Tension dripped from her voice.

He explained the situation. "I'll call you back as soon as I have any more information. I just wanted to let you know what was going on."

"Thanks. She'll be ok, Alex. You and I both know how tough she is."

Alex clenched his eyes shut, taking a deep breath.

You didn't see that pool of blood.

Then it was back to waiting. He resisted the urge to pace but couldn't stop his leg from rhythmically bouncing up and down. Several times someone in scrubs came into the room, but they always approached someone else. His anxiety steadily ratcheted upward, and he constantly raked his fingers through his hair.

His mind took off on all the stupid things he'd done since he'd met Hope. How he'd made her cry after the boat sinking and how he'd acted like a spoiled brat when he'd met Marcus after her 10K race. And finally, he tortured himself with a running film of everything he'd said during their stupid fight after her silt-out in the cave.

Does she have any idea how much I love her?

∼

After more than two hours, Dr. Grainger appeared in the waiting room. Alex rushed to his feet, wiping his sweaty hands on his shorts. She beckoned and led him into a small wood-paneled room where they sat on opposite sides of a small table. Alex's heart was hammering as he imagined the worst, and he fought to maintain a neutral expression.

"Hope is doing fine. She came through the surgery in stable condition and is in recovery now."

Alex forced a long, even exhale as every muscle he owned unclenched. Strong emotion tried to rise and he ground his teeth, determined not to show it.

Dr. Grainger gave him another gentle smile. "One of her fibroids ruptured—that's what caused the hemorrhaging. I was able to complete the surgery laparoscopically, which should please her. She was concerned about minimizing the recovery time, and there will be little scarring."

"But she's ok?"

"Yes. She should be fine." The doctor sharpened her gaze. "Hope lost a lot of blood. We had to give her several units in the OR. I plan on keeping her here overnight, and she may need another transfusion tomorrow depending on her labs."

Alex's heart was still pounding out of his chest, and maybe he wasn't hiding his emotions as well as he thought, because Dr. Grainger smiled and squeezed his hand. "Hope did really well—she's a fighter. She needs a little more time in recovery, then a nurse will come take you to see her. She'll go up to her room on the floor after that."

"Thanks very much."

Alex returned to his seat next to the ugly plant and took a few moments to collect himself. He wasn't ready to relax quite yet, but his fever pitch of anxiety had lowered a bit.

Alex called Sara and Patti with the good news, then sent Tommy and Robert a group text saying Hope was doing ok but not going into specifics. Finally, he went back to waiting, his imagination once again vivid with all the things that might go wrong in the recovery room.

Eventually, a petite nurse wearing a clownfish-covered surgical cap took him back to see Hope. "She's still pretty out of it, but she's stable. Her room is being cleaned now, so it shouldn't be too much longer before she moves up to the floor."

The nurse gave him a sunny smile as she led him into a big room with individual curtained bays. The sound of beeping machines filled the room as they walked to the third bay and she drew the curtain back a little. "There's a chair for you, and, uh, they threw away her clothes, just so you know. I'll check on her in a few minutes."

The nurse walked briskly away, and with his heart pounding in his ears, Alex finally set eyes on Hope. She lay on her back with the head of the bed slightly elevated, pale and looking incredibly vulnerable.

He bent over her and brushed his lips over hers, but she didn't respond at all. His breath hitched, and he clamped down hard on the emotion, desperate to maintain control as he stroked the side of her face. At that, she moaned and moved her head a little.

"Wake up, baby. Please."

But she settled back into sleep and tears pricked his eyes.

A buzzing noise sounded—an automatic blood pressure cuff activating. After finishing, the monitor read 105/70. Her pulse was seventy. Recalling what the paramedic had recorded this morning, he finally relaxed a little.

Alex sat in a very hard chair and settled into wait yet again, but at least able to hold her hand now. He stroked each finger, front and back, and all warmer now. Her skin was like velvet under his rougher fingers, her hand tiny within his.

Please, please wake up.

Eventually, there was shuffling outside the curtain, then it was drawn back to reveal the nurse and a burly man in light-blue scrubs. Looking at the monitor, the nurse said, "Ok, her vitals have been steady, so she's ready to go to the floor. Raul will escort you to her room."

Hope's private room was painted a muted but determined yellow. Alex stood in front of a window which overlooked the lush green mountains in the center of the island.

With a sigh, he turned and stood next to the bed, taking her hand and once again brushing a soft kiss over her lips, but there was still no response. Alex stroked her rich brown hair away from her brow, studying her beautiful face, pale as porcelain now and so unlike her normal color. Finally, he straightened and sat in a chair tucked into the corner. At least this one was more comfortable, a soft-blue vinyl that reclined.

He leaned his head back and closed his eyes, whispering to himself, "She's ok, and nothing else matters. She's earned her sleep. She'll wake up soon."

Another thought followed immediately.

God, I hate hospitals.

CHAPTER 34

It was all wrong.

There should be ocean and beach out the window, not mountains. Hope couldn't make sense of what she saw. She'd opened her eyes to jagged green mountains sheathed in swirling gray clouds. Her head was fuzzy, and her mouth was terribly parched. She swallowed, wincing at her sore throat, and turned her head to the outline of her body under a white blanket. Finally, her eyes focused beyond her feet. Alex sat in a chair, reclining with his long legs stretched out before him, ankles crossed. His eyes were closed.

"Alex?" It came out as a breathy croak, but his eyes flew open and he vaulted to his feet, rushing to her side.

"You're awake! How are you feeling?" His eyes darted all over her face as one hand brushed the side of her head over and over, the other holding her hand tight.

"I'm so thirsty."

"I'll press the call button."

There was a distant tone pinging, and a door opened. Hope glanced around, finally understanding she was in a hospital room, and a plump woman wearing green scrubs entered. There was a dull, throbbing ache in her abdomen, and the morning came back like an out-of-focus movie . . . her collapsing on the bathroom floor in a torrent of blood as a stabbing knife twisted in her belly.

"Look who's awake!" The woman seemed too perky.

"Can she have some ice chips or water? She's really thirsty."

The nurse wore a scrub top covered in palm trees and smiled at Hope from the bedside. "I'm Annie, and I'll be taking care of you for the rest of this afternoon. How about we start with some ice chips. That sound good?"

Hope nodded and the nurse disappeared, returning a few moments later with a clear plastic glass and straw. "I put a little water in the bottom, but try the ice chips first. If you drink too much, it might make you sick." She raised the head of the bed and handed the glass to Hope. "How's your pain on a scale of one to ten?"

"About a six or seven, I'd say." The ice chips soothed her parched mouth, and her voice was stronger now.

"Ok, sounds like you need some pain medication. I'll be back in a minute." Annie swept out of the room and Hope moved her gaze to Alex as he returned to her side.

"What happened? I remember collapsing on the floor and calling you for help, but nothing after that." She was still foggy and so weak.

Instead of answering, Alex cupped her face in both hands and bent down to kiss her, his lips softly touching hers for the longest time. At his kiss, her fear and confusion began to melt away.

"You had an emergency hysterectomy, but you're doing great now. They're going to keep you here tonight. You needed a lot of blood during the surgery, and your doctor told me you might need more tomorrow. I love you so much." His voice cracked on last words.

He set his jaw tightly, the emotion written all over his face. Hope's heart clutched. "I'm sorry. I can tell I scared you."

He closed his eyes and leaned his forehead against hers, whispering, "You're fine now. That's all that matters."

The door opened with a knock as Annie entered. Alex stood up, his emotions hidden again, but kept hold of her hand.

"I've got some pain medication for you," Annie said as she placed the needle into Hope's IV tubing. "This is hydromorphone, and it's going to make you sleepy." After confirming Hope didn't need anything else, she left again.

"I don't remember anything. It's so strange."

He gave her a ghost of a smile. "They pretty much took you straight to the OR."

Their eyes met and locked—Alex's eyes held a small glimpse of what he had been through in the previous hours, and his throat moved as he swallowed.

Then a massive rush of dizzy sleepiness hit her. "Oh, wow. I think I'm going to sleep for a while now."

It was dark outside the next time she woke, and Alex was back in the chair, scrolling on his phone. Hope pressed her lips together as she watched him. "Have you even eaten anything today?"

Once again, he hurried to his feet and came to her side. "No, I haven't been hungry. I'm fine."

"You're always hungry." It was after eight. Hope took his hand. "Honey, go home for the night. I'm not going to do anything but sleep, anyway. You can come back in the morning."

He stilled, his posture stiffening. "I'm not leaving you here alone."

"I'm not alone. I've got a whole team looking out for me. Besides, you need to feed Cruz."

"He fended for himself just fine before he found you."

"So did you."

He broke into laughter at that. "Touché. Ok, I'll go feed him and come back."

"No, Alex," she said softly. "Go home and go to bed. I mean it. That's an order."

He pursed his lips, narrowing his eyes. Hope stared straight back, trying to look stronger than she felt.

He finally gave in. "You're sure?"

She nodded, and he leaned over her again, stroking her face. "So, you can give me orders but not the other way around?"

"You told me point blank I was your commanding officer. I'm just doing my job here."

"Didn't know I'd regret that quite so soon." He smiled, then pointed to her. "But you call immediately if you need me, hear?"

"I promise. Now give me a kiss." Alex brushed her lips with a soft tenderness—it sent a long, rolling wave of soothing light through her sore abdomen.

Then he was gone.

Half an hour later, a new nurse came into the room. Her scrub top had different kinds of tropical fish and Hope liked her already. "My name's Lena. I took over for Annie." She glanced at the empty chair, and her eyebrows flew up. "You got him to leave? I just suggested he get something to eat, and he gave me a look that would freeze boiling water."

Hope smiled. "Sorry. He tends to get a bit intense where my welfare is concerned, but I talked him into going home."

"His concern was evident. How are you feeling? Ready for some dinner?"

"Yes, I'm starting to feel hungry."

"Let's start with some soup."

Hope finished the whole bowl of broth and was plenty full afterwards. Her phone sat on the tray table. She should call Sara, but it just seemed like too much work, and Alex had updated her.

Instead, she reclined the bed back to flat and rolled on her side. Her abdomen was back to a dull, tolerable ache. The fatigue washed over her again.

AT 3 A.M., the pain was back and woke her. This time, it was an intense thudding that radiated from her abdomen, its grasping fingers reaching for escape.

Oh, wow—time for more pain meds.

Hope eased onto her back, fumbling for the control unit that held the call button, when something caught her eye. Alex was back in the chair, eyes closed, with his head tipped back and legs out front, once again crossed at the ankles.

"Oh, you stubborn man."

A wide smile spread across his face, and he opened his eyes. He came over, and she answered with her own smile despite her irritation. Finally locating the control unit, she pressed the call button.

"It's lonely in that house without you. Even Cruz was walking around in circles. We were just following each other around—it was pathetic, so I decided to come back." He kissed her as the door opened and Lena came back in, her blonde hair still neat in its bun.

"What? You're back again?"

Alex straightened and shrugged. "Couldn't sleep."

"Uh-huh. You've got trouble written all over you. Visiting hours are only during the day, you know. Poor Hope needs her sleep. I might have to call security and have you removed."

He crossed his arms and gave her a rather frightening grin. "I'd like to see them try."

Hope snorted, then winced. "Unfortunately, he's not joking. I think we'd probably better admit defeat, Lena."

Lena saw the wince. "You having some pain?"

"Yes, it's pretty bad now." Alex's smile disappeared, and Hope held up a hand to him. "Calm down, it's normal."

"I'll get you some pain medication, honey." She was back quickly with a syringe, and Hope was ready for some relief. Alex stood back, giving Lena some room.

"Ok, fine. He can stay." She smiled at him as she administered the medication. "I've got a soft spot for the heroic types. I float down to the ED sometimes. I was one of the nurses who treated you the night you were shot. Looks like you're all healed up."

Alex inclined his head. "Good as new. And thanks—you guys took great care of me."

"Don't mention it. I'm glad you helped put that guy away." She squeezed Hope's hand. "Maria from the lab should be by around five to draw your blood. You might need another transfusion depending on your hemoglobin, so we'll wait for that to come back and go from there. Now try to get some rest." Then she glared at Alex. "And you leave her alone."

Alex grinned and saluted her as she breezed out of the room before turning the smile to Hope. She shook her head at him, already sleepy. "You really are impossibly good looking, you know."

He laughed, approaching the bed to encircle her hand. "Well, someone's obviously feeling the medication."

"No, I'm not." Her voice softened. "Thank you. I don't even want to think about what that bathroom looked like when you got home."

He opened his eyes wide as a laugh tumbled out. "You won't believe this. When I walked in the front door, there was a huge bouquet of flowers on the table and Patti had cleaned everything up. It was spotless. I couldn't believe it."

Hope's eyes filled with tears. "I don't deserve you guys."

He brushed his hand over her face. "There are a whole lot of people who love you. Dogs too. You're pretty irresistible."

She smiled, eyelids heavy as she tightened her hand around his, holding it against her cheek. "You're the best thing that's ever happened to me."

As she slipped into sleep, his fading reply was the last thing she heard. "Yep. Definitely feeling the pain meds."

Dr. Grainger came in just before 7 a.m., briskly efficient in a blouse and skirt. "You look much better than the last time I saw you. How are you feeling this morning?"

"Sore, but good, considering."

"I just looked at your labs, and I'd like to give you another unit of blood before you go home. But I think we can get you out of here this afternoon."

Hope beamed as Alex squeezed her hand. "That's great."

"Have you eaten anything?"

"I had some broth last night, and I just ordered breakfast."

"Good. I want to make sure solid food stays down." Dr. Grainger stood straight. "Here are your marching orders. I want you to get repeat bloodwork in three days to make sure this last transfusion was enough. Then I'll see you in my office in two weeks for your follow up, and again two weeks later."

She looked back and forth between Hope and Alex. "And no sex for four weeks. Minimum."

Hope snuck a guilty look at Alex, but his gaze was firmly on Dr. Grainger. "Understood."

"All right. I've left a prescription for pain medication with your discharge paperwork."

After Dr. Grainger left, Hope turned to Alex with a sigh. "Aren't you supposed to be getting ready for work?"

"You sure are eager to get rid of me, Boss Lady."

"Never. I'm just feeling guilty you're here with me instead of diving."

"Well, don't. I made arrangements yesterday—April's covering for me. Though I wouldn't mind if we started a new trend of avoiding the hospital from now on."

She smiled but didn't miss that the normally neat and tidy

Alex had a jawful of stubble and his hair was a mess. "Deal. Can you run home to feed Cruz and let him out?"

Alex rolled his eyes.

"If he makes a mess in the house, you have to clean it up. Besides, I need some clothes to go home in."

"Now that is very true. I'll be back."

∼

THE LATE-AFTERNOON SUN was drifting toward the horizon as Hope shifted position on her porch couch. She was relatively comfortable in a pair of leggings and one of Alex's sweatshirts. She had commandeered several as her favorites for cooler days, and from his smile every time he saw her in one, he didn't mind. It wasn't terribly cool outside, but she craved comfort right now.

Patti was still visible as she strode up the beach toward the resort. She had just left, full of motherly concern for Hope. The two women had sat on the porch couch, Hope's eyes riveted to the floor, unable to look at her. Her face had been on fire as she apologized to Patti for having to clean up the awful mess in the bathroom.

She tilted Hope's chin up. "Child, when you've worked in this business as long as I have, you've seen everythin'. That's not the first time I've cleaned up blood, you know." She sat back with a smile. "And there was no way I was goin' to let Alex do it. He likes to think of himself as a big, strong man. But when it comes to you, he's anythin' but."

They both smiled at that.

"Don't you worry about a thing—you just concentrate on healin'. Alex is thinkin' about someone to help in the dive shop, and I've hired a new front-desk clerk to fill in for Martine when she's on maternity leave next month. We've got it all handled, you hear?"

And Patti's endless font of warmth and common sense had eased Hope's bruised spirit even as it eased her sore body.

∽

THAT NIGHT, Hope changed into a plain but buttery-soft white nightgown and gingerly slipped into bed next to Alex, sore and exhausted. He eased her to his chest and wrapped her tightly in his arms. She'd taken an oxycodone and was waiting for it to kick in. Being cradled in his arms was much better than the pain meds. "Oh, this is where I belong."

He kissed her temple as he stroked her hair. "I couldn't handle sleeping in this bed without you last night. I got up and tried to sleep on the couch, but Cruz kept pacing around and whining. He knew something was wrong."

He'd worn boxers to bed, and Hope rested a hand on his hip. "I'm sorry for depriving you for a whole month. I tried to wear something nonprovocative tonight."

"Doesn't matter. You could wear a pair of huge flannel granny panties to bed. It would still turn me on."

She tried to control her yelp. "Don't make me laugh! It hurts."

That sobered him. "I'm sorry. I'm holding you in my arms—I don't care about anything else. Last night was the first night we've spent apart since I moved in." He kissed her head, holding his mouth against her. "I missed you, baby."

Oh, my love.

She pressed her lips to the hard plane of his chest. "I'm sorry to put you through that. I know hospitals aren't your favorite places."

"Maybe not, but I sure was glad one was nearby yesterday morning."

Hope snuggled closer to him, safe and secure, as sleep quickly overtook her.

CHAPTER 35

The balmy breeze kept the afternoon heat tolerable, but the sand was warm under Hope's feet, even with running shoes. The shoes were for traction and support, not speed. She climbed the steps onto the pier, still surprised at what an effort it was, even two weeks after her surgery. The pain had faded after the first week, but not the exhaustion.

Fatigue was her constant companion.

She glanced down with a proud smile at her other constant companion. Cruz walked alertly by her side, his toenails clicking on the wooden panels of the pier.

She had begun her rehab routine the morning after she got home with a short walk down the beach. Alex accompanied her, and she turned around after a short distance, dizzy and weak as she leaned on him for support.

Over the next two weeks, her walking distance had slowly increased, and she was surprised when the dog stayed by her side as she climbed the steps onto the pier the first time. They turned around halfway down it as fatigue caught up with her and made the slow trudge back to the house.

One week ago, Hope had nearly shouted in triumph when

she'd made it to the end of the pier, though she'd needed a rest in the swing under the palapa before heading back. She'd timed it when the dive boat was away so Cruz wouldn't get nervous with a crowd around. *I can't believe I PR'd a half-marathon a few months ago!*

Sara had called several times over the previous two weeks, assuring herself that Hope was truly ok. Her most recent call had been the previous day. "You've always been more traditional than me. I'm just worried. A hysterectomy is a pretty big deal—for many reasons. You're doing all right?"

Hope smiled as she leaned back in her home-office chair. "I am. I've known for a long time that children weren't meant for me. This was just an exclamation point. And Dr. Grainger saved my ovaries, so I don't have to take hormones. But I learned it's better not to ignore your health problems, little sister. Mine almost killed me."

"I'm so grateful Alex was there. But don't you dare tell him I said that."

Laughter bubbled out of Hope. "Don't ever change, Sara. I gotta go. It's time for my checkup."

Dr. Grainger removed her stitches without ceremony. There were just three small Xs on her abdomen—one next to her navel, and two lower. Such a small souvenir for an event that could have killed her.

The cuts were healing well, and Dr. Grainger was pleased with Hope's bloodwork and overall progress. She was on the mend.

Now Hope was able to walk wherever she needed to, albeit more slowly. She was keeping up with things from her home office as Patti assumed her mother-hen role and had expressly forbidden her from working in the lobby office.

She and Cruz continued down the wooden planks to meet the dive boat, her first public appearance at the pier since her surgery. She would let Cruz decide whether to walk all the way. The guests had already departed for lunch, so it was just the staff cleaning up. As she approached, Alex's laughter rang out. He ran to the center of the walkway and ducked as Tommy turned the hose on him, drenching his shirt. Which only made him laugh harder, bringing a smile to Hope's face. Tommy relented, and Alex straightened before seeing Hope.

His face lit up like a searchlight, and he trotted toward her. Cruz had slowed during the water fight, but rejoined Hope's side when he recognized Alex. Hope emerged from the tunnel and embraced Alex.

"You're a sight for sore eyes," he said, giving her a quick kiss.

Tommy saw her and gave an enthusiastic shout. "Hope!" Cruz scurried to the side of the pier as Tommy wrapped her in a gentle hug. "Great to see you down here."

"It's good to be back."

Alex had told Tommy and Robert her surgery was for "women's problems," which would ensure they didn't ask any further questions. And she strongly suspected Patti had given them firm orders to behave like gentlemen, not that Hope would expect anything less.

Robert embraced her next. "We'll have you back on the dive boat before you know it." He turned to Alex. "Go on, get out of here. We got this."

Alex nodded and draped his arm over Hope's shoulder as they began walking back to the house. He'd been working half-days since her surgery, leaving as soon as they returned from the morning dive trip. He looked down at Cruz, once again at Hope's side. "I wonder if he's warming up to people more, or if he just doesn't want to leave you."

"Today was my first test with other people, and he didn't run away, just stood off to the side. He's definitely making progress."

As they stepped onto the beach, a stick had washed up on shore and Alex threw it. Cruz bounded away and retrieved it, bringing it back to him for another throw. Hope smiled—the dog never brought a stick for her to throw if Alex was there. He knew who had the arm.

And she wasn't up to throwing sticks quite yet, anyway.

After entering the house, Hope watered Cindy's flower bouquet on the kitchen table. She'd brought it by in person a few days after Hope had returned home. The amazing arrangement was still going strong after nearly two weeks. Cindy had also brought lunch and valued company several times, giving Hope a welcome respite from her recovery. She closed her eyes as she inhaled the intoxicating scent of the stargazer lilies. They were her favorite.

A satisfied smile rose to her face at the neatly lined-up loaves of banana bread on the counter, ready for the guests. Her new baking hobby had been a lifeline during her recovery, providing her with a much-needed way to relax and stay productive. Alex had even helped her a few times when she'd made cookies, spooning them onto the sheets and providing "quality control" after they came out of the oven.

After emerging fresh from the shower and smelling amazing, Alex reached for Hope's hand and they headed to the restaurant for lunch, sitting at their usual corner table.

Hope poured into her seat. "The fatigue still hits me sometimes. I wasn't expecting to still be so tired."

"I know what you mean. I worked really hard on my rehab at Walter Reed, but I wondered for a while if I'd ever get my strength and stamina back."

She couldn't resist an opening like that, giving him a broad grin. "Well, I can vouch for your stamina, and you're looking plenty strong these days too."

"You behave. We've still got two weeks left."

"Counting down, are you?"

He grinned at her over his iced tea. "Why would you think that?"

Hope turned her attention to the ocean with a sigh. "I miss

swimming. I'm starting to climb the walls, cooped up in that house all day. Even with all the baking. Much worse, I'm actually finding sympathy for your behavior after you were shot."

Alex laughed, his eyes sparkling. "Feeling a little differently now that the shoe's on the other foot?"

"I'm still a *much* better patient than you were. With you, it was like being trapped in a cage with a cranky lion. At least you're healthy now."

"I am. And I intend to stay that way." He paused, his eyes serious. "You went through a lot more trauma than I did with the gunshot. Don't rush this—your body needs time to heal."

"I know." Then she grinned at him. "Besides, you're the one doing the countdown."

Alex didn't smile back. "I'll wait as long as you need to heal. I never want to hurt you, especially there."

"Dr. Grainger said my recovery is going really well, so she expects all restrictions to be lifted in another two weeks."

After Charlotte took their orders, Hope leveled a steady gaze at Alex, broaching the subject she'd had plenty of time to think about lately. "When I get the all-clear from Dr. Grainger, I want to go back in the cave. I need to face that again, especially now."

He snapped his head up. "There's no rush. It's not going anywhere."

"I know. And I also know that when you delay things like this, they have a way of not happening. The pain is gone now, and I'm up to walking a couple of miles on the treadmill. I'll have to be careful and listen to my body, but I need to do this."

He rolled his shoulders awkwardly and a rapid pulse throbbed in his temple. "We'll see what Dr. Grainger says."

∼

ALEX LAY prone on the ground with the rifle stock pressed against his cheek and sighted down the scope at the 750-yard target. His tension had begun draining as soon as he lay down in this familiar position. This was exactly what he needed to restore his equilibrium after the last few weeks.

Especially after Hope had announced she wanted to go back to the cave.

Several days had passed with some painful soul-searching on his part. He'd nearly memorized her words after the silt-out. She was right, as usual. The issues were fear and faith. He was terrified of something happening to her and didn't have enough faith in the training he'd given her.

And when the disaster did happen, it'd had nothing to do with the cave.

But the cave situation was an echo of Syria. He'd always taken the burden of command seriously—he knew his orders could get his men killed, or himself. Worse, he'd had no faith in those scouts. They'd been full of crap, and he'd strongly suspected it. And look how that had ended. He closed his eyes and relaxed his grip on the rifle.

And I almost lost her.

But he hadn't. Once again, she'd proven her steel. And, after the cave, stood up to him despite her history. There was only one logical outcome to this problem, but he was just taking a long time to come around to it.

Maybe I am a little stubborn.

He snorted, firmly turning his mind back to shooting. He'd wanted to go back to the range for some time but didn't want to deal with being recognized. And he was.

Earl in the office had flatly refused payment when he checked in earlier. "Don't even think about it."

Alex managed to keep from rolling his eyes, but it was a near thing. "I'm still the same guy I was the first time I came in here."

"Yeah, and I shouldn't have taken your money then, either. I knew you looked familiar."

There was a steady breeze today with stronger gusts,

presenting a real challenge in the longer distances. Alex shifted position slightly, leaning more on his left elbow as he concentrated on the long-range target—three times longer than what he'd shot last time. Compensating accordingly for the wind, he pressed the trigger and the bullet struck dead center. He pulled the bolt to chamber another round and hit the target again and again, emptying the magazine.

Yes!

He had three more with him and swapped out, at last sighting the thousand-yard target when the hairs on the back of his neck rose. This was the most vulnerable position a sniper could be in, and he'd always had a sixth sense when someone was watching. He turned his head slightly, catching Bill approaching in his peripheral vision.

"Don't let me disturb you. I know better than to bother an artist at work."

Too late for that.

But now that he knew who it was, Alex was able to tune Bill out and concentrate on the task at hand. He refocused and fired, hitting the target a bit low on one of the outer bands. He compensated, and the next round flew true. So did the next three. Technically, the rifle's range was 1300 yards, though she was true from much longer than that.

He'd been an expert with many different rifles, but Betsy had been his favorite—not as high tech as some, but always reliable. He quickly emptied his other two magazines in the same thousand-yard target before rising to his feet with a faint smile, finally calmed.

Bill leaned against the table that held Alex's belongings. "Just curious. What's the farthest shot you ever made?"

"Not sure. The guy wasn't walking with a tape measure."

Bill grinned. "Ok, guess I asked for that. Haven't seen you around. This your first time back?"

"I've been busy." Alex started disassembling the rifle as Bill stepped closer and inspected it with a professional eye.

"That rifle looks like it's seen some miles. Not your average civilian one."

"This rifle and I go way back." He gazed steadily at Bill. "We've been through a lot together."

Bill nodded. "That's what I thought. I'm an Army man myself. A group of us from all branches get together once in a while for a beer, real informal, and we don't talk war stories. You want to join us sometime? We've got a couple Navy guys, so you could wear blue and not feel all self-conscious and girly about it."

Alex grinned, closing Betsy's case. "Well then, I'll leave my tutu at home. I've got a lot going on right now, but maybe another time. Thanks."

CHAPTER 36

July...

The afternoon sun peeked from behind a fast-moving shower, making the damp buildings even more colorful as hot steam rose from the pavement. Alex pulled into the parking space in Christiansted. Right in front of the shop! A good omen if ever there was one, as an excited flutter ran through his abdomen.

The arctic blast of industrial air-conditioning hit him as soon as he walked into the shop, and the bright lights were nearly blinding. A small, meticulous man sat at a workbench in the corner of the shop and recognized him, brightening. After holding up a finger in the universal *wait* signal, the man disappeared into the back room but soon reappeared to hand a box to Alex.

"Here it is!" He spoke with a faint European accent, and his face radiated excitement. "I have to admit, I was *very* dubious when you said you wanted it cut down, but it turned out rather well, if I do say so myself."

Alex inspected it closely, impressed. He trailed a finger over the surface, then smiled at the shopkeeper. "Very nice. This should work—thanks a lot." He paid the man and was soon on his way back home with his secret item finally complete.

Time to plan Phase Two of my mission.

During the routine drive, his thoughts returned to the cave. It had been more than a week since Hope had declared she wanted to go back, but she hadn't broached the subject further, though it had to be on her mind.

She was giving him space.

And his experience with the group of divers he'd had this week had only solidified her point that she was capable of going back in that cave. She'd only been diving a year, but Hope could dive circles around some people in that group who had much more experience. She was a natural at it. And God knows she had determination.

She's not the one with the problem. You are.

He was driving through Frederiksted when he passed a florist shop. On impulse, he spun the wheel hard and turned into the parking lot. When he entered, the floral smell about knocked him over and made his nose itch. A local woman with a warm smile stood behind the counter, arranging spiky orange flowers in a vase.

"How can I help you today?"

"I need a dozen red roses."

"Of course. In a vase, or a box?"

Alex chewed on his bottom lip. "Uh, not sure."

Her smile grew as she set her arrangement aside. "Is there a vase at home?"

"Hmmm, still not sure."

"Well, that settles that! Vase it is. Red, right?"

He tapped the counter, trying to show confidence. "Yes. That much I'm sure of."

"Now we're talkin'! You want our regular arrangement or the

deluxe?"

"Better give me the best one you've got."

She laughed—a warm, musical sound. "Oh dear. That bad, huh?"

The image of Hope threatening to castrate him if he gave her any more orders popped into his head, and he cracked an enormous grin. "I'm not sure there are enough roses in the world, but it's a start." The florist steadied the flowers inside a sturdy box and sent him on his way with her best wishes.

When he pulled into the garage, it was nearing 5 p.m. Very pleased with himself, Alex unpacked the flowers and opened the front door.

Hope stood at the kitchen island with her hands parked on her hips, staring down with a thunderous frown. She was admonishing Cruz, who looked up at her with that sad expression only dogs are able to pull off. She turned when he shut the front door, her eyes becoming as big as saucers at the sight of the roses.

"Hello, beautiful." He swept up to her and pressed a deep kiss on her lips before placing the vase on the island in front of her.

"You bought me roses?" Her face slackened as she blinked rapidly.

"Well, I actually bought them for Cruz. But I was afraid he'd eat them and get sick all over the place, so I decided to give them to you instead."

"He doesn't deserve them anyway—he chewed up one of my flip-flops." She shot the dog a dirty look, who whined at her in abject misery, rolling onto his back.

"I sympathize. That's the look I'm trying to pull off, but he does it better. I'm sorry, baby. This is my blatant attempt at bribing myself back into your good graces."

"You've been in my good graces for a while now." She leaned over and inhaled the roses' aroma, eyes closed. "They're wonderful. Thank you, though I'm not sure what you're apologizing for." She turned back to him, and they embraced. "I love them."

He rested his cheek on the top of her head, marveling at how much smaller she was, yet so fierce. "It's all part of my master plan. If I can keep you distracted, you won't notice you're way out of my league."

She snorted. "It's the other way around, I'm pretty sure."

"No, it's not, and you were right—we're a great team. Let's go back in that cave. As soon as you get the all-clear."

She pulled back, her eyes wide, and Alex laughed. "Yes, I mean it. But after this layoff, you need to refresh your skills. We'll practice a little in the rock pool first. And I need to figure out a way to get your tank through the squeeze."

He gripped her shoulders as the smile fell from his face. "You almost died and you're not a hundred percent yet, so I need to help you with this. And you need to let me."

She gave him a smile, then her expression softened. "Thank you. I'll be fine, Alex."

"I know you will. Because we'll make this work together."

She stood on her toes and pressed her lips to his. "We've been through a lot together."

Alex circled his arms around her waist and pulled her tight. "We have. And we're a stronger couple because of it."

They shared another kiss before Hope moved to the wine cooler and pulled out a bottle of red wine, pouring them each a glass. They made their way outside and sat, watching as the sun neared the red horizon. "How was the shooting range?"

"It felt good. I shot long range again today, not quite the distances I used to shoot, but it was still a challenge. I've talked to the range boss a little each time I've been there. He's a vet too. He invited me to join a group who gets together occasionally for a beer. I might do it sometime."

"That makes me very happy. I think you should." She sipped her wine. "So, are you on maternity watch again tonight?"

Alex sat up straighter and peered out at the flag-marked area behind the house—nothing yet. "Absolutely. And it's not technically maternity watch, either. The female turtle has nothing to do with it after she lays her eggs. I'm more of the doting uncle. It should be anytime, and they like to hatch at night. It makes them harder for predators to see."

Hope studied the beach to her left. "And you found two more nests down that way?"

"Yep. I had to guess where they were because she smoothed the sand over them. But I'm pretty sure."

She poked his chest. "Just remember, you promised we could share the news of one of those with the guests. I know they'd love to see the baby turtles."

"I'm sure they would. I just want to give them the best chance possible before we're inundated with drunk tourists trampling them all to death." She dug her elbow into his ribs, making him laugh.

"They would never do that! And those people pay your salary."

"Yeah, yeah. As long as they show the proper respect to my turtles."

∼

ALEX'S silent watch alarm went off at midnight and he slipped out of bed, pulling on shorts and a sweatshirt. He'd repeated this the past two nights, staying up for a few hours, then going back to bed when there was no activity at the nest.

He stood at the railing, his jaw cracking from a yawn as he studied the quiet sand—still nothing. Tonight it was very calm. A full moon cast the beach in a pale glow as the waves whispered on the beach. It was cool enough that the sweatshirt felt good. He leaned against the frame. Standing was better than sitting for staying alert on turtle watch.

A chorus of crickets chirped around him. Alex was warm and content, happy now that Hope was on the mend. And he was ready to admit she was right. He couldn't protect her from every danger she would face.

But he'd try like hell to mitigate it.

He was watching a piece of driftwood wash back and forth along the shoreline when the sand fluttered at the edge of his vision. He whipped his head around as a small mound of sand rose inside the flagged area. He hurried down the steps and stood just outside the perimeter as all traces of sleepiness vanished.

Alex inhaled sharply as the mounded sand began to scatter and a scaly, inch-long flipper appeared, flailing in the air. It got some purchase on the ground as the other flipper threw sand around and soon a small head appeared, quickly followed by the first half of a three-inch shell. A delighted smile spread across Alex's face as the small turtle struggled free of the sand, then scampered toward the water.

He followed closely.

The nest had been dug about ten feet above the high-water line, and it was nearing high tide now. The hatchling only had to traverse eleven feet or so before an incoming wave swallowed it up.

Alex couldn't do anything more to help it. Now it was on its own.

He rushed back to stand over the nest, but nothing else happened. For fifteen minutes, he impatiently shifted from foot to foot, and was contemplating going back to the porch when the sand was disturbed again. This time he took off running toward the house, opened the slider, and burst into the bedroom.

He gently shook Hope's shoulder.

"Wha? What's wrong? Huh?" She lifted onto an elbow, looking left and right, her hair a disheveled mess. His smile widened into an enormous grin.

"Get dressed. They're hatching!"

That woke her up, and she focused on him clearly. "Really? Oh, how cool."

She threw back the covers and hurried to the closet as he waited for her, arms crossed and fingers tapping. She was soon back, dressed in black leggings and one of his Navy sweatshirts—much too big for her.

She looked amazing in it.

Alex grabbed her hand. "Come on!"

They went back to the nest, but there was only the second area of empty disturbed sand—no turtle could be found. It had already entered the ocean.

As they stood there waiting, he pulled Hope in front of him, wrapping his arms around her waist. Ten minutes passed with no activity, and Hope started fidgeting.

"Nothing's happening. Did you wake me up for nothing?"

"Be patient. Good things come to those who wait, you know."

"I just thought there'd be more action. Though standing here with you in the moonlight has its advantages too."

He smiled and held her close, closing his eyes as he breathed in the scent of her hair.

"Look! The sand."

His eyes flew open as another flipper appeared. Then, a foot away, another. Next to a flag, yet another.

Within minutes, sand flew everywhere as baby turtles emerged, one after the other, some on top of each other, and all with one purpose—to get to the sea as quickly as possible.

Hope was on her hands and knees, her head a foot above the beach as she watched the spectacle, wonder slackening her face. She glanced up at him. "How many are there?"

Alex shrugged. "Seventy-five to a hundred. The temperature of the sand around the nest determines the sex of the hatchlings."

"No! Get out!"

He grinned, rocking on his feet. "Really. Girls like it hot."

Now there were hatchlings everywhere, their leathery dark-gray shells two to three inches long. Their flippers scurried over the sand as they all scampered and fumbled toward the ocean.

Hope had been following one in particular and walked with it until it disappeared into the waves. She turned back to him with her brows drawn together. "Please tell me there aren't any sharks out there."

"I'm sure there are, and other big predatory fish." He couldn't help smiling at her stricken look. "That's the cycle of life. It's why the female lays so many nests, and why each nest has so many eggs. A good twenty-five percent won't even hatch and only five to ten percent of the hatchlings live to see their first birthday."

She came up and stood next to him, sliding her arm around his waist. "I'm so glad I got to see this. What an amazing experience."

They continued to watch the baby turtles fumbling toward life until eventually the hatchings grew less frequent, eventually becoming only sporadic.

Hope yawned. "I think I'm ready to head in. Looks like the show's mostly over."

"Yeah, I think you're right. We can still get a few hours of sleep before we have to get up."

He turned her to face him, gripping her shoulders. "I'm so glad we got to see this together. Last time, with the hawksbill, Steve and Susan turned it into a circus. There were people with flashlights all over, hollering and yelling. They probably scared the hatchlings half to death."

Alex squeezed her shoulders and their eyes held as the last hatchlings scurried over the sand toward an unknown destiny. "This means the world to me. *You* mean the world to me. You're my everything."

He brushed his lips over hers, meaning it to be a light, soft kiss, but she grabbed the back of his head and crushed their mouths together. Their tongues brushed, then she broke the kiss and buried her head in his chest as she gripped him tightly.

Her reply was muffled. "No, you're my everything, Alex."

CHAPTER 37

*D*r. Grainger's office was in a drab brick building next to the hospital. A week had passed since the turtle hatching, and Hope sat anxiously in a plastic chair, fully clothed, as she looked at the anatomical drawing on the wall of the exam room.

Dr. Grainger floated into the room and closed the door. "Your labs look great! I'm very pleased with your progress. You feeling ok?"

"Much better," Hope said. "The pain is gone, and I'm getting my strength back. I'm able to walk several miles outside now."

"You've recovered really well, so you can get back to your regular activities at this point—all of them. Just listen to your body." Dr. Grainger paused, and Hope paid close attention. "Fatigue is normal. Your body went through a major trauma, you know. Don't expect it to completely heal in a month."

Soon, Hope returned to her Jeep with an extra spring in her step, humming a tune as a smile tried to take up permanent residence on her face. She was very relieved to be leaving the office with no plans to return for a long time.

She was determined to forge ahead and getting the all-clear from the doctor paved the way. Still, she shoved down the flutter in her stomach at the thought of attempting the cave dive again. Hope was prepared to listen to everything Alex said this time, fully recognizing the role her own impatience had caused in the silt-out.

Maybe Alex isn't the only stubborn one in this relationship . . .

It was nearly sundown when she walked into the great room. Alex stood from the couch with his hands clasped behind his back, bouncing on the balls of his feet as he watched her expectantly. He was dressed up, wearing a white linen shirt and dark-gray shorts. Hope's breath caught just looking at him, and her eyes went on a leisurely trip from his muscular legs up to the broad shoulders perfectly framing the drape of his shirt. She didn't need much imagination to picture the hard planes of his abs and chest muscles. Her mouth was practically watering.

All the way home, Hope had planned on teasing him. Her grand idea was to tell Alex Dr. Grainger had sentenced her to four more weeks of no intimacy, though no other restrictions. But after one look at Alex's shining, hopeful face, she couldn't do that to him.

Instead, Hope slid up to him and made her fantasy come true by reaching under his shirt to dance her fingers up his chest, which was as hot and hard as she had imagined. She spoke in her most throaty voice. "You have any plans for tonight?"

Hope brushed her lips over his, feather soft as she whisked her tongue over his lip. Alex inhaled sharply and grabbed a handful of her hair, smashing her mouth against his as their bodies pressed together. Sparks exploded inside Hope as she pressed against the pronounced length of him.

Finally, he took a large, deliberate step backwards. "That's great news. I don't want to rush this, though. I've been looking forward to it too much. You want to go down to the restaurant?"

"Oh, yes. Let me change first."

A glance in the mirror confirmed her hair still looked good, so she headed to the closet to pick out a sundress she had in mind when her eye caught Killer Black Dress.

She regarded it for a moment, considering.

Why not?

Hope hadn't worn it since Sara's farewell dinner the previous year, and she'd *definitely* made an impression on Alex that night. She changed into a black lace bra and panties and pulled on the form-fitting tank dress before touching up her makeup. She didn't have Sara's skills in the hair and makeup department, but she did her best.

Hope finished up with some dressy sandals, pausing at the mirror for a final check. She was still pale, but the dress filled her with sexy confidence as usual. She smiled at her reflection, appreciating how different tonight was from the last time she'd worn this dress and how completely different her life was.

Alex stood at the slider, watching the ocean. He turned as she entered the room, and Hope bit back a smug smile as his eyes bulged before drifting slowly down her body and back up as she crossed the room.

Hope stopped before him and pressed a finger under his chin, closing his mouth. "Careful, you might catch flies."

"Oh my God. That dress." His nostrils flared with each deep breath.

"Well, let's get going before you get any more distracted."

They settled in at their table, and a delicious shiver rolled through Hope. Alex couldn't take his eyes off her. Their table was covered with one of her new light-blue tablecloths. She had recently made some changes to dress up the dinner service. A new centerpiece for the tables provided an additional romantic touch. Inside a clear hurricane vase sat a votive candle, nestled in white sand mixed with blue glass pebbles. The candle threw a flickering, soft light over them.

They both ordered Gerold's special, blackened mahi-mahi, and Charlotte brought them a bottle of Chenin Blanc. Her straightened black hair hung to her shoulders, and she was dressed in a black skirt and royal-blue staff polo with her name embroidered. Another change of Hope's. The servers wore a more formal uniform at night, though nothing stuffy.

Alex held up his glass. "Here's to your successful recovery. You are absolutely stunning."

"Thank you. I am very glad to have that ordeal behind us now. We have all sorts of things to look forward to."

They touched glasses, their eyes locked together. There had been an excess of time to think about her life over the previous weeks. About how lucky she was—with the resort, her wonderful friends, and most of all, this man she shared her life with. His gaze drifted to the ocean, and thoughts of where *they* were going entered her mind as well. As a wistful smile crossed his face, she opened her mouth to ask Alex what he thought about their future, but self-doubt crept back in, and she softly closed it again.

Why do you want more? You know how much he loves you, just as he knows your feelings about him. It's enough . . .

He turned back to her and cocked his head. "What are you thinking about?"

It's more *than enough. Don't risk this, Hope.* "How much I love you. And how lucky I am."

He reached out for her hand. "How lucky we both are."

A slow smile crept across her face. "And maybe some thoughts about how much I've looked forward to tonight."

He sent her a searing look, and a shiver ran through her as he stroked his thumb over the back of her hand before reaching for his glass.

She brought her own to her mouth, leaning forward to let the movement enhance her cleavage. Killer Black Dress had a daring neckline.

Alex dropped his gaze accordingly, and it stayed there for a long moment before returning to her face. "You destroyed me at Sara's party in that dress. I didn't get any sleep that night."

"Well, that was the idea." Then Hope couldn't hold in a laugh. "It wasn't my idea though—it was Sara's. But I admit I warmed up to it after putting this on."

"It was that night I made the decision to finally let you know about my hip."

"Maybe tonight will have more of a happy ending for you."

"Maybe?"

She gave him her most smoldering look. "I'd say the odds are better than even."

"Wow, you're a tough customer. I'm already wining and dining you here."

Hope slipped her sandal off and ran her foot up his bare lower leg. "Keep at it. You might eventually wear me down."

After their meals arrived, they limited themselves to suggestive looks. Alex's extraordinary eyes were on full display. Hope dropped her right shoulder, and the tank strap of her dress slipped off to reveal her black bra strap. Alex was in the process of lifting his fork and froze. He swallowed hard as his eyes were riveted to her shoulder.

She had never played the seductress before as she did with him. Alex made her feel safe down to the center of her being, and that brought out sides of her she'd never explored before.

And she loved his reactions.

Hope was the only person who saw the unguarded Alex, and that gave her a confident, new sense of freedom and power.

He shifted his gaze from her breasts to her eyes, his look blistering. Hope wanted to climb across the table and attack him as she sent a scorching look back.

A slow smile crept over Alex's face.

AFTER DINNER, they strolled hand in hand down the beach. Just before they reached the porch, Hope couldn't wait any longer and pulled Alex to her. She ruffled his hair and pressed his head down to hers, kissing him wetly as she dragged her nails over his shoulders. He groaned, pulling her tighter, then pushed her away and grabbed her hand. They rushed up the stairs as her wind chimes sang in the night breeze.

Alex opened the slider and led her straight to their bedroom, his hand tight on hers. There was no moon tonight, but enough ghostly light entered the room to illuminate it in a pale glow.

He spun around, then took a deep breath, stopping.

Instead of the frantic passion she expected, he approached her gently, cupping her face in both hands. He kissed her softly, their lips melding against each other as he stroked the back of her right shoulder. Breaking the kiss, Alex leaned forward over her shoulder.

"There it is. I couldn't stop thinking about your tattoo that night. You sat across from me, so I couldn't see whether your dress covered it. I spent half that night thinking about doing this."

He spun her around and pulled her dress and bra strap off her shoulder, then ran his open mouth over her tattoo, his tongue trailing a hot wet stripe behind. He traced his head back and forth, and Hope felt every movement deep in her center, her knees weakening as a soft moan escaped.

With a lazy smile, he turned her back toward him, moving back to her mouth as they pressed together. Hope unbuttoned his shirt, running her hands up and down his chiseled chest before sliding the shirt off his shoulders.

Alex's hands danced over her back, searching. "Does this thing have a zipper?"

"It's a side zip." Hope reached under her arm and started to tug the zipper down when Alex grabbed her hand, holding it tightly as their eyes locked.

"Oh, please don't deprive me of this. This was what I spent the other half of the night thinking about. Well, one of the other things—we'll get to the rest."

He smiled against her mouth and slowly drew down her zipper, the sound loud in the confines of the room. Stepping back, he watched as he slowly slid the straps of the dress off her shoulders and it fell to the ground. Hope stood before him in her black lace bra and panties. His breath caught, and her own response deepened, throbbing now.

She slid her eyes down his chest and rippled abdomen to the very prominent bulge in his shorts and kissed him again, circling her tongue as she palmed him with one hand. A groan escaped him, and he pushed against her hand, pressing them together.

Hope broke the kiss, stepping back and drilling him with her eyes. She unbuckled his shorts and pulled them and his boxers to the ground, staying on her knees and enveloping him. She drew him in and out, and his breath deepened steadily until he pulled her to her feet, fisting a handful of her hair and crashing his mouth hard into hers.

"Tonight's about you, not me. Let me please you, Hope."

"Oh, my love. You have no idea how much you do." Every line of his body was familiar, but the forced abstinence made him feel new. The still air was filled with their deep breaths.

Alex was hard between them as their tongues circled. He unhooked her bra and she shrugged it off as he cupped her breasts, softly circling with his thumbs. Hope's blood pounded in her head as he lowered, moving his lips over her breasts. His tongue made her gasp.

Alex lowered to his knees, just watching as he ran both hands slowly over her abdomen. He kissed each of her three scars, feather light, before meeting her gaze. "You kissed mine. Now it's my turn." He turned back to her abdomen. "You're so beautiful." He left a trail of loving kisses from scar to scar.

Next, he slowly pulled her panties down, his mouth touching every inch of skin revealed. Hope groaned as his tongue darted out. "Oh my God, Alex."

He threw one of her legs over his shoulder and settled in.

Hope tipped her head back, panting as the waves of sensation rushed over her.

Then she became very aware the one leg she was standing on was getting weaker by the second. "I can't stand up much longer. I'm about to collapse."

"Well, I've got a cure for that."

Alex stood up and walked her backwards until her legs backed up against the bed. He ripped the covers back and softly pressed her down on the mattress before resuming his prior position. He always knew exactly what she needed. She buried both hands in his hair, driving him closer as her climax built.

Finally, it exploded, radiating from her center to her toes and up again.

Alex kissed his way to her abdomen. He left a wet trail across it before moving more slowly in the other direction, moving his tongue in slow circles. But this was different from his earlier passion—hesitant, almost shy.

Hope moaned and tugged on his arms. "Honey, I need you. Come here."

He lifted to face her with wide eyes, his chest expanding with the force of his emotion. "I almost lost you, Hope. I'm so scared of hurting you."

Pure white light floated through her. Alex wasn't a small man, in any respect. But that wouldn't be a problem tonight. "You won't. You just saw to that—I am *very* ready for this. Come to me, love."

He gently climbed up, and Hope guided him in. He closed his eyes and kissed her with a tenderness he'd never displayed before as he began slowly moving within her. He opened his soft lips and danced his tongue across hers.

Alex trailed kisses across both her closed eyes before rising on an elbow above her. "This is ok?"

His eyes were so filled with concern that a smile rose on

Hope's face, unbidden. She reached behind him, urging him on. "It's more than ok."

She shifted a bit, opening wider, and he moaned in response but kept the same slow rhythm. Alex's lips traveled all over her face, kissing her eyes again, then moving across her forehead and down each cheek before finally coming back to her mouth as his breathing quickened.

He moved to her ear, whispering, "I need you so much," before pressing his mouth against her hair, making a deep hum in his chest but still keeping a gentle, tender motion.

Tears rose to her eyes, and Hope wrapped her arms around him, pulling him tight. As she rubbed her face back and forth against his shoulder, the sensations built within her once again, and their breath became ragged.

Finally, she dug her nails into his shoulders and cried out as he did.

They collapsed together, Hope brushing her hands over his back as she swallowed the lump in her throat. Alex lifted up on one elbow and smoothed her hair with a finger, and they just stared at each other, drinking in every detail.

Neither said those three words. They'd already said it all.

CHAPTER 38

Hope took a nervous breath as she screwed the regulator onto her tank, her headlight bobbing around in the blackness of the smaller room. She closed both hands into fists to calm the shaking. Now that she was finally back in here, her nerves did their best to claw their way out. She kept a neutral expression, not wanting to worry Alex. She was determined to make it all the way through this time.

A week had passed since she'd received the all-clear. The previous afternoon, they'd spent a couple of hours in the rock pool, making sure Hope was able to take her scuba kit on and off in the water. In the zero-gravity environment, her recent surgery didn't cause any problems as long as she kept her movements slow and deliberate.

They had continued into the cave, where Alex deployed his idea for the squeeze. Prior to leaving, he had attached an extra-long hose assembly for his regulator. He scrambled into the squeeze feet first, cradling the rebreather between his legs as he scooted backwards.

He ran a portion of the climbing rope he'd bought several months earlier through the shoulder straps of her BCD. Then they inched along, with Alex tugging her BCD. Hope only had to army-crawl forward on her elbows and knees.

They'd made it all the way through without mishap.

Hope could only imagine how exhausting it must have been for Alex, but as usual, he was stoic about it. As soon as they reached the room where he'd found the pendant and coins, he rested, then insisted they turn around at that point. Above his headlamp, the red light of a camera blinked in a slow, steady pattern. She had purchased one of the popular waterproof action cameras along with a head mount, and Alex volunteered to wear it.

"We always wore helmet cams, so I'm used to it, and I've seen enough divers with these that I've got a decent idea how to use this. And it's a good idea. If we do find anything, we should have video documentation."

They repeated the exhaustive maneuver on the way out and were soon back in the rock pool, high-fiving each other. Hope had gotten a good night's sleep and was as prepared as she could be.

Now she took one final glance at her scuba tank and stood. "Ok, I'm ready."

With the camera's red light blinking, Alex came over and double-checked her setup, verifying everything was ready to go. Hope prepared to enter the cool water and turned off her headlamp, switching to her handheld light. Alex kept his headlamp on at all times and frequently turned toward her, but had never shined the beam in her face. He didn't even think about it—the correct motions were second nature to him.

How many nighttime missions have you completed?

She walked up to him and placed her hands on his shoulders, pulling him down for a kiss. "Teamwork, right?"

A pulse throbbed in his temple. "Yes, ma'am. Do you think we could maybe skip the sightseeing on this trip? I would very much prefer to get you through this passage and into the big cavern as quickly and painlessly as humanly possible."

She grinned at his excessively polite tone. "Why, yes, I think that's an excellent suggestion." Then she sobered. "Compared to what we just went through with the squeeze, this should be much easier, especially for you. I just need to keep my fins out of the mud, right?" She met his eyes, his uneasiness oozing from every pore.

"Please keep your fins out of the mud. Let's go."

They descended and swam into the passage. Hope ensured she stayed well above the silt layer and kept the green guideline well in sight, fully focused on her task. As they proceeded down the tunnel, Alex's headlight bounced all over the walls. His head was in constant motion this time—keeping tabs on her position behind him.

After entering The Closet, he turned around to face her. He pointed to his eyes, wanting her to keep eye contact with him. As he held his hand out, she reached hers forward to grasp it, and he squeezed it tightly.

Alex back kicked across the room, his long sweeping strokes keeping them well above the floor. Hope softened as their gazes held—he wasn't taking any chances today. Soon he moved his gaze to the walls around him, judging his position. He asked if she was ok, and she returned the signal with a nod. He nodded back and gave her hand one final squeeze before turning around to enter the passage on the far side.

Relief washed through Hope as she left the small room and entered the new tunnel. It was dark gray, and similar in size to the channel on the other side of The Closet. She exhaled a disappointed sigh that the black mud layer continued here too.

It also exuded the same ominous, foreboding aura, but she kept a tight rein on her emotions and made sure her fins stayed sideways and well above the mud. She alternated her gaze between Alex in front of her and the bright-green line below, welcoming his slow, deliberate pace.

Alex angled to the left as the passage bent but maintained the same diameter this time before tilting upwards. Soon they passed a tank he'd staged. Finally, the walls broadened and Alex was out, turning to hover motionless, facing her as she exited the tunnel.

Alex stretched his arm out and pulled her toward him. His laughter came through clearly as he embraced her and gave her the thumbs-up. She grinned back, the warmth and pride welling up inside her as they surfaced, both shouting as their calls echoed around the chamber.

Hope pulled her mask down around her neck and smiled at Alex. "See. Told you I could do it!"

He gave her a kiss. "You don't have to prove anything to me."

"You did all right yourself."

He grinned and tipped his head back, visibly relieved. She did likewise, and her mouth dropped open.

The cavern was a cathedral, filled with natural wonders.

She broadcast her flashlight up. The ceiling towered above her, and masses of multicolored stalactites grew from the expansive crown. The water ended in a smooth rock plateau that reached farther than she could see. Several stalactites almost met matching stalagmites rising from the stone floor. Thick columns were scattered throughout, their joining completed.

This made The Closet look like a drab afterthought. Her gaze wandered back to Alex, who floated with a smile, his eyes glittering at her reaction.

"This is incredible! You didn't say anything about this, just the ceiling in The Closet."

"I wanted to surprise you. Since we're in the air here, I figured it was safe enough."

"Thank you—this is some surprise." Finally tearing her gaze away, Hope observed where the green guideline came out of the water and was tied off. "I take it that's where we get out?"

"That was the easiest exit I could find, and the slope's gradual."

Alex removed her kit, slinging it over one shoulder as he

steadied her from the water with the other arm. They climbed onto the flat shelf of rock, and he set her tank and his rebreather on the rocky ground. "You doing ok?"

"Yes—really good. And very glad to be past The Closet." Hope could see slightly even without the headlamp. "There must be some holes to the outside. I can see light and it doesn't smell as stale." They scrambled up the stone slope to a broad plateau. "We don't really know where to search—this cavern is huge. Should we split up?"

"No. We stay together. We're still deep in a cave here, you know." He paused, then turned to her with a softened gaze. "However, I defer to your far greater font of common sense. Where to?"

She smiled and gave him a quick kiss, acknowledging his effort. "Barnaby wrote that he put the box in a corner, so maybe it's in a more open area. How about we just follow this for a while?" She pointed to a ribbon of rock on the floor, rippling like a creek frozen in time, then looked closer. "This is amazing."

"I did some research on caves. This is called flowstone. Apt, huh?"

They followed along the flat surface. It was multicolored—primarily golden, but also had ribbons of dark red and black running through it. The river of flowstone wove around and through a forest of columns, which Hope and Alex wound around as the ceiling arced high overhead. She stopped next to a column and tipped her head back. It soared at least a hundred feet.

Hope laughed, turning to Alex. "I feel like Alice in Wonderland!"

"This is really incredible."

"Why didn't Barnaby say anything about this? I hope we don't have the wrong cavern."

"I suppose he could have gone off that other passage in The Closet, but the way we came was the most obvious," Alex said.

"Hopefully he didn't say anything because he was so sick and tired of being on this island all alone."

They continued, and a sheer dark vertical wall appeared out of the darkness in front of them. It rose higher than their headlamps could illuminate.

"Pick a direction," Alex said.

"Let's go right."

She turned and walked along the wall, her beam bouncing around as she looked for obstructions. Stalagmites as large as trees reached from the floor at scattered intervals. Alex walked beside her and in their combined light, another tall, dark wall slowly materialized out of the gloom, perpendicular to the one they were following. Alex moved to her right around a thick column of stone and continued forward a short distance away.

It was very dark here except for their lights, and Hope approached where the two dark-gray walls joined. Her beam followed down the natural vertical crease where the walls came together, illuminating the dark corner to the floor.

Hope froze at what lay before her.

It had once been a wooden box encircled by supportive iron bands. But over the centuries in the cool, damp environment, it had partially disintegrated, spilling its contents onto the flowstone ground.

Goosebumps rose at the golden reflections being cast back at her.

"Alex."

A multitude of coins tumbled over the area, as well as several gold chains and many black, circular coin-like objects. And in the midst of it all, brilliant gemstones twinkled in her light—emeralds, rubies, and sapphires. Two golden chalices lay nearby.

Alex was still some distance to her right and hadn't reacted—she'd hardly whispered his name.

Hope cleared her throat and spoke louder. "Alex."

The light became brighter as he turned his head toward her.

"Come here. Now."

He hurried over and his sharp gasp echoed in the silent cave as his headlamp traveled to the floor, further illuminating the sprawling mass. He hunkered down on his heels as she dropped to her knees beside him, one hand gripping his thigh.

The box must have originally been about three feet long. Shards of wood could still be seen, and the top was somewhat intact. But the bottom of it had disintegrated, creating the tumbled mass of treasure as the action camera recorded everything.

Hope was so stunned she didn't know what to think. Her heart thumped in her ears as she took it all in. This was worth a *lot* of money.

How do you even go about selling a treasure? But that was a thought for another day.

"How are we going to get this out of here?" Hope asked.

"With lift bags."

She raised her brows at him.

"Standard scuba equipment for lifting anything heavy, though it's easier when you use them to lift the object straight up to the surface. This is going to be trickier. A lot trickier."

"Look at all this!" She hefted a golden chalice. About eight inches tall, it was inlaid with what had to be emeralds and diamonds, and her beam highlighted every facet—the workmanship was incredible.

"Yeah, I can hardly believe it." Alex reached for one of the black discs. "This is probably a tarnished silver coin. It just needs to be polished up a bit."

At the same time, they turned their heads toward each other. Alex's chest moved with rapid breaths. His eyes were enormous, and no doubt her expression was similar. Simultaneously, they started laughing, and the sound bounced throughout the large chamber.

The couple sat on the floor and separated the trove into piles

—gold coins, silver coins, gemstones, jewelry, and other items, such as the cups. They also uncovered gold and tarnished silver dinner plates.

Very intriguing were many small ingots of what appeared to be solid gold. Hope picked one up, amazed at the weight of it. "I can't believe he carried that chest. It wasn't very big, but this must have weighed a *lot*. Our Barnaby was a determined man."

Alex just nodded, still stunned.

"Can we get this out of here in one trip?"

He shook his head and his expression became more thoughtful. "No. I need to think about this. Why don't you grab a couple trinkets to take back? We need to get going."

For the first time, Hope felt the cool dampness of the cave—it was trying to seep into her bones. Time to go back. She chose the ingot she'd been holding as well as the two chalices. Alex took several of the tarnished coins and a light-green emerald the size of his fist, and they made their way back to the rocky slope. She started toward her BCD to zip her finds into the pocket when Alex stopped her.

"I'll carry them. The extra weight will affect your buoyancy, and I don't want you worrying about that. I can adjust mine on the fly easily. Let's head back."

He took the items from her and placed them in the pocket of his rebreather, chewing on his lip as he regarded the neatly divided piles of treasure. Many of them.

CHAPTER 39

*L*ater that evening, Hope couldn't hold back a smile as she watched Alex, who had taken over the kitchen table. He had moved a pile of documents and drawings of the coral-restoration project to make room for his open laptop and a large pad of paper that sat before him. Several pages were already torn off and scattered around the surface as copious notes, calculations, and drawings covered each. Hope got queasy just looking at them.

Alex was definitely the right man for the job.

After returning from the cave, Hope had placed the items they'd brought back into her home-office wall safe, then settled in the great room, thinking about their next steps. Meanwhile, Alex was working out how to get the treasure out of the cave, occasionally tearing off a page to add to one of his piles. Finally, about eight o'clock, he sat back and rubbed his eyes, sending a big smile her way.

"I think I've got it figured out. It'll take multiple trips for sure, but I can get it all out of there."

Hope removed two beers from the refrigerator, handing him one as she took a seat next to him and they toasted.

He took a drink and regarded her, serious now. "This is going to be really boring and tiring grunt work. What we found might be exciting, but getting it out of that cave won't be."

He glanced at the papers on the table before returning his gaze to hers. "It's also going to be highly technical. The weight requirements coming out will be massively different because of the gold. That's going to affect buoyancy in a very big way in that silty passage. I need you to let me do this alone. Are you all right with that?"

A smile swept across her face, even as she experienced a guilty pang at how worried he was about stepping on her toes. "I guess I did make an impression on you, didn't I?"

"Yes. You did. I'd love for you to accompany me to the cave, but I need to carry the treasure out myself."

"Honey, I've watched you poring over your notepad for hours now. I think carrying the loot is solidly within your domain. I'm smart enough not to overdo it. I'll come along to the pool for moral support."

"You're a lot more than that."

She leaned in to kiss him. "So are you. And there's one other big item we need to decide—what to do with it all. I've been thinking about that while you were working on your fun little project." She frowned at the pages filled with his meticulous handwriting. "Though I suspect you actually enjoyed that."

A smile lit up his face. "I did. It's fun to have something challenging to solve. What's your idea?"

"Well, we can't store all that gold and silver here in the house."

"Definitely not. That's a huge security risk."

"Agreed. So, a simple solution. You and I go down to Virgin Islands Bank in Frederiksted and open a large safe deposit box—jointly. We're a team on this."

He stared at her with a determinedly neutral expression. "You sure about that? It's your treasure."

"Wrong. It's *our* treasure."

"Not in the eyes of the law. In fact, if Barnaby had dropped that box in the ocean and we'd found it, you'd be in for years of legal hassles and the government would still take a huge chunk of it. But since the cave is wholly on your land, you own it free and clear. We have to verify that with a lawyer, but I'm pretty sure."

"It's our treasure, Alex. Period. Full stop."

A crooked smile cracked his face. "Ok, Boss Lady. I know better than to argue with you." Then his eyes softened. "I'm incredibly proud of you, Hope. You were great in that cave."

"Thank you. I'd be lying if I said I wasn't nervous about it, but I needed to face my fear. And having you there gave me the courage to do that." She rose and walked to him, settling on his lap to give him a long, lingering kiss, still amazed at the change their lives had just taken.

∽

Hope sat at her lobby desk, a fierce welling of pride and happiness rolled through her as she studied the new, finalized website. Two weeks had passed since discovering the treasure, and getting this project finalized had been her major endeavor. Steve had seen an earlier version, but now it was wholly functional.

Since moving here, Hope had been unhappy with their website and the resort brand as a whole. Neither had been updated in a very long time, and she wasn't sure the resort logo ever had.

With the resort doing well financially, she'd finally had the resources to hire a PR firm in Christiansted who worked with her local website company to design a cohesive new look and modern logo. It still retained vestiges of the old one, so long-time guests didn't feel alienated.

She had decided on shades of blue for the overall color scheme. The logo had three, plus the crescent beach the resort was named after. Each page of the website featured the new logo and one of the three blue hues. One page was dedicated to their new environmental focus, and all the staff members were listed under the *About Us* tab.

The resort was now fully modern and represented her vision beautifully.

Hope stretched her shoulders, enjoying the slight ache. Since her surgery, she had made a regular routine of having Selena give her a massage at the spa. It had helped her recovery too, or at least had put her in a more relaxed, healing frame of mind.

Hope turned to Patti to enquire about her ongoing, thorny project. "Is your new dishwasher working out better?"

Patti shot her a rueful glance. "*Much* better. She's been a dream. I wish I'd never hired Byron—it was awful firin' him. Sometimes having such a big family can be a curse. His mother still won't speak to me."

Hope laughed. "I'm sure it will blow over, eventually."

Patti gave her a warm look. "You're lookin' so much better. I'm very happy you're on the mend now."

"That makes two of us."

Patti's eyes glazed in a faraway look. "I wonder if we'll hear from Steve again. I know he had mixed feelings, seein' how well we're doin' without him."

"That's up to him. I told him he'd always be welcome to visit, and I meant that. And he and Alex still have some things to work through. But that's between them."

Patti nodded before turning her attention to a stack of comment cards the guests filled out upon departure. "You sure made a lot of people happy with that turtle nest and the lecture Alex gave about it in the dive classroom. The guests *loved* that."

"You wouldn't believe how protective he was about those hatchlings! I had to really twist his arm to let the guests see it."

Patti grinned. "I'm sure you're up to any arm-twistin' Alex needs."

. . .

After leaving for the day, Hope walked barefoot down the beach, holding her sandals in one hand. Alex and Tommy were preparing *Surface Interval* for tonight's night dive, so he wouldn't be home until after eight o'clock.

Looking the opposite direction, she admired the four southern bungalows as she passed by. All were painted with the premium stain, and beautiful handmade wooden signs adorned the doors, displaying each bungalow's namesake flower. And all four were booked solid.

Cruz waited on the porch, bouncing up and down. He came in with her as she stopped at the kitchen table, lifting a silver coin in her hand and inspecting it closely.

She'd made a trip to Frederiksted for silver polish, and the half dozen coins they'd brought back had cleaned right up. Like the gold coins, they were irregularly shaped and embossed with a cross on one side. A quick internet search confirmed her guess that they were Spanish reales, otherwise known as pieces of eight.

Hope shook her head, still not able to fully believe it.

Knowing discretion was the better part of valor, Hope had accompanied Alex to the rock pool but only cheered him on as he brought the treasure out of the cave by himself. The exercise of walking back and forth was good for her, but the literal heavy lifting was a job for him.

Alex meticulously loaded two lift bags to carry on each side of himself, so he stayed evenly balanced in the silty cave. During the first trip, she had waited for him on the sandy beach. He appeared out of the rock pool, raising a bulging lift bag with each arm, and a wide smile crossed his face as she applauded from shore.

After shucking off his gear, he opened the champagne bottle Hope had brought and she poured it into the two golden chalices. She needed both hands to raise hers as they toasted their victory. Then they'd gone home and spent a wonderful night together, drinking more champagne from the chalices. Later, Hope had worn nothing but gold necklaces to bed, including the pendant

Alex first discovered. She had woken the next morning, sore and giddy—the necklaces were still in place.

In the end, it took half a dozen trips to bring out all the treasure, two bags at a time.

The day after their discovery, she had driven them to the bank in Frederiksted, where they rented a safe deposit box and were now also the owners of a joint checking account, a requirement of the bank.

Next, they had opened a second box and account at another bank, so they could divide the find. Alex insisted on accompanying her if she were depositing anything in the box. For her own protection, he said. And she wasn't about to argue. After all, the small gold ingots alone were around five ounces each and worth close to ten thousand dollars apiece, just in gold value.

She hadn't inquired if Alex had been armed on these excursions. She already knew the answer to that.

They were sitting on their find for now. They needed legal counsel before making any decisions, and Alex was very concerned about the cave and its inherent dangers if word got out, attracting inexperienced treasure seekers.

They made the final deposit to the box at the bank two days ago, and for now, they were done. The thrill of the cave had worn off for Alex. It had become a routine job. One he gave his full concentration to, understanding the dangers. But he didn't take pleasure from it anymore.

After dinner, she settled in the great room with her latest adventure novel, Cruz curled up at her feet. Alex came in just before eight, his entire body broadcasting happiness. She broke into a smile as her eyes took him in. Her tall, strong, beautiful Alex.

She could hardly believe he was real—or how much she loved him.

Alex sat on the couch, and Hope gave him a deep kiss. "You look wonderful today."

He raised a brow. "I look the same as any other day."

"Exactly."

He tucked a lock of hair behind her ear. "I can't tell you how happy I am that you're doing so much better. You're not pale anymore."

"I've turned the corner. Looks like you had a good dive."

"Fantastic! We found two octopuses that put on a great show. I'm still not sure if they were fighting or mating. It was intense. They changed color and texture constantly. Wish you could have been there."

She grinned at his wildly gesticulating hands. "Sorry I missed it."

He nuzzled her neck. "Mmm. Let's go for another night dive. They're so different—I want to be with just you. I'll carry your tank so you don't strain anything. We'll do a nice, easy dive."

"Sounds great. Just tell me when and I'll be ready."

"No time like the present. How about tomorrow?"

"Perfect."

CHAPTER 40

The next afternoon, Hope pulled on a rash guard as Alex popped his head into the closet. "I'm going to pull my Land Cruiser down to the resort to load our gear. I'll come back up here after I'm done."

"We're not taking the boat?"

"Nope, this one's a shore dive."

Hope finished dressing with a pair of board shorts and grabbed a sweatshirt too—it could get chilly coming out of the water at night.

An hour later, they were on the highway, passing through Frederiksted. Hope relaxed in the passenger seat, happy to let him surprise her with their destination. The sun had set and there was a muted orange glow to the west, but the ocean view disappeared as they turned east and headed toward Christiansted.

Thirty minutes later, they crept down a rutted dirt track that opened onto a wide north-facing bay. Alex passed the marina parking area and continued down the bumpy road. Fully dark now, there was no moon, and stars sparkled above the surface of the bay. Hope looked out the window, content and anticipating the dive as the dark mangroves moved past her window.

Alex backed into a packed sand pullout that fronted the bay, then began removing their scuba gear from the car. "Do you know where we are?"

She shook her head, gazing around the quiet area.

"This is Salt River Bay, just west of Christiansted. I got the idea to dive here when I read Barnaby's letter. Over the years, the Salt River has filled in the bay, but several hundred years ago, it was a good, deep anchorage, and pirates loved it. So much so, at one point the British Navy tried to build a fort here, but it's been lost to the jungle over the years. The rumor is that Henry Morgan designed it."

"You're kidding!"

He laughed as he tugged her BCD over a tank. "A few years ago, I actually came out here and tried to find it. Bushwhacked all over the place, getting eaten alive by mosquitos. Never found anything. But Morgan has more of a history here on the island than just the rum factory."

Alex finished assembling their gear and turned to her. "This is a popular place for diving, and the night dives can be really good. The parking lot we passed is where the dive shops bring their groups—that's why I continued. We should have this area to ourselves."

There was almost no breeze, and the water softly brushed back and forth along the sand. "Well, we couldn't ask for a better night."

He nodded. "We'll enter the water here and swim out along the bottom. There should be stuff to look at in the sand, and we don't need to go too deep, probably only forty feet."

Alex kitted up, then pulled her BCD and tank over his right shoulder. He took her elbow and they entered the ocean. When they were waist deep, Hope put hers on with the water supporting its weight.

They descended and finned just above the sandy bottom. Hope cast her light about. The bay was a featureless sandy plain, gently rippled by the wave action. There was a soft surge tonight, rocking Hope back and forth in an easy, relaxing motion as she swam. She caught movement out of the corner of her eye. Alex whipped his hand back and forth in the dark water, then stopped.

That's weird. He's always stressed keeping your hands still.

They descended along the gently sloping bay to forty feet before turning left and swimming on, keeping their depth constant. Shining her beam around again, Hope still saw nothing but sand and an occasional fish darting away from the light.

Many creatures made their homes in the sand, including jawfish who carry their eggs inside their mouths until hatching. So she made a determined effort to find something—anything—in the barren plain. But no jawfish were to be found.

Why did we come here?

The water was beautifully clear. There just wasn't anything to see, so she just tried to enjoy the motion of the surge and the weightless environment. Not every dive could be spectacular.

With a sigh, she turned to Alex. Once again, he rapidly waved his hand back and forth. This time, sparks of white light exploded in the water around his hand.

What was that!

Hope started at the sight, and Alex widened his eyes, turning to her. He signaled her to settle onto the sand after checking to make sure they weren't disturbing something's house. He helped her to her knees and settled next to her in the customary half-kneeling position he used when teaching.

Alex pointed to his eyes, indicating for her to watch him as he again moved his hand rapidly, a river of white and blue stars bursting into life. Eager, Hope followed suit, holding the light with her right hand as she whipped her left back and forth, the tiny sparks of light amplifying the faster she moved her hand. She was grinning now and placed her hand next to Alex's as they moved them together, creating a large wave of light sparks that scattered about them before fading.

Then, as if there had been some signal, the water around her exploded with blue and white waves of light as the surge moved back and forth. Whenever Hope moved her hand, additional tiny light-blue twinkling stars lit up the water in their wake. The sparkles of light became more numerous, moving through the swells of water.

As Alex swept an arm in front of him, the water burst into a ribbon of blue radiance after his movement before slowly becoming dark again. Hope did the same, long sweeping motions that lit up the black water like a long tape of blue fire, surrounded by the bright sparks. With a grin, she began rapidly drumming her fingers, watching blue and white stars appear like fireworks before fading away.

She was in awe of the spectacle.

Something drifted in front of her. Hope's heart drummed as a jellyfish neared. About four inches long, it consisted of a clear elongated bell with tentacles drifting after, all softly pulsing with light. Hope immediately stiffened with her arms close. Alex squeezed her arm and gave her an ok when she turned to him.

He held his hand out as the jellyfish swam toward him. It brushed softly against his palm—it didn't sting. As it made contact, the creature exploded into light, ribbons of color running up and down its body.

Hope was stunned.

The jellies were now everywhere, light of every hue imaginable pulsing and vibrating from their translucent bodies. The rolling waves of white and blue surge continued around her with ripples of aqua, royal blue, and turquoise.

The water had become transcendent with light.

The jellyfish danced all around them, beating with color that traveled up and down their bodies, from the top of their mantles to the ends of their tentacles. Long ribbons of illumination lit up the water as the surge moved gently around them.

Hope knelt in stupefaction—there was color everywhere.

Slightly to her right, a large section of sand glowed pale blue, pulsing with the gentle motion of the sea.

Hope's breath deepened at the sheer wonder around her.

This was unlike anything she had ever seen or even heard of. Everywhere she saw flashing, multihued lights—white, blue, red, and purple. She was inside a galaxy. Stars and planets exploded all around, a nebula every time she moved her arm. She relaxed her jaw in openmouthed wonder as she ratcheted her head down, up, left, right—everywhere there was color. She didn't know where to focus.

Holding out her hand, Hope's heart soared as a jellyfish landed on her palm, pulsing regularly with light and content to rest for the moment. The colors raced up and down its body in multiple lines of constantly changing color. She lowered her hand and the jelly continued on its way, joining the countless others in the water now. The ocean was bursting with swells of kaleidoscopic light, the multicolored jellies sparking everywhere now.

Is my mask leaking?

No. Tears were sliding down her face at the sheer unearthly magnificence of what she was witnessing.

She glanced over at Alex and there was enough light to make out his face. He was completely still, his eyes fixated on her as if memorizing the moment. Blue and white ribbons exploded around his head, and her love for him welled up from the depths of her.

They just stared into each other's eyes, and she never wanted this moment to end.

Alex hadn't moved since the spectacle started. He was still half kneeling with one fin flat on the sand before him. He held his flashlight at his hip, and her gaze followed the beam, revealing the dive slate he held on top of his outstretched thigh.

The light illuminated his slate and the four words he'd written.
Will you marry me?

Hope froze, blinking rapidly and not believing what she'd

read. Her flashlight dropped to the sand as both hands flew to her mouth.

She flicked her eyes to his, then back down to the slate—the words were still there. Hope just stared at the slate, pressing her hands against her regulator. Her breath was coming faster and faster, bubbles rising through her fingers as tears spilled freely from her eyes.

Is this really happening?

She lifted her gaze again, riveted to those crystal blue eyes. Eyes that encompassed her whole existence. All the while, countless flashing luminaries exploded around him.

Finally, Alex raised a brow, his expression equally expectant and exasperated. Hope had probably been staring at him for at least a minute, but hadn't actually answered him. She laughed, nodding her head up and down, nearly whipping it so there could be no mistaking her intent.

Instantly, Alex set his lit flashlight on the sand and clipped the slate back on his BCD, ribbons of blue following his movements.

Unzipping the pocket of his BCD, he pulled out a small, hinged box and opened it. Hope's heart nearly stopped when he withdrew a solitaire diamond ring nestled inside. Alex pulled it out and grasped her left hand with both of his, sliding the ring on her third finger.

Hope blinked, clearing the tears from her eyes. The light was dim, but the ring looked like white gold. The diamond was large and square cut. Alex removed his regulator as he lifted her left hand, kissing the ring on her finger as their eyes locked together.

His touch seared through her, and as Alex lifted back up and replaced his regulator, Hope flew into him, the water exploding in waves of luminous blue as they tumbled into the sand with her on top. The bay around them still exploded with light.

His laughter was as clear as the flashes of light reflected in his mask. She leaned her forehead against his and closed her eyes, just living in this one moment of a dream come true as he stroked up and down her arms.

Eventually, Hope opened her eyes and lifted away, rolling off him. The twinkling lights became less frequent—the jellies were moving away. The couple sat side by side on the sand, slowly waving back and forth in the multicolored surge as they watched the show slowly fade. Alex held her hand as he stroked her ring finger with his thumb.

Finally, the remaining bursts of light extinguished all at once, and it was over.

Hope sighed, feeling the loss, but she had gained something of immeasurably greater value.

Alex moved, tugging on her hand, and they swam back to shore. They stood in the waist-deep water.

"Oh my God. Alex, I . . . I don't even know what to say."

He gazed at her with a small, shy smile. "Well, I'm still waiting to hear you actually say yes."

"*Yes!*" Hope threw herself into his arms. Her shout echoed off the water around them as their lips came together.

Finally, he pulled away. "You kept me waiting long enough down there. I was starting to worry I'd made a terrible miscalculation."

Her laughter bubbled up as she pressed her hands to her cheeks. "I'm sorry! I was so shocked I couldn't react at first—I had no idea that was coming. The whole thing was just so incredible!"

Alex's smile was enormous.

"What was all that light? I've never seen anything so extraordinary!"

"Bioluminescence. They're small, little critters that emit light. Different ones are different colors. The jellyfish were comb jellies—totally harmless. This bay is one of the best places to see this. But it doesn't happen all the time, mostly just in the summer."

His grin widened as he slung her BCD over his shoulder. "I

know a marine biologist who studies this bay, and I've had him watching for a good display. He texted me yesterday and wouldn't guarantee anything, but he thought tonight would be—and I quote—*epic*."

"Epic doesn't even begin to describe tonight." Hope stroked her left ring finger. She was still amazed. "Alex, what a beautiful ring. It's perfect."

Even in the dim glow of their flashlights, pride glinted in his eyes. "Your ring is the other big part of the story. The diamond was one of the first things I found in the cave. It was set in a different ring I found near the coins and the emerald pendant. I picked it up and zipped it into my pocket, but when I got a chance to look at it, it was a man's ring and the diamond was gigantic. It didn't look like anything you would like."

Hope gaped at him, then snapped her mouth shut. His grin could have split his face.

"I took it to an artisan jeweler in Christiansted. He looked at me like I had two heads when I told him I wanted the diamond cut down and made into something more modern, but it turned out pretty well. I had him set it in a white-gold ring. He was able to make some smaller stones that are part of the wedding band back at the house."

Hope stood still, just admiring him—his strong jawline and his eyes glimmering with warmth and so much more. He was all she wanted in the world. "Alex, I love you so much."

"Well, that's good! You're going to be spending a long time with me. And I love you more than anything."

They came together again, their lips meeting in a long kiss, promising a lifetime. It was Hope's turn to pull away. "This isn't a dream, right? You really want to get married?"

Alex smiled. "I do."

He held the crook of his elbow out to her. "Come on, let's go back to shore. We've got some big plans to make."

I HOPE you loved that proposal in *Rising Hope*, but don't stop now! Hope and Alex's story reaches its powerful, uplifting culmination in *Forever Hope*.

Order Forever Hope today!

★★★★★: *"I really don't know where to start with the praise. Each book in the series has been enthralling and captivated the interest from beginning to end."* -Amazon reviewer

Hope and Alex... Will their fate be triumph or tragedy?

HOPE COLLINS INCHES toward her greatest dream as her date with destiny draws ever closer. Alex Monroe grapples with one last ghost from his past, stunned at who this final piece of the puzzle is.

Together, they uncovered a great secret, which will now cause

danger for both. A secret that also could change their lives forever, as well as those they love. Since Hope moved to St. Croix, strangers have become friends, and are now family. Alex has learned his purpose will always be within a team, and he isn't meant to live a solitary life.

Can Hope finally achieve her highest wish? Will Alex triumph over the past at last?

Is their fortune to stand together forever and lead Half Moon Bay Resort into its new life?

Forever Hope* brings Hope and Alex's story to its incredible, emotional culmination, and lays the foundation for the next installment in the Half Moon Bay series. It features all the lovable characters, blazing chemistry, irresistible setting, and happy ending readers have come to love. Dive in today!

Forever Hope: Half Moon Bay Book 4

∽

WANT MORE of Hope and Alex? How would you like a free short story featuring them? Sign up now for my Beach Read Update (www.erinbrockus.com/vip.html), and I'll send you an electronic version of my short story *Tropical Hope*.

This is a quick, fun read that is set between books 1 and 2 of the Half Moon Bay series. Hope and Alex are trying to reunite after she has been off the island for several days, but obstacles keep getting in the way!

My Beach Read Update subscribers hear about all my free content, plus exclusive offers and sales. I'd love to have you along! Sign up to download this exclusive bonus today.

If you're already on my list, I've got you covered! At the bottom of each newsletter is a link to all my free content for subscribers. Just find your last email from me to read this bonus, as well as any others you might have missed. Or you can simply sign up again—you'll have your bonus in a flash.

KEEP READING for my Author's Note, and a preview of *Forever Hope*, Book 4 of the Half Moon Bay series, and the culmination of Hope and Alex's story . . .

AUTHOR'S NOTE

Ahhhh . . . I hope you're feeling all warm and fuzzy inside, and eager for book four! I *loved* writing that final chapter. Bioluminescence is a well-documented phenomenon at Salt River Bay. In fact, there are two areas on St. Croix that feature it. The island is one of the best places in the world to experience the marvel. Now, I must admit I amped it up a bit for the sake of the novel. Come on—he proposed! I hope you'll forgive me.

One of the great things about writing fiction is being able to take a true account and change the strands to fit your story. As I was researching pirates for *Rising Hope,* I came across an account of a pirate who decided to switch ships. So he enclosed himself in a barrel *with his dog*, rolled into the Caribbean Sea and washed over to the other ship. Fortunately, the other pirates fished him out of the water and made him one of their own (his dog too, presumably).

As soon as I read that, I knew I had to find a way to use it! Barnaby's story ended up being a little different, and I left the dog out. It's funny how fact can be more unbelievable than fiction. Though if he'd had a dog with him, maybe Barnaby's exile might have been less lonely.

Writing a novel can be a difficult slog that feels like pulling teeth sometimes. But occasionally, the words just flow out of their own accord and it's magical. Barnaby's letter and Alex's proposal were like that.

Barnaby Morgan is a completely fictitious character, though Henry Morgan was real, of course. And he was stationed at St. Croix while serving in the British Navy and designed a fort at Salt River Bay that has been lost over the centuries.

The cave scenes are loosely based on my experiences diving cenotes in the Yucatan peninsula in Mexico. That is an incredible adventure. The water is so clear, it looks like air, and wonders abound everywhere your dive light illuminates.

I was very pleased that Steve got a chance to come back and make amends—or try to, anyway. We didn't really expect Alex to just fall over with forgiveness, now did we?

I have a request to make. If you enjoyed *Rising Hope*, would you leave a review at Amazon or your favorite platform? Reader reviews are the lifeblood of independent authors and ensure I'm able to keep writing more books. Even a line or two helps tremendously.

This was a more insular novel in that our lovable side characters didn't get as much of a role. Both Hope and Alex had some major things to work though, so there wasn't room. But don't worry—they'll be back in force in the next book, along with a few new ones too! After all, to paraphrase the last line of the book, Hope and Alex have some big plans to make.

Erin Brockus
February, 2022

Turn the page to read the first chapter of *Forever Hope*, Book 4 of the Half Moon Bay series . . .

FOREVER HOPE EXCERPT

July...

HOPE COLLINS WENT from asleep to awake in an instant. Its weight was the first thing she noticed. The *difference*—yesterday morning compared to today. It wasn't a heavy thing, but its import was tremendous. She opened her eyes as a smile slid across her face. On the other side of the bedroom was a wall of floor-to-ceiling windows, and streaming light caught her eye. The white sand beach and ocean of the western shore of St. Croix were brightly lit by the morning sunshine.

What time is it? She glanced at the clock, which informed her it was after 7 a.m. Her smile became a smug grin.

Guess we did have a pretty late night. Well, Alex will be long gone by now.

Finally, she couldn't deprive herself any longer. Hope raised her left hand and the grin turned into slack-jawed wonder as she gazed upon her engagement ring. After returning home the previous night, she had inspected it closely. The showstopper was a large princess-cut diamond, surrounded by a square of smaller, similar-cut diamonds. A white-gold band held the ring firmly to her finger. Even in the soft morning light, the diamonds glimmered. It was perfect.

But today was a workday for Hope, just as it was for Alex Monroe, the dive-operations manager and head dive guide of Half Moon Bay Resort. And as of last night, also her fiancé.

Her breath caught at the thought.

My fiancé. We're getting married! *I'm getting married!*

But workdays generally meant Alex rising before the sun. *Well, I have a few minutes before I need to get up. I'll just snuggle up with his pillow.* Turning on her side, Hope yelped as she came face-to-face with a pair of crystal blue eyes and an enormous grin.

"Like it, huh?"

The hand in question was now pressed against her bare chest as she tried to quell her racing heart. "You scared me to death!" Then her smile reappeared. "I didn't think you'd still be here."

"I thought it might be worth hanging around to see what you'd do when you woke up. Definitely worth it, even if you do sleep until noon." Alex faced her, raised up on one elbow with his head resting in his hand. Morning stubble lined his chin and his short, sandy hair was sticking up like someone had run her hands through it. Repeatedly.

She smacked his chest. "Give me a break. It's barely seven." She kissed him, morning breath be damned. "And I don't like it—I love it. Mr. Monroe, you really knocked it out of the park with that proposal."

"Meh. It was all right, I guess." His grin got bigger.

Last night he'd taken her on a night dive to Salt River Bay, on the north shore of the island, and proposed to her underwater amidst an extraordinary display of bioluminescence. The water around them had been an explosion of illumination, provided by countless numbers of light-emitting sea creatures. Hope still couldn't believe it had really happened.

She brushed a finger over the ring. "I'm amazed at how well it fits."

"A woman who worked at the jewelry store was my hand model. She was about the same size as you."

Hope shook her head as amazed laughter burst through. She'd had no idea his proposal was coming. Her experiences with men had kept her from dreaming too big, but Alex had proven time and again he was worth dreaming for. He rolled onto his back, and she settled on his chest. "I can't believe how lucky I am."

Alex's chest shook as he laughed, exuberant and long. "Ok, let's get this straight. I'm marrying a woman who owns her own oceanfront resort and has made it a resounding success. She just happened to find a cave which contains a treasure worth who-knows-how-much. Not to mention she's brilliant and drop-dead gorgeous. I'm just a dive guide."

"Oh, god. Not this again." Hope counted on her fingers. "Dive guide, rescuer of multiple persons—myself included, defender of justice against employee thugs, expert diver capable of finding hidden treasure, and sexier than hell. Am I forgetting something?" She slapped her forehead. "Oh yeah! Former Navy SEAL and war hero. Alex, shut up."

"Yes, ma'am." He turned, pressing the length of his body against hers.

"Uh-huh. And there's the real reason you stayed in bed so long." She pressed back, stretching like a cat.

He ran a finger down her arm. "I've told you before. I've got no self-control around you."

"Then I guess it's a good thing I don't either. Let's start this day in style."

An hour later, Hope breezed into the lobby office where general manager Patti Thomas was at work. She sat at her own desk and woke her computer. "How's it going?"

"Fine," Patti replied, frowning at her screen as she drummed her ebony fingers on the desk.

"Any more problems with Princess Tinkerbell?"

Patti laughed, a deep, rich sound, before she continued in her lilting accent, "No, nothin' since the Cockroach Crisis yesterday."

They had a very high-maintenance guest named Annabelle Smythe. Her boyfriend escaped on the daily dive trip every morning, leaving her free to terrorize the staff. The previous day, an errant beetle had dared to race across her front porch, and she had stormed into the office, demanding Patti fumigate the bungalow immediately. Fortunately, Patti convinced her bugs were occasional visitors, and nothing could be done about them.

Patti typed some more, then groaned, clutching a hand to her salt-and-pepper halo of hair. "Annabelle sent us that detailed itinerary of her activities, and I've been tryin' to keep ahead of any problems that might crop up. But now I *cannot* find it."

Hope brought up the email. "Really? It's still in my inbox."

Patti pointed to her terminal. "Take a look. Nothin'. She probably found a way to retract it, so she could complain some more."

Hope rose and leaned over Patti's computer, verifying there was no email before looking closer. "Oh, look." She pointed at the screen. "You're in the deleted folder, Patti."

Patti inhaled sharply as she grabbed Hope's left hand, pulling it close to her face. Her eyes grew steadily bigger as they met Hope's.

"Oh. Alex and I have some news." Hope grinned just as the power went out, plunging them into dim twilight. Both women glanced at the television on the wall, which normally showed landscape photos of St. Croix but was now black.

"Wonder how long it will last this time?" Hope said as she

marched toward the front desk. Several areas of the resort were linked to backup generators, which became active immediately upon the occasional loss of power. The front-desk computer was one. Martine, their front-desk agent, sat on a stool behind the counter, her very pregnant abdomen pressing against the counter in front of her.

"Is your computer still up, Martine?"

She nodded, pulling her black braids into a ponytail, already preparing for the heat. Hope gave her a thumbs-up and continued, heading out of the lobby to the restaurant just behind. As she walked through the swinging doors into the kitchen, the lights cast a brilliance over the clean room. Sous chef Pauline was cutting up a pineapple.

"Looks like all's well here?"

"Just fine," Pauline said, her black hair pulled back into a tight bun. Gerold Harrigan, their executive chef, had hired Pauline several months previously. She was a local from Christiansted, and grateful to learn under the tutelage of such a talented chef. "The fridges and freezers are workin' just fine."

"Ok, sounds good."

Hope headed back to the office. As soon as she opened the lobby door, a raised voice radiated out. A tall young woman wearing a white terrycloth resort bathrobe stood in the middle of the lobby, both hands propped on her hips. The left side of her long blonde hair was perfectly flat-ironed and glossy, but the right side was a dull, frizzy mess that stuck out everywhere.

Hope bit down hard on the inside of her cheek to keep from laughing.

"How can the power just go out? I need it back on now! Greg and I have a photo shoot this afternoon. I can't go looking like this, now can I?" She glared at Patti, who stared back with her usual even, calm expression.

Hope took a deep breath and approached. It was her turn.

"I'm so sorry, Annabelle. We live on a small island in the middle of the ocean, so power outages happen from time to time."

Annabelle turned her blazing eyes to Hope. "Why wasn't I informed of this ahead of time? I never would have come to this third-world hellhole if I'd known that!"

"Well, many of our guests think it's part of the charm of discovering a new place. But don't worry, we'll make sure you look perfect for your photo shoot. We have several outlets that are powered off the backup generators, just in case. When is your session?" A quick glance at the clock informed Hope it was 11 a.m.

"It's at three o'clock. Greg is on the dive boat now. And that damn dive guide better not keep him out late again. Yesterday they took forever because of some stupid rare fish or something."

"Yes, a pod of pilot whales is a pretty rare sight," Hope said. "Greg was very excited when I saw him."

Annabelle rolled her eyes. "I don't understand the appeal at all."

Of course you don't. Your hair would get wet.

Patti broke in. "If the power's still out after lunch, bring your hair supplies and find us. We'll make sure you look incredible for your photos, ok?"

"Well, I'd better, or there will be hell to pay." With that, Annabelle huffed, spun around, and marched out of the lobby.

"Is it too early to drink yet?" Hope asked.

"I may join you." Patti turned to her. "Is everythin' ok elsewhere?"

Hope nodded. "I didn't go down to the pier to see if the air compressor is still powered. I don't have a clue how the thing works. Alex can look at it later."

At Alex's name, Patti grabbed Hope's left hand. "We got interrupted by the power failure! You two are engaged?"

A smile threatened to crack Hope's face as she nodded. Patti wrapped an arm around her shoulders as she steered them back to the office, beckoning to Martine to join them. "Come on then, child. We need to hear all about this."

Order Forever Hope Today!

ALSO BY ERIN BROCKUS

HALF MOON BAY SERIES:

Associated Short Stories and Novellas:

Tropical Dawn: A Half Moon Bay Prequel Novella

Tropical Chance*: A Second Chance Half Moon Bay Novella

Tropical Hope*: A Half Moon Bay Prequel Short Story

* Subscriber exclusives

Main Novels:

Finding Hope: Half Moon Bay Book 1

Defending Hope: Half Moon Bay Book 2

Rising Hope: Half Moon Bay Book 3

Forever Hope: Half Moon Bay Book 4

Half Moon Whim: Half Moon Bay Book 5 (Standalone)

Half Moon Ember: Half Moon Bay Book 6 (Standalone)

Half Moon Aqua: Half Moon Bay Book 7

Crowning Hope: Half Moon Bay Book 8

STANDALONE BOOKS:

In Too Deep: A Second Chance Romance (Flamingo Island Series)

Beached in Bali: A Friends to Lovers Romance (Vagabond Series)

ABOUT THE AUTHOR

Dive Into a Tropical Romantic Escape!

Erin Brockus writes steamy, small town romance set in exotic, balmy locales. Her books provide the perfect beachy escape from everyday life, and she features mature, relatable characters you can't help but root for. Count on plenty of breezy adventure with a focus on the ocean, especially scuba diving.

Two of her greatest passions are scuba diving and travel, which combine to form the inspiration for her characters and stories. Sipping a cocktail on the beach after a morning of diving is her idea of the perfect day. Erin has even been known to pull on a drysuit and explore the cold, murky waters of the Pacific Northwest. She is also an avid runner and cyclist.

Erin lives with her husband, a scuba instructor, in the middle of Washington wine country. She is currently submerged in her next island escape.

Made in the USA
Monee, IL
02 June 2023